THE DIVE

THE DIVER

SAMSUN KNIGHT

UNIVERSITY OF IOWA PRESS, IOWA CITY

University of Iowa Press, Iowa City 52242
Copyright © 2023 by Samsun Knight
uipress.uiowa.edu

Printed in the United States of America

Text design and typesetting by April Leidig
Cover design by Kathleen Lynch / Black Kat Design

Printed on acid-free paper

Library of Congress Cataloging-in-Publication Data
Names: Knight, Samsun, 1992– author.
Title: The Diver / Samsun Knight.
Description: Iowa City: University of Iowa Press, [2023]
Identifiers: LCCN 2023007506 (print) | LCCN 2023007507 (ebook) |
ISBN 9781609389277 (paperback; acid-free paper) | ISBN 9781609389284 (ebook)
Subjects: LCGFT: Thrillers (Fiction) | Detective and mystery fiction. | Novels.
Classification: LCC PS3611.N568 D58 2023 (print) | LCC PS3611.N568 (ebook) |
DDC 813/.6—dc23/eng/20230509
LC record available at https://lccn.loc.gov/2023007506
LC ebook record available at https://lccn.loc.gov/2023007507

You are a soul carrying a corpse,

as Epictetus used to say.

~

DEEPWATER

A scuba diver is on a deepwater dive with her husband, one hundred thirty feet below. The red frequencies don't make it this far down and so everything around is green or blue, the seaweed and the shipwreck and the husband and the algae, the schools of fish and the jutting rocks. The shafts of sun that do reach this deep are so dispersed as to seem an inherent glow, original to the setting, less falling from above than staying where they are, where they always are. Breathing steady, breathing slow.

They're in Lake Michigan, diving after a shipwreck from some de-cade in the 1800s, and the scuba diver and her husband are outfitted in these big bulky dry suits to deal with the freezing cold, baggy jackets and baggy pants that look like ski gear—the underwater equivalent of winter clothes. Nylon hoods cover their heads and surround their faces, leaving only just enough room for the goggle-masks over their eyes and the respirators plugged into their lips, connected by a thin rubber tube to the steel cylinders of oxygen on their backs. The masks suction their cheeks as they drift. The husband is swimming a little above and a little ahead of the scuba diver, and the wake from his flippers brushes her bangs back from her face, as though tucking her hair behind her ear, and for one endless moment she has the impression that they are the only humans in existence.

The shipwreck is from the era of the early railroads and the Erie Canal, when the markets of New York were newly accessible to Chicago and, by way of Chicago, much of the Midwest, and commercial fleets suddenly populated both Lake Michigan's surface and its depths. This particular vessel is a schooner, one of those skinny ships with two masts and many more sails, and because of the cold and the pressure and some other miracle of circumstance it's almost perfectly preserved down here, filmed with a thick layer of algae but otherwise just about the same as it was almost two hundred years ago. And everything inside it, too. As she approached from above, drifting down at a snail's pace to allow time for her ears and mask to pressurize, the scuba diver had amused herself by imagining the wreck as a ghost ship. But once they arrive at the deck and swim into the ship's chambers, she is surprised to find that it actually is: a skeleton floats in the first room they enter, still despairing the massive hole in the hull. Its skull seems to make direct eye contact with the scuba diver precisely because it has no eyes. Her husband takes out an underwater camera and gestures for her to pose for a photograph next to the dead man and she reluctantly allows herself to drift to its side, removes her respirator, and grins. In other rooms they find other skeletons, and each time the husband insists on snapping a similar shot.

The spookiest part of the ship, though, turns out to be the hold. In a rather glib twist of fate, the vessel had been carrying a full shipment of brand-new porcelain toilets when it sank, and so the hold is still lined from wall to wall with the uncannily familiar commodes, ranks of ceramic basins gaping up at the scuba diver and her husband. She can't help but think of birdlings when she looks at them: open beaks eager for the food of their mother's gut. She cannot say why this unsettles her so deeply, unsettles her even more than the actual skulls and bones, and she also cannot fathom why all of the merchandise is exposed like this—why on earth the toilets are unboxed, not packaged at all for the voyage, and, given this, how it is they remained in their tight arrangement even throughout the disaster and the sinking and the two hundred years since. The husband is obviously not so bothered. He shakes his belly to imitate laughter and takes more photos. This only heightens the scuba diver's discomfort. Hovering about ten feet above the legions of toilets, about five feet above her husband, watching him mug for a selfie, she turns in an idle circle while she waits for her nerves to settle. A large part of what's wrong is that she does not understand what's wrong.

Until her air supply abruptly cuts off for no apparent reason, and what's wrong is that she cannot breathe.

~

When the scuba diver was first getting certified for diving, about two years prior, she became comfortable breathing underwater much more quickly than the husband. In their first pool dive, lying on their stomachs on the bottom of the shallow end, the husband returned to the surface for air four times before the instructor finally coaxed him into trusting his respirator for more than two breaths below. But even after he figured out how to breathe comfortably, the exercises continued to torment him—the training naturally centered on the skills required to recover from every possible mishap, and this constant reminder of disaster was torture to him. His eyes shrank into his face and his hands fluttered constantly at his sides, picking at his wet suit, toying with the straps of his mask. He had to try three times before he correctly pressurized his ears and mask on the way down, and six times before he managed to properly simulate losing and locating and replacing his goggles at the bottom of the deep end.

Something about breathing underwater in the pitch dark of your own closed eyes, he told her on the drive home, gave him the terrifying feeling that there was no world outside his own mind; no world to escape into; no escape.

For the scuba diver herself, there was no such feeling. There was no feeling to it, really, at all. While she'd experienced similar jitters when she first descended, when she drew those first few breaths beneath the surface of the pool, she simply refocused her energy on her breathing as per the instructor's advice, keeping her inhales steady and slow until, as promised, the jitters slowly and steadily receded. She did not convince herself that the danger wasn't real; she didn't think about danger at all. Throughout the session, she watched her husband flounder with a mixture of curiosity and pity, because she understood that they were not experiencing the same emotions—that his brain was being inundated with a larger dose of anxiety than hers, and had that much more to overcome.

If anything, she told him in the car, it was more impressive and coura-
geous that he pushed through, given the amount of fear he was fighting.

~

The procedure for when your air supply runs out is as follows: (1) exhale steadily; (2) slice your hand across your throat to gesture to your
partner that your air is out; (3) locate your partner's alternate respirator;
(4) breathe from your partner's alternate respirator; and (5) exit the dive.

The scuba diver fails the first step at once. She holds her breath—just
for an instant, just for that first moment when she realizes that she is
not receiving oxygen—and then the sense that she has messed this up,
that she is messing this up, that she's gotten the procedure wrong and
the procedure is now done wrong, all of this overwhelms her so quickly
that she forgets to stop holding her breath until the arrival of a secondary panic, the secondary realization that she's still holding her breath,
and even after she finally starts exhaling a little stream of bubbles all
she really wants to do is weep, although of course all she really wants
to do is breathe. She has never felt panic expand this quickly. She never
knew that it could. But once it does, the possibilities of what else she does
not know immediately become just that much more threatening. Before,
none of the described dangers of the world applied to her—disasters
happen to other people—but now that she is one of these other people,
every danger, known or unknown, may apply.

If she does fall apart all at once, however, she gathers herself back
together just as quickly. She forcefully reminds herself, once the stream
of bubbles is flowing from her lips, that she has achieved step one: that
the procedure is back on track: that she is not, in fact, failing. She has not
failed. The steps are working and the steps will work. Her heart beats
and her heart beats and she keeps breathing out, as though she might
at any moment be able to breathe in, and she swings her flashlight back
and forth over the husband's face to get his attention and slices her hand
across her throat to communicate her situation and she swims over to
him and he swims over to her and she plunges her hand into his dry suit

for his second respirator and yanks the broken one from her mouth and replaces it with his spare and breathes, and breathes.

Bubbles flow up along the sides of her face, up through her hair, up to the ceiling of the ship's hold and through the gaps in the hull, up toward the surface.

Directly beneath them, the army of toilets softly gleams beneath the glare of their flashlights. A particularly thick cloud of algae floats over from where her husband disturbed it and turns their flashlight beams even greener for a moment, and then passes on.

The scuba diver breathes, and breathes.

The husband makes a hand signal to ask if she's A-OK and she gives the same hand signal back, to confirm that she's A-OK. She shakes her head from side to side, meaning to shake her head at her own ridiculousness, at her ridiculous panic, but her husband is confused by this and asks again if she's A-OK, and she makes the A-OK signal once more. She wants to kiss him. He clasps her forearm in his.

After he draws her close to his body, however, she can't help but peek at the gauge on his oxygen tank and notice that he's almost entirely out of air, too.

~

Authorities would later determine that faulty pressure gauges were to blame for the mishap on the lake floor. The couple's oxygen tanks were otherwise up to inspection standards, but the needles on the pressure gauges were simply stuck at 3,000 dpi—the pressure level of a full tank of oxygen—and thus misled the fill station into thinking the tanks were topped off, when in fact they only held ten or fifteen minutes' worth of air. Only after the tanks were just about zeroed out did the needles finally swing back down and reveal the true quantities remaining.

The local newspaper, covering the incident and its investigation in the days that followed, likened the tragedy to the *Challenger* explosion in 1986. In that accident, the newspaper's most ambitious young journalist wrote, the entire spaceship imploded because of a malfunction in one of its smallest components: a single broken O-ring, a tiny circle of rubber that sealed the cabin's smallest cracks from the outside, which failure allowed a minuscule amount of air into the spacecraft and thereby prevented the chamber from properly maintaining its pressure in ascent until the chamber collapsed under the massive force of the movement and the fuel tanks ignited and the crew members were incinerated on live television, midair.

It's almost always the simplest parts of a complex system, the journalist wrote, privately ecstatic that the editor was willing to let such sweeping language go into print, *that are overlooked.*

~

It is impossible to interpret the expression on the husband's face through his mask and goggles, with the respirator plugged into his lips and the nylon covering the rest of his skin, as he takes the pressure gauge from the scuba diver with his free hand and looks at it for himself. His other hand's grip on her forearm slackens and she drifts an inch away from him, and then another inch. They are still close, but they are also farther apart than before. He brings the gauge right up to his goggles and shakes it, and then shakes it once more, and then brings it back down from his face and looks up at her.

Based on the shorthand for reading the gauge as they both understand it, a single person would have about thirty seconds' worth of fresh breath left. Which is to say, about fifteen seconds for each of them, together.

It's important to note that this is actually enough for them both to safely reach the surface. Through controlled and careful swimming and very long, slow exhales, they can space out this remaining oxygen and reach the surface without gasping for breath, and even have enough time to slow their ascent at key moments to allow their bodies to decompress. There have been many recorded instances of individual divers entirely out of oxygen who make such controlled emergency exits from the depths with no lasting damage to speak of. The scuba diver does not yet have reason to panic.

Until, that is, the husband makes a complex gesture with his fingers

8

that the scuba diver does not understand and then reaches over and plucks his secondary respirator from her lips like it's just that easy, because it is just that easy, and then makes another gesture, and turns to swim away.

In retrospect, the husband could have meant a very simple thing with this movement. Later on the scuba diver would spend hours, days, deciphering the most likely meaning: when he'd placed a fist over his chest, the gesture for breathing, and then pointed at his mouth, presumably to indicate his respirator, he may have only meant to communicate that they needed to share his single respirator on their ascent now, to ensure that they didn't go through the air too quickly. But what the scuba diver sees in that moment when he takes his spare from her lips is the gesture for breathing and then the gesture for himself, to indicate that just he is breathing now, that he is leaving her behind to drown because only one of them can make it back up to the surface, and once that interpretation enters her mind there is simply no room for any other. The panic that she'd only seconds ago subdued comes roaring back and claws the rest of her thinking apart and she ceases to recognize this person before her, ceases to presume that the features of her husband lurk beneath this mask and hood and diving apparatus and sees this body instead as what it is, as just another competing consciousness seeking to satisfy the demands of its flesh, and she imagines she can feel the weight of all the one hundred thirty feet of water above her, can feel it pressing into her, compressing her, because truly she can, because truly it is and her husband is long disappeared, was never there to begin with, and this body and its tank of oxygen is moving away from her and her head is pounding and her whole body is pounding and she is going to die, she is going to drown here, she is going to choke on water and suffocate and her body won't even rise all the way to the surface because she'll be stuck in this hold and she'll stay here, floating, dead, until she rots into another skeleton on the ghost boat, stuck in the toilet room and how long has her husband been a stranger, has he always been willing to leave her to die, has he always been prepared to let her drown as soon as the choice arrived, and her whole body is pounding and she is going to die and this stranger hates her and she hates this stranger more, more than anything or anyone she has ever hated before, this nylon suit of flesh floating to the exit and leaving her behind, and she frog-kicks her legs out behind her and catches him in the door from the hold and shoves her elbow into his throat and removes his primary respirator from his lips and takes a long breath, the last breath, and then kicks off from his chest, knocking his head against the lintel and sending him back down into the hold and herself propelling upward, and she rises and he sinks.

~

Another potential piece of the puzzle is gas narcosis, the journalist would later try to add. While the medical community still doesn't understand precisely why, there is a well-documented phenomenon of intoxication that can occur when divers descend beyond one hundred feet below, wherein they feel not so much drunk as intensely hungover: headaches, dizziness, disorientation, irrational thinking, and in some cases, border-line insanity.

There are even some recorded instances, the journalist would describe in one of the portions that the editor eventually cut, *wherein divers apparently just decide to die. Bodies are recovered with plenty of air remaining in the tank and nothing at all wrong with the equipment, and it appears the diver simply removed their respirator from their lips and let water fill their lungs.*

Although it may be only the most fleeting of lapses, the journalist would be sure to clarify, *since once the lungs begin to fill with water—especially if there is not air immediately available, when the diver starts to involuntarily cough—it does not take very long at all, in fact, to drown.*

~

The scuba diver is about fifteen feet from the surface when she looks back down. The grip of panic finally slips when she reaches the rest point, the requisite pause in ascent for reducing the risk of decompression sickness, and without really thinking about what she's trying to see, without really thinking at all, she glances back the way she came.

She realizes that she had expected to see her husband behind her only when she does not.

Unconsciously, her hand rises to the button on her buoyancy device, preparing to descend, to go back down to get him. Even though she already knows, as her thumb hovers over the button, that she will not. She still doesn't have any air in her oxygen tank; she has not taken a breath for the entire ascent, but only maintained her same small stream of bubbles, as per procedure. She cannot return.

The wreck rests in the blue depths, the exact same as before, as always, the mid-nineteenth century lurking in a drowned vessel on the lake floor.

A stray current brushes the scuba diver's bangs from her face and her body sinks back down a few inches. A painful lump begins to form in her throat.

She ascends the remaining few feet to the surface and breaks back into the open air.

～

On their second day of scuba training, the husband finally found his bearings. He awoke that morning before the scuba diver and prepared a fresh cup of coffee and a bowl of sliced fruit before she even came downstairs, and sang along with the radio all the way to the pool. She told him that he was intolerable and kissed him on the lips twice while their car waited at one red light and then again at the next. At the second stop, he wrapped her into his arms and didn't notice the light had turned green until the cars behind them started honking. He nailed every training exercise on the first try, same as she, and the instructor declared them the best pair of students he'd ever had. They flew to the Bahamas to complete the open-water portion of their training and subsequently went diving at least once every couple months for the next two years. They got a mortgage and bought a house but decided to put off having kids for another year, to allow them more time to explore the world.

It was on a speedboat, flying over the surface of the Pacific for a reef dive, that they decided they wanted to have only one kid, at the very most, unless it took two tries before they got a girl.

~

The scuba diver heaves herself up the ladder enough to lay her torso on the boat's floor, but feels too weak to bring her legs all the way up after her. Her fins sway with the lapping of the waves against the boat's hull, pulling her body a half inch back toward the water, pushing her that same half inch back out. The boat tilts toward her, tilts away. Her face is pressed flat into the floor, her nose squashed and her teeth pressing into her lips, biting from the inside. The sun heats her dry suit in seconds and beads of sweat break out across her brow, slide down the side of her face, pool where her skin meets the fiberglass.

Two hours later a local stevedore will find her passed out at the helm of her boat, run aground near an industrial pier, essentially beached on an outcropping of rocks. She will still be wearing her dry suit, with even her oxygen tank still strapped to her back. The doctor on call in the emergency room will declare her a victim of severe dehydration and heatstroke and at immediate risk of decompression sickness, and will keep her in the hospital for forty-eight hours before releasing her. The police will attempt to interview her in bed twice, and each time, they will fail.

The second time the officer comes to the door she will not pretend to be asleep but will simply stare at him in silence, with slightly open eyes and slightly parted lips, until he leaves.

A particularly large wave slaps against the backs of her thighs where they still hang down over the speedboat's ladder and she is suddenly seized with the need to not be here, to be away from here, to be miles away from this place and this day, and she rears to her feet and flops her way to the boat's tiller and dislodges the anchor and roars the engine into gear, still in her full dry suit, still wearing her empty oxygen tank on her back, still half sea creature and half survivor, like the last woman in existence, and she guns the boat toward shore.

PETER

I first met Evelyn Forrester in Evanston, Illinois, toward the end of August 2009, when she came to the law firm where I was working to look for representation. At first, I thought that she was there to arrest my boss. It was early on a Wednesday morning, only ten minutes or so after seven a.m., and because of my angle of approach to our office's front doors—the law firm was just a little single-story structure at the far end of a strip mall, one of those generic side-by-side storefront locations that might have housed a video rental store otherwise—I wasn't able to see at all into the waiting room until I was already right in front, fitting my key into the lock of the double door and by then she was already staring straight back at me, standing beside the empty receptionist's desk with a manila folder wedged underneath her elbow and a single eyebrow raised. I jerked back without turning the key. But the right-hand door edged an inch or so inward anyway, apparently already unlocked.

At that time, I'd only been working at the private law practice of Masterson, Masterson & Zell, LLC for about eight weeks, nine at most, at the very bottom of the food chain as the newest (and only) paralegal, and I'd never once encountered anyone else at the office before I arrived; the door was always locked when I got there, as a rule, and there were rarely even many cars in the parking lot when I crossed over from the bus stop on the far side of the highway. I could only think of one possible explanation, a suspicion immediately hardening into certainty at the very bottom of my gut. Both because she was standing in our office before we were open—the telltale skeleton-key access of the FBI investigator—and also, I think, because of the implicit authority of her beauty, the flawless side part in her long black hair and the pointed directness of her stare, with no trace of a smile on her lips as I blinked at her and then kept blinking, each of us waiting for the other to explain what we were to do next.

"Hello," she said finally, her voice floating through the inch-wide gap between the edge of the right-hand door and the jamb. "Are you Masterson, Masterson, or Zell?"

I opened my mouth to speak and then swallowed instead, and glanced over my shoulder. My whole body felt simultaneously hot and cold, frozen and sweating. In some ways, it was a relief to get shut down by the feds after only eight weeks on the job, both as a vindication of all my intense discomforts over the past two months of working at MM&Z, LLC and also as a final release, a way out that left no room for any indecision. I wiped my palms on my thighs, stepped forward, and pushed the right-hand door the rest of the way open.

"No, but—I'm Peter," I said, my voice catching in my throat. I coughed into an elbow and tried again. "My name is Peter, I mean."

She returned my smile distantly, impassively, as if observing the both of us from above.

~

The last time I'd lost a job, it had taken me almost seven months to find a new position. It was right at the very beginning of the recession, just after the news stations had all started playing the same wall-to-wall coverage of collapsing Dow Jones graphs, zoom-outs of whole streets of empty houses and crying fathers, important people sweating in their cars and unimportant people looking scared on the sidewalks, leaves turning from green to yellow, yellow to brown. The phrase "global financial crisis" was still just one term among many that October, as the news anchors tried to find a name to make it all seem understandable, if not yet understood. It seemed too abstract to really think about until I was also fired. And even then, I'd only been working part-time at a small press in downtown Chicago, a placeholder job that I'd taken mainly for the off-hours access to their printing equipment, and after

I was let go, I tried to dull the insult by repeating to myself and to my art-school friends that I'd never really wanted the work anyway, and also by making a secret copy of the office key so that I could keep using the printing equipment in the small hours of the night. At the time, my friends and I were all collectively obsessed with making the first issue of our new critical theory / graphic novel-ish art magazine, the *Movie Review Canoe*, and it hardly seemed like a bad trade-off, really, to have to dumpster-dive a little more than before and to adjust my sleep schedule so that I could sneak into the press between midnight and six, laboring away at the lithograph machine with all the urgency of a heist that's already gone wrong, but that we still-just-might pull off with a little extra sweat and gumption. It felt meaningful, in other words. Only then the market fell even further, and the entire small press was shuttered on the same day that my older brother killed himself back home; and I went to stay with my parents for two months and then found, upon returning, that the magazine project was dead, and my friends no longer felt like my friends anymore. By the time that I finally got another job interview the following June, after moving out of the apartment I'd shared with that whole friend group and into a decrepit one-room studio on the opposite side of downtown, I'd been applying to jobs more or less nonstop for six full months in a row—all through December and all through January, February, March, April, and May—and this single callback felt so precious that I barely believed it was genuine. I lifted a used suit from a thrift store that same afternoon and arrived for the interview fifty minutes early the following morning, and then came into work a full hour early every morning afterward, even before they gave me a key to let myself in.

Naphtha—a sometimes-girlfriend from the School of the Art Institute of Chicago whom I'd been sleeping with every few months or so, on and off, since the end of my freshman and her sophomore year—described the paralegal job to her roommates as just the latest stage in my "regret spiral," something that I was doing in order to purge myself of my youth and guilt and energy, or at least something that would leave me feeling purged. But while I liked the sound of the phrase, it didn't even begin to capture the strange mixture of obeisance and panic that consumed me there, in the used-carpet musk of that strip mall law office: as I fled from the stranger in the waiting room to my window-less office in the back and then collapsed into my broken swivel chair, burning with fear that John Zell was about to fire me as soon as he arrived, the chair springs creaking loudly underneath me and my shoulders hunched almost up to my ears, my fingers laced together above my head. I needed this job with more certainty and more desperation than I'd felt about anything or anyone for as long as I could remember, and with at least as much terror as when I'd first fallen in love. I didn't know if I would survive another seven months of being unemployed. A tiny knock sounded on the doorframe and I almost fell out of my seat with surprise, my hands gripping the very edges of my armrests, while our receptionist Willa stuck her head into the open doorway and peered in through small eyes.

"Pete. What's going on? Where are the coffees?" She wrinkled her nose. "Also, why did you ask that woman in the waiting room if she was here under a search warrant from the FBI?"

I pushed myself back up into a normal sitting position, already out of breath. "That wasn't—"

"Also, why is it so dark in here?"

"—that was just, the door was already . . ." I trailed off, my skin cold under the evaporating sweat on my temples, and started over. "It's always this dark in here, the overheads give me a headache. I can see fine, anyway, with the light coming in from the d—ah."

The fluorescents thrummed to life above us after Willa punched the switch with the bottom of her hand. I lifted my arm to shield my eyes. "Grow up, Peter," she said, turning to go. "John will be here in less than twenty minutes. Just don't be late with his coffee, okay?"

"Shit." I squeezed my eyes shut and stood, took my phone out of my pocket and confirmed the time. "*Shit*." I pushed my phone back into my pants and nearly ran after her, my head down and my gut clenched with dread. Even before I turned the corner, I could sense the non-FBI-agent sitting on the lobby couch in my peripheral vision, her ankles crossed and her stare calm and steady, prickling on the back of my neck as I strode past and shoved the glass double door open with my shoulder. The humid summer air pushed into my hair and over my skin as I emerged into the sun.

~

"It is a mistake, though, in a larger sense," Naphtha said, a smile flickering at the edge of her lips while she waited for me to smile back. "This job, I mean. Cosmically."

I took a sip from the edge of the jar, taking the tiniest mouthful of the bitter green liquid before swallowing it down. "How sure are you guys, actually, that this is real absinthe?"

Anderson James, Naphtha's roommate since as long as I'd known her, snorted and took the jar from me with both hands. "You don't have to have any if you don't want any," he muttered, cradling it close to his chest as he eased back into his beanbag chair.

"Seriously, though, P. You're damaging the world. You're damaging yourself, also, but especially you're damaging the world. Like a gear in a gun's trigger mechanism. No?"

I folded my legs, leaning my head and torso very far to one side as I rearranged myself. We were seated in a rough circle beside the kitchen table/work desk/rectangular slab of treated oak in the warehouse where Naphtha and her roommates had been living for the last four months, establishing their various artistic practices and hosting parties and sleeping in loosely curtained-off places on the floor. In the darkness outlined by their floor and table lamps, with the walls looming up on either side and only the intimation of a ceiling in the shadows above, the place felt like a church that had been hollowed out of ritual, a canvas erased of a painting. I said something generic about the pleasure of working hard for the sake of working hard, the satisfaction of exhaustion, the simplicity of feeling deadened at the end of the day, but with my voice low and my eyes on the ground and avoiding Naphtha's narrow gaze, trying to signal the conversation to move on. Byron Garcia—always Naphtha's nicest roommate—nodded along sympathetically, pausing only to drink deep of the green jar that AJ had passed along. He began to ask a soft-voiced follow-up when Naphtha cut back in with a hum of displeasure.

"But that's bullshit, right?" she said, gingerly lifting the absinthe from Byron's cupped palms. "It's like — these Halliburton guys who talk on and on about how early they get up, and how late they stay at the office, in order to orchestrate the looting of Iraq. As if the action of self-sacrifice has any positive valence just by the fact of self-sacrifice, without any reference to what you're sacrificing for. The means justifying the ends. People in the *shape* of good Christians, only without the faith, and without the good. Industrious, hardworking Nazis. Right?" She took another draught of the green liquid and then quickly set it down on the floor beside her camping chair, pressed a wrist to her mouth, gulped again, and coughed. "Right, though?" she wheezed.

"The poison residue of the Christ narrative in Western culture," AJ mumbled, grinning.

The warehousemates laughed, Naphtha's coughing fit increasing as she added a chuckle to the mix. I smiled weakly.

"Well, I don't know," I began, my shoulders high as I crossed my legs. "The practice of how you live, and how to live well, that's still —"

"But. Come on, P." Naphtha turned her head so that she could look at me sidelong, while Byron rose shakily to his feet and stumbled over to the shower curtain around his sleeping area. He snatched the curtain back to reveal a pack of cigarettes and a lighter on the floor next to his pillow. "Don't your bosses, like, kill people? You said?"

"No, that's —" I bit down on my tongue, squinting. Byron lifted the pack of cigarettes into the air in a gesture of offering and both AJ and I raised our hands, and he took out three cigarettes to bring back over. "They just, scare people, sometimes. Or, *they* don't, but. These 'private detectives' that they hire."

"But that's so nakedly evil."

"They tell people that they're going to kill them," AJ offered, "but they don't actually."

"I mean," I said, setting my jaw to one side.

"As far as you know."

"They lease henchmen, basically. Right, P?"

"Well." I accepted the cigarette and then leaned forward to accept the flame also, puffing while he lit the end. "I guess, I could start poisoning their coffee, maybe."

"You should."

"Set the office on fire in the night."

"No, I like Nap's idea," Byron said, chewing his words in one side of his mouth while he lit his cigarette in the other. "Be a lazy Nazi. Take it down, with sheer incompetence, from the inside."

I accepted the jar of absinthe back from AJ and blinked at a particularly bulbous aspect of the blackness above us, trying to decide if I was hallucinating at all. For about as long as I'd known her—but especially in the last year or so, and when I'd been working so feverishly on the art magazine with my friends—Naphtha and her roommates had always been the image of exactly the type of people I'd wanted so desperately, so obsessively to impress: the category of faces whose imagined disapproval set my whole body into disequilibrium, sweat slipping between the fingers of both hands. Even when she dumped me, repeatedly, every few months or so; and even more so when she always took me back. I took another tiny mouthful and swallowed, squeezing my eyes shut while I pushed past the taste, and then opened my eyes and saw the shadows opening wider and deeper above me, flexing into a curve and then inverting, like the skin of a wave as the crest pulled the surface smooth.

~

I waited in line at the coffee shop for twenty-seven minutes and forty seconds before I was able to put in an order with the barista, and nine more minutes after that before I was able to leave with the food and drinks. Whenever I got there at 7:15, it never took more than six minutes for every step combined; but that day, after arriving at a criminally tardy 7:42, I was forced to endure thirty-six minutes and forty seconds of cold, anxious shifting back and forth in the crowd of strangers, listening to the other names as they were called with an increasing sense of indignation and plain resentment, my hairs standing on end at the back of my neck. I felt vaguely like weeping, but only in the way that someone nauseous feels like throwing up. After they called my name I snatched the coffees and the breakfast sandwich and the baglet of hash browns and sprinted for the door, beelining through the crowd and then leaping across the highway in long strides, catching my breath on the median for less than three seconds before plunging across and into the strip mall complex that housed our office and through the parking lot and then edged open our double door using only my fingertips and the point of my shoe, the food and drinks precariously cradled in my arms until I collapsed it all together onto the front desk, my chest heaving, spilled coffee burning across the tops of my fingers and along the sides of both palms. I could hear Willa saying something to me, but my breathing and my heartbeat were together too loud to make it out. A strong hand gripped my shoulder and I jerked myself back upright.

"You're late, Pete!" John Zell said, speaking through an audible grin as he reached around me for his breakfast sandwich. "And you look like shit, too, with those sweat stains. Did you run to work?"

I huffed out an imitation of a laugh, but in the context of my heavy panting it sounded much more like a cough instead, and then I started coughing in earnest. John Zell released my shoulder from his hand and bit deep into his bacon-egg-and-cheese, his smile fading. Willa said something else that I didn't catch and that he completely ignored.

"Sorry," I said, still covering my mouth with my elbow as I cleared my throat. "Sorry about that. Won't happen again. I was—"

"I don't suppose you happen to have another suit, or something else you could change into."

"Oh—"

"There's a client here this morning. Fucking drop-dead gorgeous. She's waiting in my office right now. Willa, do we have any extra shirts or jackets that might fit Pete? In the closet?"

"Why would we have an extra shirt in the closet?" Willa monotoned, without taking her eyes from the computer monitor on her desk.

"Fuck you, Willa. Work with me." He picked up his half-caf skim-milk latte from the cardboard tray and took a slurp, his eyes lighting up as he swallowed. "Hold on. What size are you, Willa?"

"You can't fucking ask me that, John."

"Take off your blazer and give it to Pete."

I lifted my small coffee from the tray and stepped back while they descended into a hissing match, turning to squint at the sunlight coming through the floor-to-ceiling windows along the front wall of the lobby. The strip mall had already been about a quarter vacant when I'd first started working there, but in just the last few weeks two more retailers had announced clearance sales, leaving the big department store now flanked on both sides by soon-to-be-empty storefronts. Like a herd of starving bison in winter, I imagined, with the strong watching in silence as the weak slowly sank into the snow. John Zell slammed a hundred-dollar bill on the front desk and Willa shot to her feet, so quickly that she almost lost her balance, but with her eyes bright and her nostrils flared. John stepped back while she shook her arms out of their sleeves and thrust the orange-red blazer out in my direction.

I looked at the jacket, then looked at John.

～

The first time I ever walked into John Zell's office, I was too preoccupied with the possibility that I might have terrible body odor to really hear the words that he was saying to me. At that point, I'd proudly gone without wearing deodorant for some years, ever since that one week at art school when everyone, it seemed, had been talking at length about how antiperspirants created a dependency in your armpits through years of accumulated adjustments to your body's chemistry and you wouldn't even smell bad if you just stopped using the corporate fixes, as long as you regularly showered. For years afterward, I never thought twice about it, until I arrived at my bus stop on my first morning of work at MM&Z and ran into one of my old roommates, eating a bagel on a bench and smelling like an entire subway car full of sweaty people. After I got to the office that day, I excused myself twice in the first five minutes to wash my armpits in the bathroom and even then, with the hand soap from the dispenser beginning to itch along the length of my obliques, I still felt intensely nervous that I was an aroma. The room was narrow but very long, with a row of high windows across one wall to let in all of the morning's sunlight but none of the view of the parking lot, two couches lined up end-to-end underneath and a pile of Persian rugs in the very center, at least five or six, that I always stood quite close to because I felt the dust would lend an excuse to my clothes for being slightly dirty. I never showed up without a shower after that first day, but I always remembered that anxiety whenever I stood there, and it's hard to say what the exact difference is between remembering an anxiety and feeling it, sometimes. On the day that I met Evelyn Forrester, with Willa's orange-red blazer cinched tight around my waist and my body still hot underneath, I followed John at a generous distance and then hung back at the door while he introduced me, and raised a hand without looking up from the carpets when he said my name.

"Thank you," Evelyn said, as though in reply. She'd risen from her seat at the far corner of the far couch, but without approaching, and she shook her head when John offered the chair across from his desk. He stood for a moment, deciding how to respond, and then motioned for them both to sit down at their opposite corners of the long room.

She laid her manila folder flat on her lap as she arranged herself back on the couch corner. "I'd like to hire you to help me with a sister-in-law problem," she said, enunciating each word as if she'd practiced the phrase in front of a mirror. "I hear you're the ones to call."

I shuffled the rest of the way into the room and closed the door behind me, trying and failing to keep the knob's mechanism from making its loud clack. She'd caught me off guard with this positioning: I'd planned to be as far as possible from both of them, but now she and I were on the same end of the room's rectangle, perilously close. John leaned magisterially behind his mahogany desk and gave her his own practiced reply, and she glanced instead at the shaft of sunlight coming through the high windows while he spoke, squinting as though seeing something in the floating dust motes. She shook her head no. I decided to take my chance and zipped across the floor to the seat that she hadn't taken next to John's desk, lifting it to the side so that I wouldn't interrupt their line of sight.

"I want to say, 'it's hard to explain,' but I guess these types of situations are always hard to explain," she said, directing a pained smile at the window glass. "My sister-in-law murdered my brother, only no one suspects her, and now she's trying to make large withdrawals from the family trust. I want you to make her stop."

John Zell grinned, holding a pen like a bridge between his two thumbs and forefingers. "That didn't take so long to explain," he said, trying hard to get her to return his level stare.

She exhaled, granting him only the barest glance before she returned her eyes to the sunlight. I imagined meeting her ten thousand years in the future, adventuring into the heart of the galaxy as the only two people left in the universe, holding her hand as we perished together on an exploding moon. John asked a follow-up question and she rubbed her eyes with the back of her wrist, the manila folder crinkling underneath her fingers' grip.

"Well. She told me that she killed him," she said, one eye open and red with broken veins while she rubbed the other, "is the main reason."

I blinked back into the present moment, surprise catching in my throat and then coughing once more into my elbow. Evelyn lowered her arm, both eyes a little red now and the corners of her lips curling down, as she waited to go on. John slid a legal pad and pen across the surface of his desk toward me and I snatched them up and started jotting down notes.

"I was the first person she spoke to, from Robert's side," she continued, "after the accident. It was a diving accident, officially. Scuba diving. They were underwater and their oxygen tanks ran out before they were supposed to. I don't remember all the details." Here she opened the manila folder for the first time and lifted out a single piece of paper, holding it meaningfully aloft. John nodded, his eyebrows high, and gestured to me without breaking his stare at Evelyn. I trotted across the room to accept the piece of paper from her extended hand. CHICAGO MAN BELIEVED DEAD IN LAKE MICHIGAN DIVING ACCIDENT, the headline blared at the top of the printout. "She was still sorting out her feelings about it, evidently, when I saw her at the hospital. She told me that she had panicked underwater and elbowed him in the throat, and then took the last breath of oxygen from his tank. Then kicked him. So he drowned." Her features seemed to steadily contract as she was speaking, her eyes narrowing and her brow low and her lips pursed, as if she were biting down on something hard. I retreated to my seat slowly, without turning my back. "And she told me all of this—but totally distraught, do you know? Just crying, and crying. And she gave me the impression, I felt sure at that time, that she was going to tell this to the police, too. That she was going to turn herself in."

"That's a type," John Zell said, commiserating.

"She's a fucking sociopath."

Fucking sociopath, I wrote down on the legal pad, arranging myself back in my seat.

"But. She got her bearings before she talked to anyone else, apparently. My mother thinks I'm a complete bitch now for wanting to go after the grieving widow like this, and over something so 'mean' as money. For wanting to go after her daughter-in-law, I should say." She took out a pack of cigarettes and a Zippo lighter from the inner pocket of her pantsuit jacket, shaking her head in disagreement, and then slid a cigarette from the pack and into her lips and lit the end in a single fluid movement, and then snapped the lighter shut. She inhaled.

"Sorry," she said, blinking through her own smoke.

"I actually, I do have a bit of a cold, so," I started, but in a tiny voice, giving ample space to be ignored. John Zell shot me a glance, but Evelyn made no sign of having heard at all. She took another deep draw and then exhaled in twin streams of smoke through her nostrils.

"Go ahead," John Zell said. "Now, you mentioned—"

"She doesn't want there to be any more bad feelings, of any kind," she continued, shifting in her seat so that she could smoke more comfortably.

"My mother, I mean. Anyone bringing bad energy, you know — they're toxic, as far as she's concerned. And she's committed to this idea that she has a new daughter, now, too, in Marta. She thinks I'm just jealous." The thin trail of smoke from the end of her cigarette seemed to change phase in the flat shaft of sunlight above her head, the gray spreading through the white like dye through liquid. But she seemed to see it differently, or to see something different, as she squinted up toward the high windows once more. "I know that there's no chance that I can get the police interested in the criminal side of this again," she said, "because I've already tried. They're not even looking for his body anymore, after they couldn't find him the first time. And I've talked to another lawyer already, and I know that there's really limited options, legally speaking, for freezing her out, especially with my mother on her side." She sniffed and ashed the cigarette on the floor, rubbing her nose with the back of her wrist. For the first time, I realized that she was visibly sleep-deprived: that her mannerisms and her posture and her rubbed-red eyes were those of someone on the edge of complete exhaustion, of a mind keeping a body awake past the point where it starts breaking. I couldn't tell if I'd been too prepossessed by her attractiveness to notice before, or if she'd just now decided to let it show. "He told me, essentially," she went on, "this other lawyer, I mean — that the only way I could really make her go away, legally speaking, is if I got her to go away on her own. If I convince her that it's not worth it to fight me on the money stuff, essentially, and she walks away. In his words." She ashed her cigarette on the floor again and then let it fall, tumbling onto the carpet with its ember still alive, while she closed her eyes and then opened them. "Then he gave me your card."

John Zell leaned back and laughed, glancing over at me if he expected me to be laughing, also. I looked at him with a blank stare and then looked down at the legal pad, at the brief sketch I'd made of the smoke's movement through the sunlight. Evelyn bent down to pick up the cigarette from the floor.

"Guilty as charged," John Zell said, restraining a smile, his hands out and open on either side.

~

Riding home on the bus that night, I was feeling in my pocket for my phone and my wallet and my keys—the three essential items that I'd lost far too frequently, throughout my life, and that I now checked with a compulsion as soon as it was too late to go back wherever I'd just left—when I found Evelyn Forrester's printout of the online news article, folded into a tight square between the halves of my flip phone. It was more unnerving than it should have been, probably, to find. All that afternoon and evening, I'd gone through the article and compiled contact information for both the journalist and his sources and also our target, making lists of all the public and private information that I could find and then, after normal working hours were over, calling them one by one on their home phones; but I had no memory, I felt certain, of ever folding the piece of paper and putting it in my pocket to take with me. I couldn't shake the uncanny sense that someone else had placed it there for me to find. I opened the phone to remove the printout and then carefully unfolded it, shifting in my seat so that I could reread without revealing the text to the stranger sitting next to me, tilting the page toward the bus window and then leaning my temple against the plate glass, the tempered material cool against my forehead while I scanned the words.

When John Zell first introduced me to my role at Masterson, Masterson & Zell, LLC, he had explained that their law firm was in the business of providing legal services to the moderately wealthy of a type that were usually only available to the mega-wealthy. Almost all billionaires and multimillionaires, he explained to me, kept people called "fixers" on retainer, who acted essentially as legal guard dogs—or as attack dogs, should the situation require—to protect the territory of their clients' estates and their clients' persons. It was the type of hire you made, he said with a smile, around the same time that you hired a private chef for your second home. And in the same way that people with only a few million dollars couldn't quite pay for a private chef but could well afford to eat daily at fancy restaurants, MM&Z, LLC provided high-quality one-off "fixer" services to a broad range of clients for a fraction of the cost of a full-time retainer. A handful of ex-cops served as the ground troops and I was to be the entry-level intelligence officer, organizing the information that they gathered and condensing and collating the important parts for briefs and motions, separating out the most salient and damaging information so that John Zell could use it or bury it, depending. I listened without comprehending, imagining a battlefield from World War One, biplanes bursting into flame as they crashed to the ground. He seemed quite pleasantly surprised when he asked if I had any questions and I told him that I had none.

"Not asking questions is good," he said, glancing over my shoulder at the door.

It wasn't until I spent my first morning of work there, reading through thousands of pages of emails illegally obtained from a client's ex-wife's email account, that I started to feel a sinking in my stomach. I had been given two colors of highlighter to use, red and yellow, with red for information that would be embarrassing if made public and yellow for any clues that might lead to embarrassing information, as well as sticky notes for places and times we might want to photograph with our hired investigators. I spent the first hour just reading the pages, unable to set any colors down. The voice of the ex-wife, read aloud to the inside of my head, took on the same cadence and intonations as my mother's, and as I read her terse schedulings and reschedulings and complaints to the PTA, her chain emails with her coworkers and her forwarded horoscopes, for some reason I couldn't stop imagining her as a strange woman in my mother's clothes, with different features but the exact same sweaters, the same shoes, and the same style of wearing her hair. At nine, John Zell stopped by my windowless room and suggested that I sort the emails by sender and by recipient, arranging them so that the correspondence with the ex-wife's lover was at the top and then work from there. I looked at his hands, gesturing intentionally as he spoke, and then looked at the stack of printed emails, plainly unmarked since I'd sat down at the desk an hour earlier. I nodded without meeting his eye.

But as much as I was frozen with dread, I was also—and increasingly so, as the day wore on—a little curious. As much as it was profoundly immoral, and shameful, and illegal, and vaguely humiliating, it was also undeniably interesting, learning about a person from the inside out. And surprisingly intimate, too. Especially after I followed John Zell's advice and reorganized the emails into a loose sort of narrative, I began to find myself rather starkly engaged by the twists and turns of the ex-wife and her lover's affair, by the dates and the details and the plain vulnerability of their asymmetric relationship, the apologies from her side and the silences from his, the differences in capitalization. She was so lonely, I realized. At the end of the work day, I highlighted two paragraphs that described afternoons when the kids were implicitly unsupervised while the two lovers fucked and afterward I felt physically awful all over my body, in my legs and in my chest and in the pit of my gut, all the bus ride home and all that night at Naphtha's, even as I kissed her clitoris until she came on my tongue. But the following morning, I woke up to my phone's alarm and went straight back to the office nonetheless, and I sat down at my desk and picked up both colors of highlighter and categorized the rest of the correspondence as quickly as I could, returning the sheaf of annotated emails to John Zell's desk before lunchtime; and then that afternoon, I spent long stretches of time staring at the shadows on the walls, imagining the ex-wife sitting on a park bench with her hands pressed flat between her thighs, bent forward either in thought or in the complete absence of thinking, still wearing my mother's sweater but with her hair down now, falling around her shoulders and frazzling out over her ears. Breathing out. I wanted to imagine myself apologizing to her or making some form of anonymous apology, or least some brief encounter where I secretly alerted her to the circling hawks, but for whatever reason I could only picture her alone, isolated and in public, unaware that she was being observed.

I woke up only just before the bus doors opened at my stop, jerked awake by the lurching gears as we pulled to the curb and my neighbor rose from the seat next to me and shuffled toward the door. I cleared my throat and then stood, my body stale with sweat and my mouth covered in dust, it felt like, with a crick in my neck and a crumpled sheet of paper in my left hand that I shoved into my pocket as I strode, running my tongue over my lips and slipping out through the doors just as they began to close. It would have been heart-pumping, leaping out between the squeaking hinges, if my heart rate hadn't been so stubbornly low from my accidental nap; but as it was I had to stand and sway for a moment afterward on the edge of the sidewalk, breathing heavy through the simultaneous exhaustion and adrenaline while I waited for my blood flow to equilibrate. Beside and above me, the streetlamp's halo shone overbright on the top of the bus stop's awning, casting the broken windows of the warehouse adjacent into an even darker shadow than usual. The sky low and moonless behind. I caught a yawn in the back of my throat and swallowed, licking my teeth, and turned to walk the rest of the way to my apartment building.

I need to know that you're someone I can trust, the ex-wife had sent in an email to her lover, and then later on to her ex-husband, and then again, later still, to the head of the PTA.

The street was deserted, but it felt even more deserted when I stepped out and into the middle of the car lane, ambling toward the empty tenement with my hands loose outside my pockets, my fingertips tapping out the rhythm of my steps against my thighs.

The survivor wakes up, and then wakes up again, every ten to fifteen minutes or so, for the first three days after.

During her initial recovery, while she's still in the emergency ward, she never rises from her bed except to stumble to the bathroom and back. She pulls the thin hospital blankets up to her neck and then pushes them back down to cover her feet, tangles them into tight knots around her ankles, shoots upright in her bed and yanks the knots loose, leans back onto the pillows and then turns into the pillows, breathing in the spaces between. Sunlight filters through the gauzy curtains, mornings like midnights, the glow of the streetlamps outside. Doctors appear and fade. Policemen, her sister-in-law. Her husband's mother holds her hand and she vomits, or experiences the sensation of vomiting, even though no liquid extrudes. She falls back asleep, and then asleep again. The deadening weight of exhaustion and then the free fall, lurching back into waking with a sound like a scream.

The hospital releases her on the third morning after and her head lolls against the cab window on her ride home, her eyes opening and closing, and then she collapses onto her living room carpet, her face smushed against the fibers, her dog's tongue licking against her ears. It takes her five cycles of consciousness, lapsing in and out between sleeping and waking, before she finally realizes that the smell around her is dog urine, pungent and drifting from a dark spot in the carpet. She forces herself up and finds the dog's leash hanging from a coat hook by the door.

The first full hours of sleep feel like paradise for as long as she remains unconscious. Then she awakens, breathing, lying lengthwise on her couch with a small pillow wedged between her knees, for some thirteen hours more.

The initial sensation is not one of sense, exactly, in the usual meaning of the word. There is neither touch nor taste to it, nor sight or sound. It's neither peripheral nor focused, visible nor in-, or even within her field of attention. It's more like a shift in the shape of her attention itself. The sunlight or lamplight streaming softly through the front window above the couch, forming a square of illumination along her and beside her, across the cushions and the floor.

I arrived at the restaurant exactly half an hour late, as John Zell had instructed me to, but I still had to wait at an empty table for ten minutes more before the journalist showed. It wouldn't have bothered me nearly so much, I don't think, if I hadn't just received such a strange voicemail from my mother; but as it was, I drank the entirety of my water glass in the first minute and then chewed all of the soft cubes of ice in the next five, trying to decide if I had time to stand up and give her a quick call back or if I'd only have to hang up a few seconds later when the journalist finally got there, and then I felt increasingly frustrated when a few more minutes passed and it was apparent that I could've made the call at that earlier moment but still didn't know if I had time to make it now. Even though my mom wouldn't have been able to answer from the airplane, anyhow, if she'd really been serious—but this only made my frustration more acute. I was glaring in the general direction of the journalist for some time before I finally registered that I was in fact glaring at the journalist himself, standing across the table from me with his hand on the back of the opposite chair and asking if I was Mr. Singer, from MM&Z. I stood and shook his hand. He looked at me for a long time before sitting down.

"Sorry," he said, shaking his head, "but I think—have we met, before?"

I raised my eyebrows, then scootched back in my seat as the waiter appeared and slipped menus down onto the table before us, murmuring about the wine menu and the smaller card with the lunch specials. I couldn't focus on a word he said. The journalist—Mason Kantor, twenty-five, recent graduate of Northwestern with a major in communications and an up-and-coming beat reporter for the *Lake County Herald*—was slighter than he'd seemed in his online photographs, with longer brown curls and far more antsy, crossing his legs twice in the brief duration of the waiter's introduction and then once more after we were left alone, his eyes darting over my face and then over my clothing, my shoes. I knew for a fact that we'd never crossed paths, but I didn't want to spook him with the source of this certainty. He leaned forward onto his elbows and laced his fingers underneath his chin.

"Did you go to Lake Forest High? Class of 2003?" he asked, flirting with a smile. "I think you were in the year below me. I remember you, I think."

"Oh," I said, tilting my head to the side. It was probably just a rather involved way to point out that I looked younger than he did, I decided, and to pretend a closer intimacy than we'd actually earned; I wondered if he was one of those people who kept a bag of conversational tricks, like the men who practiced how best to insult women in order to get them into bed. "No, I don't think so," I said, taking a sip of my refilled water glass.

"Jason. Right? Jason Schultz?"

"Peter."

"Well, sure, but. That's not really your name, though."

I set the water glass down. "Um," I said.

"And you went to art school. Didn't you? At SAIC, right?"

I straightened in my seat, staring across at him and then up at the waiter, who'd appeared in a flash at my elbow to refill my water from a pitcher. "Thanks," I said.

Mason Kantor observed me with the same flirtatious smile, leaning back from his elbows only to ask the waiter for a mimosa, or rather two mimosas, one for us each. I watched him with a frown. When arranging the meeting, I'd made sure to emphasize that the lunch would be on the firm's expense account, but the tone of his voice still pissed me off. "Anyway," he said, crossing his legs again with a different smile than before.

"Anyway." I cleared my throat. "You are the author of the article published in the *Herald* on July 30, 2009, about the presumed death by drowning of Robert Forrester during a deepwater dive in Lake Michigan. Correct?"

"That's correct."

"And you've also been conducting a number of follow-up interviews, related to this event, since."

His face cleared, expressionless, while he considered how to react to this. "I've been trying to make something longform," he said, looking away from me. "Still not sure if it'll hold together on its own, but. Sort of an *Into Thin Air* type of thing." He narrowed his eyes. "Is it the mother who hired you? Is that where this is coming from?"

I glanced to the side, trying to see what he was squinting at, but there were only other couples and groups of three around similar circular tables, drinking and laughing loudly at one another's jokes, silverware scraping against plates. John Zell had cautioned me, multiple times on Friday morning, against a journalist's instinct to turn every contact into a source: speak like a robot, he told me, and if things start to head in a different direction than you want them to, just shut down. "I've been given to understand that you managed, on at least one occasion, to interview the widow, Marta Winters, for your article," I continued.

Mason Kantor glanced back in my direction, and then abruptly switched his smile back on as the waiter reappeared with the drinks. "Thanks," he said, accepting both mimosas and then passing me one. He took a long sip from the flute.

"We're prepared to pay up to five hundred dollars, per item, for any interview transcripts, recordings, documentation, or notes."

He inhaled sharply and then swallowed, licked his lips, set the flute down next to his appetizer plate. "It's the sister, isn't it. The jealous younger sister." He looked up at me with an opaque expression that slowly clarified itself into an open-mouthed smile, his tongue pushing against the inside of his bottom lip. "You are aware, right, that I'm going to have to include this in my piece."

The sides of my neck burned. I looked at him and then looked down at my glass of mimosa, untouched, and carefully picked up the stem between my forefinger and thumb.

~

My mother called me from the tarmac two hours later, just after three o'clock on Sunday afternoon. I hadn't had time to get my car towed and working again so I had to borrow Naphtha's ancient Ford hardtop, with the hood like the swell of a whale and the thick wake of exhaust that slowly filled the cabin whenever you were stopped and so required the windows to be cracked to keep from suffocating. Given my shitty lungs,

I kept them rolled all the way down, the summer humidity baking the inside of the car as I sat in traffic for forty minutes and then slid up to the curb at Terminal 3. My mother sat on the bench, exhausted, while I lumped her bags together in the back seat and then helped her to her feet and into shotgun.

"Sorry, thank you," she said, tipping her head with relief against the headrest. "I've been having a bad sleep week, this last week. The fatigue comes on a little bit randomly. Sometimes."

In her voicemail message from three a.m. the night before, my mother had explained in a breathless ramble that she was getting on a flight that morning to catch a particularly auspicious moment—astrologically and geologically—for a séance with one of the best soothsayers in the world, a once-in-a-lifetime celestial alignment that she'd have to wait eighty years for if she missed this one and so had to go that following evening, in Chicago, with me. When I'd called my father that afternoon, he'd laughed me off and sworn she was at home, probably just with her phone off or in the charger. He'd have her call me after he got back from the grocery store and saw her, he said. I clicked on the left-turn signal and asked her where we were going and she handed me the address of a hotel and then fell promptly asleep against the side of the car, her head knocking regularly against the plastic siding as the hardtop bumped and rolled.

She came to after I pulled into the hotel parking lot, but only fully awakened after we carried her things to the hotel room and she took a cold shower, shrieking as she stepped under the water and then singing as she dried off, first "Danny Boy" and then "White Christmas." She emerged with her hair in a towel and a dress pinned over one shoulder, beaming, her eyes ringed with red.

"So what's wrong, Mom?" I asked, clicking through the channels of the hotel TV.

"You're excited to speak to your brother, too. Admit it. It's going to work, Peter."

I switched to the Weather Channel and my mother walked over and took the remote, turned the TV off, and handed me my shoes. I put them on slowly, tying double knots in each set of laces. I didn't know how to explain to my mother that I both believed in psychics and believed that she was wrong to, at least right now — that she was effectively indulging in self-harm. She led me down the hallway to the hotel exit with one hand on my shoulder and one hand massaging the back of my neck, murmuring about the recent communications she'd been receiving from Henry's spirit through the little dreams she had after she woke up and then briefly fell back asleep in the morning, when the sunlight was resting on her eyelids and the dream-memories didn't fade as quickly afterward. He was a prism of love, she said to me, every time he appeared. She buckled her seat belt and ran her hands over the dashboard with a confused expression, then twisted around in her seat.

"What on *earth* is this car, Peter?" she said, in either marvel or disgust, as if this were the first time she'd ridden in the passenger seat. "This must be from the dark ages. I think I remember this model from my childhood."

"It's possible, honestly. I borrowed it from Nap. You remember Naphtha?"

"That's your girlfriend?"

"No. Although," I said, tipping my head to the side.

"That sounds like a chemical. I think that is a chemical."

"She's not really my girlfriend. At least, I don't think she wants to be."

She looked at me for a long moment, her eyes watering, but more likely as a physical side effect of the sleeplessness than from any sudden overreaction; unless that reaction, too, was a side effect. I watched as she removed a sheaf of printed-out directions from Google Maps and then smoothed them against the glove compartment, pushing the bottom of her palm across each sheet of paper before handing it over. I recognized the name of the shopping mall printed under *Destination* and laughed, and made a comment that she ignored.

"You should be with someone who wants to be with you, Peter," she said seriously, her eyes still glistening at the corners.

～

In truth, though, I could have chosen to see Naphtha a few different times over the last few days if I'd wanted to. She'd sent me two separate text messages during the week before, one late at night but another in the middle of the afternoon, and both of which I let sit for over eight hours before responding with a terse apology and nothing else. The first time I was actually asleep, and didn't feel anything at all after I woke up and saw that I missed it, but the second one I saw and decided immediately to pretend that I hadn't, flipping my cell phone closed and returning to my work with only the faintest glimmer of satisfaction, a smile twitching at the corners of my lips before I cleared my throat and pushed my phone back into my pocket.

I wished that I could have told myself that I was distancing myself from her because she treated me like shit, and in particular because of how relentlessly she'd humiliated me in front of her roommates the last time I was there. But that was belied, frankly, by the months of same or worse that I'd already withstood beforehand, and that had only ever seemed to make me want her more, and more anxiously, before. If any-thing, Naphtha's consistent disdain seemed like the most plausible ex-planation for why I'd stayed in touch with her, however intermittently, in the midst of moving out of my old apartment and cutting ties with every one of my former roommates, and then letting go of my whole extended group of college friends: I could never drive her away because she was always driving me away already. Even the gratification of letting her text messages slide was textured by the fear, if I chose to think about it, that there would be no one else to call anymore, if I also fell out with her.

But for the first time in a long time, that week I chose not to have that thought. Because I was too preoccupied, essentially—because the insides of my eyelids were still imprinted with the afterimage of Eve-lyn Forrester and because I was increasingly fascinated, the more I dug into it, by the mess she'd asked us to simplify. Most of the work that I'd done at Masterson, Masterson & Zell, LLC had had a similar fascinating quality, but of a type that usually left me loathing myself; but with this drowning story, I could hardly tell if the people involved even counted as victims at all. The dead husband seemed like he'd been a classic asshole—Harvard College, McKinsey, two years in Cape Town before moving back to the States, with a set of "adrenaline sports" hobbies that all, it appeared, cost at least twenty thousand dollars to enjoy—but he'd also died doing one of those hobbies, and fairly miserably, so. The rest of the Forrester clan was cast of a similar mold, indisputably part of a larger systemic evil but also, individually, probably fine. Neither innocents nor aggressors, entirely, and certainly not of the pure-fucking-evil type of our usual clients.

And the widow, the accused Marta Winters, was even harder to place. On paper, she was a perfect counterpart for the late Robert Forrester: one year younger, Brown University, Class of 2001, an English major with a Distinguished Senior Thesis on the semiotics of color in Coleridge and Keats, then three years at three different addresses in Manhattan before enrolling in law school at the University of Chicago, where she met her husband at a mutual friend's wedding in her 1L year. But then her husband drowned next to her at the bottom of Lake Michigan, and she left him there—whether or not she caused the drowning herself, she had to have at least seen that he was dying and chosen to leave—and now she had, indeed, successfully withdrawn four hundred thousand dollars from her late husband's apportionment of the Forrester family fund in the last three weeks, in segments of roughly two hundred thousand dollars every ten days since his death. It was too strange to look away from. Evelyn was particularly incensed that Marta had skipped the funeral, three days after Robert's death, claiming to be too grieved to be around other people; but Marta did, in fact, seem to be truly grieving, leaving her house only once in the three days that our detectives had been staked outside and with her garbage composed mostly of used tissues and microwave dinners and hand towels stained with snot and a truly astonishing quantity of candles, mostly little tea candles but also many larger wax bulbs and scented cylinders, alongside empty containers of Xanax and bottles of wine, and occasional pamphlets for support groups and various Gnostic churches around town.

I understood well enough that there'd be a clearer antagonist in the story after our detectives started their campaign of concentrated harassment, trying to make her life discreetly unbearable until she re-lented to Evelyn and went away on her own. But in the meantime, while we were still in the information-gathering phase, paging through the photographs of her scattered garbage and summarizing the debris into bullet points for later reference, I felt only comfortably perplexed, my fantasies revolving evenly between myself and Evelyn Forrester at a bar together, myself and Evelyn Forrester in the back seat of a cab together, and myself and Marta Winters walking past one another on a crowded sidewalk, sharing a lingering glance.

~

My mother pointed me to two parking spots that she well knew I couldn't fit into, I felt, before we found a space much farther off with two cars that I could more comfortably angle the big hardtop between. She claimed complete innocence, but I understood clearly enough that she'd been criticizing my parking ability. I'd always sucked at parallel parking, and she should know better than to set me up with tight-squeeze spots, I told her. She didn't reply but hissed dramatically through her teeth as we walked back over, loudly laboring through the whole quarter mile from the parking spot to the pedestrian mall.

The shop was underneath a florist's, petunias drooping over the edges of the descending staircase and petals pooling around the wel-come mat along with a smattering of brightly colored plastic straws. We went past it two times, going both ways, before we realized finally that the printed-out Google Maps directions were precisely correct, and we stepped down tentatively, my mother and then myself following, waiting to be scolded for trespassing by an employee of the flower shop. But at the bottom of the stairs, the sign was in fact plainly legible: JESSICA APOTHE-CARY AND FORTUNE, carved artfully into a wooden board and hanging from two rusting chains above the doorway, perfectly motionless in this windless space beneath the aboveground breeze. My mother gripped my hand and beamed, the same smile she'd worn after coming out of her ice-cold shower that afternoon, and then removed a small vial of liquid from her purse, dropped it on the ground, and crushed it under her heel.

"Post hoc," she said, her eyes closed and her fingers still gripped tighter around mine, as a powerful aroma of soap lifted up from the ground.

I opened my mouth to speak at the same time that a dark-haired woman opened the door from the inside and my mother took a sharp inhale, appreciating. I paused, the tip of my tongue perched against my teeth. The silence seemed portentous until my cell phone started to buzz in my pants pocket.

I waved for them to go ahead when I saw it was from my boss, and I stepped back up the stairwell while my mother and the medium disappeared together through the darkened door.

"Where the *fuck* are you?" John Zell's voice blared from the speaker, even before I'd lifted the phone all the way up to my ear.

I straightened, blood draining from my face and from my stomach, and instinctively took a step back up toward the ground level. I began to stammer out a reply but John Zell was only interested in shouting me down, it seemed, for not heading straight back to the office after my Sunday lunch with the journalist, his voice breaking out at such a pitch that it fuzzed into static in the earpiece, and I had to keep the phone held out a few inches, my whole body twisted into a wince, while he both made clear that I was fired and insisted that I come into the office even earlier than usual this week, six thirty at the latest, every single fucking day.

Some ten feet above me, the bells attached to the florist's door tinkled as a customer either came or went, the sounds of people talking as they walked along the road above. I watched the movement of their shadows with my heart pounding in my ears. A car honked and the wind scraped a medley of plastic trash along the pavement, pushing the plastic top of a coffee cup to the edge of the stairs and then over. I blinked as it rolled down.

I lifted the phone back to my ear after the noise had died down only to realize, belatedly, that John Zell had already hung up. I looked at the screen for a long moment, at the duration of the call blinking and then disappearing into my phone's usual background, a grainy photograph of the Andes, my skin tingling along the backs of my arms.

I pushed my cell phone back into my pocket, leaned my shoulder into the doorway, and followed my mother inside.

~

The smell of the basement room was the most arresting, in retrospect, but it didn't come upon me until later, because my mother's cloud of soap was still strong enough in my nostrils when I entered that I couldn't parse anything else. The walls and ceiling were all covered by sheets and Persian carpets, hanging loose and low and coloring the lights arranged behind them so that the room had the feeling of a child's clubhouse with a colored disco ball, with glass beads twinkling and metal gems sparkling in the soft yellows and reds and dappling a circle of pillows on the floor and a low table rimmed with tea candles, a breadboard leaning against its legs. And a strange churn of sounds, too, that I deciphered at roughly the same rate that the smell began to finally insinuate itself into my consciousness: the shifting rhythm of straw and grains and fur and feathers, the distinct odor of feces, the squeaking of wheels. The medium smiled and reached up from her pillow to hand me a stick of incense, the thin stream of smoke rising from the point of ember at the end, and motioned for me to take the pillow next to my right foot. I held the stick in front of my mouth as I eased down, inhaling.

"As I was just telling your mother," she said, twisting her smile into a frown, "I am the Lady Jessica. There are few rules to this space, but they are important, and I require them observed: You must be quiet when I ask you to be quiet, and you must take your energy with you when you leave. You agree?"

My mother recrossed her legs underneath her, shifted her pillow forward and then back. "We agree," she said, distracted.

"I agree," I confirmed.

"Good. You came at the right time. Your mother called me last night and it was important, because it was the right time." She lit another four incense sticks and placed them into invisible holders on each corner of the small table, then waved her hands to waft the smoke around. "Do you know what you're looking for?"

My mother looked at the Lady Jessica and then at the sheet-covered walls, finally noticing the squeaking. "We need your help making contact with my eldest. Henry. I need to speak with him." She pinched the tip of her nose and then twisted her nostrils delicately to the side, something she'd always tried to train Henry and me to do instead of scratching. "He needs to tell me something, I mean."

The Lady nodded. She was wearing an open crimson blouse with sequins in each of the buttonholes and tiny black glasses perched on the very end of her nose, attached on either end to a drooping gold chain, the metal glinting bright along the sides of her cropped black hair. She leaned backward and pulled back a colored sheet to reveal a glass cage roiling with rabbits, white and gray, tucked neatly into a roughly two-foot space between the hanging sheet and the wall, pushing their pink noses at her hands as she unbuckled the mesh top. She lifted a smaller rabbit out by the scruff of its neck and then held it tightly underneath her elbow as she clamped the lid of the glass cage back in place. "Tell me about your son," she said.

My mother crinkled her eyes at the rabbit, her mouth twitching toward a smile. The medium paused for a moment and then passed it over to her, watching the animal carefully through her tiny black glasses as it wriggled into my mother's palms.

"Oh, isn't that," my mother said, arranging the bunny with some difficulty into a football carry and then petting its ears roughly with her free hand. "Henry was a suicide," she said, tilting her head far forward to try and look the rabbit in the eye as it squirmed. "He was twisted into a knot, do you know what I mean? All his life. But he just needed to—"

"This is a recent death?"

My mother lifted her head and the rabbit pounced forward, bounding off my mother's chest with a swift kick and only barely caught between her palms in time; and even then, it twisted around and gave her a pair of deep scratches along her right forearm. The Lady Jessica took it back quickly, calmly, without asking and without acknowledging my mother's whimpered thanks. In the Lady's arms, the animal's gray fur seemed to turn slightly pinker in the light, its whiskers glimmering.

"A little less than a year ago," my mother said, now extremely flustered, brushing her hands off on her pants. "He died, I mean. But his spirit has remained. It's been causing my husband considerable difficulty."

The Lady Jessica nodded. She placed the rabbit on the breadboard and then took out a band, a stretchy sort of white elastic, and fit it around the rabbit's midriff so that it was strapped quite tightly to the wooden surface. "Henry Singer," she said.

"That's right," my mother said, in the same moment that the Lady Jessica took out a pocketknife and then plunged it into the center of the rabbit's chest. "Oh, my *God*."

The smell of fear wasn't something I'd ever identified separately from other smells, previously, but sitting in a room filled with caged mice and caged rabbits in the moment when another rabbit was disemboweled generated a sudden choke of scent that was unmistakable: a hard manure tang—but mixed with something else, something almost like a soda's fake grape flavoring—that briefly overpowered my nostrils and set my eyes wide, even with the thread of incense before my nose. The Lady Jessica pulled the pocketknife down the center of the rabbit like a zipper, opening its gut, then reached in and pulled out a fistful of intestine and spread it, like she was wiping her fingers, across the remaining parts of the breadboard. The disemboweled animal squirmed, its individual squeaking lost in the overpowering cacophony of squeaking around us. Both my mother and I seemed to be frozen in our seats. My whole body tingled, hairs vibrating on my skin.

"Henry Singer," the Lady Jessica said again, still nodding.

I hadn't actually ignored the Lady Jessica during my first few minutes in the basement room, but nonetheless I had the feeling that I was only seeing her for the first time now, in this moment, her pockmarked face wrinkled in concentration and her thin nose flared and her fingers pushing through the gore on the breadboard as though searching for something, blood smearing up her arm and along her red sleeve. In all the hubbub of my mother's antics and then John Zell's phone call, I hadn't taken proper note of the steady gleam in her eyes, I decided, or the small bells that she wore attached to the ends of her pants and that now tinkled, almost inaudible under the animals' increasing noises of panic, as she shifted her legs into a kneeling position. My mother gripped my shoulder with both hands, leaning hard.

"Henry Singer," the Lady said for a third time, separating a single thread of intestine from the mass and setting it to one side. "He was hanged."

My mother sniffed sharply, astonished, tears standing out in her eyes. "Yes."

"Hung himself."

"That's—yes."

"You were not the one, though. You did not recover him."

My mother was breathing like the animals around us now, it seemed to me, her chest rising and falling and her eyes sparkling, her mouth wide. I'd felt something similar before, myself; the first time I encountered a psychic who told me the truth, I felt abruptly naked, defenseless against their judgment in either direction. But this woman frightened me in a different way this time. "His father," my mother said, and then stopped to swallow, clear her throat. Her hands were shaking, I noticed. "His father found him, afterward."

The Lady Jessica took a deep breath. The rabbit on the breadboard did not seem to be alive in its eyes but its legs continued twitching, shivering side to side and one of them kicking, an irregular rhythm against the wood and rattling, slightly, the low table's legs.

"You can call to him," my mother whispered, helpless with anticipation. "Henry. You know how to, I mean."

"Sorry, can you," I interrupted. "That bunny is still alive, and it's really—it's really bothering me. Can't you, just?"

"Quiet, please." She rolled her head toward her right shoulder, as though peering around the edge of one of the rabbit's exposed hip bones. "He felt unloved," she said.

My mother's breath choked in her throat. "Oh, no," she said, shaking her head slowly, then quickly. "No. That's not—"

"Okay," I said, holding a hand out. "Let's slow this down."

"He was loved. You—and he knew that. You know? He was. He is loved."

45

The Lady Jessica looked at each of us in either eye, staring directly into my right eye and then my left and then my mother's, one after the other, until we both stopped trying to speak. The terrified pealing of the caged animals around us had not actually receded but it had begun to fade in my consciousness nonetheless, an intensely anxious white noise underneath the pounding of my heartbeat in my neck, the continued dryness of my tongue in my mouth. The Lady Jessica took another deep breath and motioned for us to do the same. My mother rubbed her eye with the back of her wrist.

"I do not think this is going to work," the Lady said, twisting her frown back into a regretful grimace. "I am sorry."

"Oh, no, no," my mother said, blanching. "We didn't mean, I was only—"

"No." She held up a hand.

"—but I was just—"

"It is not going to work, because Henry Singer," she said.

I narrowed my eyes. I had hated this woman, I was only then beginning to realize, from the first moment that my sinuses had cleared.

"Oh," my mother said.

"I am not receiving, here, an invitation," the Lady Jessica continued, as if regretfully, gesturing at the bloodied mess on the breadboard, the disemboweled rabbit that had only then stopped twitching. "I have called to Henry Singer, and I have found the Henry Singer who died by hanging at twenty-six years old, and was found by the father, in a California garage. But I have not felt the opening from the other end, from him." She took another breath, resigned. "Henry Singer has not opened himself to this space."

My mother ran her hands through her hair and then pulled them back forward, pushing the strands of her hair now down and around her face.

"Fuck you," I said.

Both women sniffed, turning to look at me. But I couldn't see anything, it felt like, other than the head of the dead rabbit on the table between us, its empty eyes staring out at the space behind the hanging bedsheet where it had lived the last of its brief, terrified life.

"Henry doesn't want to talk to us? That's really your reason?"

"Peter." My mom dug her fingers into my biceps through my shirt's cloth.

"My mother just lost a child, and you're full of *shit*, so you tell her that her kid feels unloved and doesn't want to talk to her. That's your reason why."

I could feel the Lady Jessica staring evenly at my right eye, and then my left, but I refused to meet her gaze.

"It's honestly." I barked out a harsh laugh. "It's honestly pretty plausible, though. You know? It does sound like something he would do." I licked my lips and looked up at the hanging sheets, at the orbs of yellow and red that showed where the lightbulbs were burning just behind them. "Fuck you, too, Henry."

At that moment, the lights flickered, the bulbs going on and off above and from every side. I stood so quickly that I banged my head against the ceiling, shouting that the medium had pressed a button to make the lights flash to try and scare us, but by then my mother had already started screaming so loudly that no one could hear even their own voices, and she kept screaming until I finally wrapped her in my arms and lifted her through the door and back outside.

～

My mother and I argued for a long time on the drive back about when exactly the rabbit had begun to smell so incredibly bad. The Lady Jessica, true to her word, had made us take our bad energy with us, thrusting a plastic bag with the rabbit's bloody carcass into my mother's hand just before she slammed the door, and it was only then that we noticed the stench—which, my mother decided, was proof that it hadn't smelled like a days-old rotting corpse until after I'd cursed at Henry and he'd invested the rabbit with the smell of his own decomposed body in order to revenge himself upon us. Or, I repeated, we hadn't noticed the smell until we were out of that noxious basement room, and it was the only thing that stank so strongly outside. But we were just shouting past each other at that point. I dropped her off at a hardware store near her hotel so that she could buy a shovel to bury the creature and then I sat in the parking lot for a long time, my shoulders hunched and breathing through an open mouth, before I switched the ignition back on and took the car back to Naphtha's.

After I parked and came in to drop off the keys, Nap greeted me from the warehouse's spavined couch with a wolfish smile, calling me a name without looking up from her ancient Game Boy Color; but then she saw how spitting mad I was, and she set aside the Game Boy and sat up straight. I paced back and forth on the floor in front of her with my hands gripping the air, every muscle in my fingers flexed with intention as I gestured, describing my mother's decision to visit and then the Lady Jessica's basement and the cages of animals, the smells and the squeak-ings, the way she smeared the breadboard with gore, the little bells around her ankles. Naphtha was entranced, but in exactly the wrong way. Byron took a break from making pasta in the kitchen/general-area-near-the-stove and joined her on the couch to listen.

"But that's so fucking incredible, though," Naphtha finally interrupted, her eyes wide with wonder. "What a piece, you know? I want to see this performance."

"It was fucking evil, Nap," I said, shaking my head. "This woman, she's — to the extent that she's able to actually guess, essentially, about my brother's suicide — there's a responsibility, you know? That comes with that. With being so convincing, I mean. She can't just do this to people. My mom is fucking falling apart at the seams already. Her kid fucking died, less than ten months ago. And I don't know if she's ever going to recover from this feeling, now that my brother also fucking hates us from the afterlife. It's just such a phenomenally shitty thing to do to someone."

"That sucks," Byron said, nodding. "Are you okay, though?"

"Well, sure, but," Naphtha continued, wagging her head from side to side, "just the performance aspect, though, I mean. The fucking *sooth-saying.* She straight-up gutted a bunny on a breadboard and then *saw the truth in its intestines?* That's legitimately incredible. Like a moment of pure religion. Magic exists and God is real, and I can find Him in this bunny's guts." She threw her head back in a laugh, the couch creaking in distress underneath her as her weight shifted forward and then back. "Hell, fucking, *yes.*"

I clenched my teeth. "It's honestly illegal, I think," I said, blinking. "You can't just torture rabbits alive like that."

"Cruelty to animals," Byron agreed.

"You guys can't be serious, though." She turned to look between me and Byron and then back again, incredulous. "This is, like, looking at a Jackson Pollock and feeling bad for the punctured paint can." She threw her hands up in the air. "This is art! That was real, living-and-breathing art that you just experienced, P! I'm sorry that it was so fucking awful for your mom, but—"

"Nap," Byron said, noticing.

She looked again between the two of us, and then back at me. But I only shook my head and lowered myself, still shaking, to the ground. I covered my face with my hands.

"Oh, shit," Naphtha said, inching toward me in her seat. "I'm sorry, P. I was only—"

I sank my head as far as it would go between my knees, my arms entirely folded over the back of my head, either to contain or to conceal my ragged breathing. Naphtha leaned forward and put her hand on my shoulder. I wanted to shrug her off, but I just didn't seem to have the energy.

Byron stood and went to the other end of the room and then came back fifteen minutes or so later to where Naphtha and I were then lying side by side on the floor, staring up at the ceiling in silence, and placed a pot of macaroni and cheese down beside us, along with two forks.

INTERVIEWER: But you described the hobby as--

MARTA WINTERS: It was his hobby. All our shared hobbies, really,
                 were his.

INTERVIEWER: All of them?

MARTA WINTERS: It was always a fault line between us. He always in-
                 sisted that we should be perfectly content to do things
                 separately. You know the saying? "Before you can be
                 with others, first learn to be alone." I want to say it's
                 Arendt. Hannah Arendt? Do you know?

INTERVIEWER: The philosopher?

MARTA WINTERS: Maybe not. He took it as a principle. But in practice
                 all it meant was if I wanted to do things together,
                 then I had to agree to do what he would have done
                 anyhow. If I wanted him to do something with me that
                 only I wanted to do, it became this, like I didn't know
                 how to be alone. Like wanting to do things together
                 just for the sake of doing things together, it didn't
                 even make sense to him. Or it violated his principle.
                 Do you know what I mean? He wanted to do his things
                 and wanted me to be happy doing mine without him.
                 And if I wanted to have us-two-together things, then
                 I was welcome to join his. He was very sensitive about
                 it, sometimes.

INTERVIEWER: And the adventure sports, the--

MARTA WINTERS: Was his. All of it. It was all his.

John Zell called me into his office first thing after he arrived on Monday morning, five after eight. I went in with his breakfast sandwich and a tray of four coffees, both his usual go-to and his sometimes-favorites, just in case, stepping through the door and across the long office and then setting the tray on the edge of his desk while he squinted intently at his massive computer monitor, as if he were already concentrating too intently to make time for me in this second or third minute of his morning. Only after I withdrew to the chair across, perched on the very edge of the seat with a legal pad and pen on my knee, did he finally glance at the tray. He slid over in his office chair and took a sip of the nearest cup, grimacing, then looked down his nose at where I was sitting.

"So," he said, his chest expanding as he drew himself to a height in his chair. "Peter. You do still work here, after all."

I pressed my lips together and lifted them, an imitation of a smile, halfway up my cheek.

"Did you know that I was here yesterday?" He took another sip of his coffee and then held it against his chest, the steam rising under his chin. "At the office. I came in."

During this first part of the morning, John Zell always looked a little like a compressed version of his normal self. Never a particularly tall or physically imposing man, he seemed at once smaller and paler before he'd taken his second sip of coffee, his jacket loose and rumpled around his shoulders and his skin not quite fitting over his face, wrinkles around his nostrils and surrounding his mouth and his eyelids lower, it seemed, over his gray eyes. Only his dark hair, gelled into a receding swoop from his forehead and over his ears, was the same as ever. But he always worked hard to make up for this deflation with an extra edge to his usual viciousness: lips curled back from his teeth as he detailed the abject humiliation he'd endured at my hands the day before, after he found himself stood up by his own useless fucking underling and left to sweat in the empty office for two hours and he slammed the desk with the flat of his palm, leaning toward me with his teeth bared, as though to make sure that I could smell the stale curdle of his breath.

"I'm not going to let you fuck up this case on me, Singer," he said, exhaling into my face. "I'm not going to let it happen. If I have to breathe down your fucking neck every single day of this week. Do you know how many women there are like Evelyn Forrester? In Chicago, I mean?" He leaned back, shaking his head as he took another sip of coffee, this time from a different cup than before. "In New York, sure. London, maybe. But Chicago? Chicago, Illinois?" He barked out a single harsh laugh, unwrapping his bacon-egg-and-cheese.

I looked down at the legal pad in my lap and then back up at his desk, at the strings of melted American still attached to the paper wrapper as he leaned forward into his first bite. "I guess, not many," I ventured quietly.

John snorted, chewing. "None," he said through his mouthful, holding up his forefinger and thumb connected into a zero sign. "Fucking none. Believe me, I'd know." He swallowed and shook his head again, peering up at the sunlight coming through the windows, lamenting this injustice from on high. "Evelyn, even—I'd bet you a million dollars that she has a place in Manhattan. I'd bet you a million bucks she was just stopping here for her brother's funeral, and only stuck around to get the murderer's hands out of the family cookie jar. A million dollars, I mean it. At least a pied-à-terre. I'll even give you two-to-one odds." I turned to look over my shoulder at a knock on the door and he slapped his hand on the table again, a loud crack, and then flapped his wrist in pain. "Three-to-one. But you still won't take it, right? Because you know that I'm right."

I started nodding and he snorted again, disgusted. Willa opened the door and stuck her head in the gap, asking about some client on line one, and without a blink of hesitation John picked up one of the extra cups of coffee and flung it at her, the liquid spraying over the carpet—I jerked to the side just in time—before it splattered on the wall beside the doorframe. Willa disappeared, the door already slammed shut by the time John started shouting after her to get someone in to clean it up.

"*Fuck*," he swore, sliding his chair away from the sudden splash of spilled coffee on his desktop. He gestured urgently at my legal pad and I tore off two sheets of paper and he snatched them out of my hand, wiping ineffectually against the spreading puddle on the surface. "I want to know where the fucking money is going, Pete. This Marta woman. No one takes out four hundred thousand dollars in twenty days just to look at it. We find the money, we find our opening." He managed to establish a rough boundary to the spill with the crumpled paper, but then the sheets were shortly soaked through and began seeping coffee themselves. I tore off four more sheets and held them out. He leaned forward and grabbed my whole legal pad. "You got the interview transcripts? There wasn't anything in those?"

"Oh," I said, watching him push the yellow-lined paper at the spreading liquid. I cleared my throat. "Not really. They just talk about her husband, mostly."

"Bullshit."

I bit my lip, wincing. "It's not a very directed conversation. Some stuff about death, life, religion. There's a pretty long part of it where it sounds like she's just crying, on the tape."

"*Bull*shit. Wait." He nodded and then shook his head. "Weren't there some church pamphlets? In her trash?"

"Oh," I said, turning my head to the side.

"That's it. That's fucking it." Holding a mass of soggy sheets far out in front of him so that the drippings landed on the carpet between his legs, John Zell carefully angled his wheeled chair over to the garbage can and then dumped them in. "There's got to be some shill behind this. Some pastor. Don't you think? Bleeding her. Or it's related, somehow." He kicked off the wall to roll back over to his computer and then tore off a fresh handful of papers, laying them flat now to soak up the spill directly. "I want you to go to ground on this, Peter. No more desk work. See if there are any old Gothics nearby, talk to the neighbors, see where they go on Sundays, see if they won't say more to a fresh-faced kid. Figure out where two plus two aren't making four."

He held out a sopping-wet handful of paper sheets and I looked at them for a moment before reaching out and accepting them into my hands, holding them dripping above the carpet. John ticked his head to the side and I stood and carried them over to the garbage bin. "You want me to go with the Garys?" I asked, dropping the wet bundle on top of the last.

He passed me another handful of soaked pages and then turned back, with considerable relish, to his breakfast sandwich. "We're going to destroy this woman, Peter," he said, smelling the cheese and bacon in his hands, his forehead wrinkled but his eyes wide. "Burn the village, kill the children, salt the fucking earth. *Carthago delenda est.* And then, who knows." He took a bite and then swallowed without chewing at all. "Maybe I'll even let you keep your job."

$$\sim$$

At that time, at the start of my third month at Masterson, Masterson & Zell, LLC, I'd only ever interacted with our firm's on-call private detectives, Gary Weingarten and Gary Schnell, in very particular and prescribed circumstances: namely, when they arrived at our strip mall office with "case materials," usually printed photos in a manila envelope or something less savory in a black plastic bag, and dumped them on the floor outside my door. We'd been introduced once, technically speaking, but neither Gary had seemed to accept the introduction, so I wasn't sure if they actually had any idea who I was; Willa had spoken their names aloud to me one morning in my first week and pointed at their heads in turn as they strode past on their way to one of the Mastersons' offices, but they'd barely glanced in my direction and I'd been too distracted by the spattering of dried mud all over their pants and their boots, their general affect of NFL linebackers on their way back to the sideline after successfully flattening someone much smaller to the ground. Apparently, they weren't actually so interchangeable—Gary Schnell was a sixty-one-year-old ex-cop from the Cook County PD, Willa explained to me, while Gary Weingarten was only in his forties, having served ten years or so in the U.S. Navy before taking on a stint as a bouncer and then as a private bodyguard before this—but they both gave me the exact same feeling whenever I found myself in the room with them, and despite the obvious age and size differences, I always had trouble finally telling them apart.

"You're the guy?" either Gary Weingarten or Gary Schnell said to me, leaning over his elbow in the passenger seat of their remodeled police van, peering down at where I was sitting on the curb.

"Peter," I said, rising to my feet. I'd been waiting for them outside our strip mall office for about an hour and forty minutes by then and my hamstrings twinged as I stood, my tendons catching somewhere just beneath my right knee. I shook my leg out for a moment before stepping gingerly over to the window, pulling the straps of my backpack tighter over my shoulders as I walked. But before I could approach, either Weingarten or Schnell pushed open the passenger door and hopped out and past me, his boots crunching on something that appeared to be stuck to the bottoms of his soles as he led me around to the back and then threw open the rear doors and motioned for me to climb inside. I took a step back and blinked into the interior dimness, the blinking lights on the black metal boxes and the fuzzy static on the little screens, the low bench against the van's right wall.

"John didn't mention, huh," Gary observed, studying my expression.

I lifted my lips up my cheek in a half smile, trying to decide if this meant that the Garys and I might be on the same team against John Zell, or if this was a test to see if I'd blame the boss by default. I slid my backpack onto the corrugated floor and then turned and hefted myself up into a seat on the ledge, then pivoted my hips to lift my legs in after. "He gave me the general idea," I hedged.

Gary snorted. "On the way," he said, slamming one door shut beside me, "we'll fill each other in." I crab-walked backward up onto the bench by the right side just before he slammed the second door shut and I was briefly plunged into a cave-like darkness, with only the red and green and blue blinking bulbs and a shaft of yellow light from a small interior window to the cab, before two overhead fluorescent tubes flickered on along either side and the car started, the passenger door slammed shut up front, and I was lurched into motion as the van began to move.

I shielded my eyes with one arm while I gripped the edge of the seat with another. A knuckle rapped on the little window from the cab and I uncovered my eyes and, with some difficulty, slid closer on the bench. Then the knuckle rapped again, and I saw that the latch was on this side. I undid the catch and slid the plastic panel over.

"So, new guy," a surprisingly high-pitched voice called out from the driver's side, from a face I could only see a small piece of in the rear-view mirror. "We hear you got first listen on the Kantor interview. That right? What do you think — did she kill the husband, after all?"

I squinted in the sunlight, taken aback by both the brightness and by the driver's light, friendly tone, entirely unexpected after my never-ending morning. Through the small gap, I could see easily through the windshield to the street unfurling beneath us, the trees along the sidewalks and the shadows beneath the leaves, disappearing.

"I don't really know if there's that much of a difference either way, to be honest," I replied, gripping the bottom of the little window into the cab with all the fingers on my right hand, just barely managing to keep my balance as the van bounced. "You know what I mean? No matter what happened when they both ran out of air, she still left him down there."

The driver looked at me directly, the rectangular reflection of his eyes in the rearview mirror staring straight into mine as the van slowed toward a red light. His expression was too incomplete to read. "There's a difference," he said.

"This interview," the larger Gary asked from the passenger seat, leaning forward into view without taking his eyes from the road. "You have the recording with you?"

⌁

Earlier that morning, I'd spent a long time listening to the interview on my headphones, first on my bus ride to work and then once more after I arrived, in the hour and a half before the rest of the office got there. I'd known well enough that I didn't actually have to be there so early, despite John Zell's insistence over the phone the day before, but after I found myself awake before sunrise anyhow — breathing, my eyes and mouth open, in that towering darkness beneath Naphtha's warehouse ceiling — it had felt reassuring to have a motion to go through, a reason for rising and gathering my things from the dark floor beside her mattress and then catching the bus just as the black sky was washing out into gray, the glow of the other cars' headlights slowly fading as the rest of the world became already visible around. I'd sat in the window seat farthest to the front on both the first leg of my trip and after my transfer, leaning the top of my head against the cool glass while I stared out at the sliding city and listened to the burned CD audio, the steady murmur of the journalist's and then Marta's voice over and underneath the rumblings of the engine and the regular bumps and jitters of the bus along the road. Chicago always felt like more of a home to me when there was no one at all on the sidewalks. I got off the bus at my stop and took my time walking along the side of the highway, kicking a stone with my shoe as I listened to Mason Kantor's voice lilting upward at the end of each question, the soft friction of Marta Winters shifting in her seat next to the microphone, and then I arrived at the strip mall office and fitted my key into the lock. At that point, I'd already seen enough photographs of Marta Winters that the image of her shouldn't have been at all malleable in my mind — I knew that she was a brunette with somewhat mousy hair, frazzled at the sides except in the most formal of settings, when she managed to tame it into a wavy mane that nonetheless still curled out around her neck and her shoulders; I knew that she had green eyes and wore contact lenses, that she was five foot three and favored blue overalls or white pantsuits, that she wore high-heeled boots in university and platform shoes in law school and, most recently, banana-shaped slippers around the house; I knew that she had freckles across her nose and a toothy smile in her driver's license photo — but at the same time, when I heard her voice in my ears, I couldn't seem to keep any of those details in my mind. Swiveling back and forth in the chair in my windowless back room, listening to the whole conversation for the second time that morning, I'd found that I was imagining someone, instead, who seemed both smaller and larger, with nervous movements but a steady gaze, who caught your eye and held it. Someone who watched you while you spoke, as if understanding, but looked away as soon as she noticed that you'd noticed her staring. Someone acutely observant, who acutely disliked being observed.

After I located the CD in the back of the van, though, and then passed it through the cab window to the Gary sitting in the passenger seat, it was only the first Marta, the mousy woman from the photographs, who came through the speakers. We listened in silence while driver-Gary navigated us to I-94 and then merged into traffic, the turn signal clicking underneath the voices and then the thrum of the engine as he accelerated, all the machinery in the back clattering as we bumped and bumbled along the highway's right lane. I felt extremely uncomfortable, listening to the tape with these two men who I was increasingly leery of, in large part because I felt at least as scummy as they were, having already listened through twice on my own. But the Garys gave no hint of any feeling in either direction. Marta was just beginning her long, meandering discussion on the inconsistency of memory when she broke down for the first time into crying, heavy breathing and heaving sniffs, and passenger-Gary pushed the FM button to switch back to the radio.

"Well," the Gary in the driver's seat said, ticking his head from side to side over the abrupt twanging of the country station. "Maybe this will be easy-peasy, then. She's already falling apart on her own."

"You think this is enough?" the other Gary asked, still leaning just out of my view.

"I didn't say that. This journalist kid knows who we are. And I don't know if there's anything really juicy here, anyway, to get a tabloid to bite." He turned his reflected stare again in my direction, an eyebrow raised. "What do you think, new guy?"

I sat up straighter, watching the cars slide together in my vision as the van pivoted onto the nearest exit ramp. "Oh," I said, glancing at his hand turning the steering wheel. "About tabloids?"

"About what this journalist would do, if we used this recording to blackmail the widow over taking her story to the press. Threaten to make her famous across the state of Illinois for murdering her husband

and making off with the cash, unless she plays ball." He eased down the highway ramp and onto Fullerton, approaching the Chicago River from the west. "She seems broken enough already on the tape, frankly. She might not call the bluff."

"Well, but what about," I said, watching the gray-blue water glimmering in the high noon sunlight. My tongue felt too large to form syllables. "I doubt the client would like it, you know? The Forrester family, being part of a tabloid story. Right?"

The Gary in the passenger seat sniffed, shifting his head to the side. "I still say we break in. Make her know she's not safe."

Driver-Gary barked out another laugh, loud and booming, at the same time that the country song on the radio crescendoed into a honky-tonk solo. "You always want to break into people's houses," he said, grinning.

"Tell her we'll tie her to the bed and burn the fucking house down with her inside if she doesn't do what we say," the other Gary clarified.

The driver laughed again, quieter this time, glancing over his shoulder to smile at me. The wrinkles around his eyes were kindly, like a grandfather's. I noticed only belatedly that my fingertips were gripping the edge of the interior cab window so tightly that they were white underneath the nails.

"Or, this nice young man will get the neighbors to trust him, help us find the smoking gun, and we'll get to do it the easy way," the driver said, his smile widening as he turned back forward. "You have any experience knocking on doors?"

~

I stood on the sidewalk for a long time, my hands loose at my sides and my eyes squinting underneath the sun, after the Garys dropped me off at the corner of Marta Winters's neighborhood in Lincoln Park. My mouth was still dry, but it seemed like it had been dry for days at that point and I didn't pay it much attention, watching the old police van disappear around the corner and then watching the other cars driving through the intersection afterward, the pedestrians walking their dogs in the tree-dappled sunlight, the traffic light changing from red to green and then back to red again. I felt the urgent need to hide but I didn't know where, or how. I understood perfectly that I had no excuse to be so shaken, hearing the Garys talk about what they were planning to do to Marta Winters; I'd known for a long time what Masterson, Masterson & Zell, LLC really was, and what we did to people. But it had felt different, all the same — strikingly different — to ride in a car with the two men who actually did it, and to hear them actually talk about doing it. It wasn't so much that I'd imagined anything else as that I hadn't really imagined anything at all when it came the final details of execution, and when I was in the car with them, listening to their descriptions in those easy tones, with the practiced casualness of the regular violence, it suddenly became real to me, concrete and visual, for the very first time. And it made me want to disappear. I couldn't stop imagining the thick-necked passenger-seat Gary breaking into my parents' home and terrorizing them, stealing their documents and threatening to burn them alive, and then the older driver's-seat Gary barking out a loud laugh while he blackmailed them into silence afterward, and I felt both intensely resentful and intensely anxious, hating them and hating myself in almost equal measure, unsafe on the sidewalk and unable to escape, now, from this day that I'd trapped myself inside. Before dropping me off they'd given me a fake police badge and an earful of advice for how to be a good cop at the door, how to get strangers to open up off-the-cuff, and in the echoing silence of my mind as I stood on that street corner I heard their words repeated, sinister and bleating, reminding me to look people in the eye and keep looking even after they looked away and to ask for a glass of water right away in order to accustom the person to saying "Yes" from the start. I squeezed my eyes shut and opened them. The light changed again and I turned and stepped back from the middle of the sidewalk to make room in advance for a new cluster of pedestrians, crossing after patiently waiting for the light on the other side, to walk past.

I recognized her in the crowd at once, but it took another moment before I accepted this recognition as possible, let alone correct. Sandwiched awkwardly between a pair of shining-haired businessmen behind and an older couple pushing a double stroller in front, but unmistakable even with her frizzled hair mostly covered by a broad straw sun hat, Marta Winters accelerated and then slowed down twice as she crossed the road, looking for a way around the slower walkers. She stalled as the businessmen pushed past both her and the family together, almost bumping into one group and then the other before she finally stepped all the way to the side, directly in front of me on the sidewalk, to let the aggressive men go on ahead; her straw hat tipping back and falling behind, pulling tight on the cord around her neck. She looked nothing like her photographs. There were dark bags underneath her eyes but she didn't seem tired, her eyes searching as she took another step to the side. I only realized that I was staring when she glanced at me and I looked, too quickly, down—but then I glanced back up, still too quickly, and saw her look away. She was wearing a black messenger bag and a dark dress, shapeless and blue, that flowed around her knees as she stepped back toward the larger group of pedestrians. My tongue surged at the back of my throat.

"Um," I said, reaching a hand up in an ambiguous gesture, something between a raised finger and a wave.

But Marta Winters made no sign of hearing except to widen her eyes and take another quick step away, pulling her straw hat back down over her hair as she moved on.

I stepped back, burning. The flow of pedestrians quickly ebbed into just a single old man in a dirty checkered suit, working his way past with a cane. I dropped my hand back down to my side and tapped my thigh with my fingertips, pulled my phone out of my pocket and flipped it open and closed and then pushed it back into my pocket, ran my hand through my hair. The old man stopped in front of me and asked if I could spare any change and I took out my wallet and gave him a ten. He pulled his head back into his shoulders and looked me in the eye before saying "Thanks," but took himself quickly away after he noticed my expression. The sunlight was hot on the back of my neck, hot on the backs of my arms. I stepped off the curb to look down the street where Marta Winters had gone and then sat down on the edge of the sidewalk, pushing at my temples with my palms, feeling the heat and the pressure and hearing the words of the Garys again in my ears, *burn the fucking house down with her inside.* I rocked backward and then forward, pressing my chest into my knees, gazing always in the direction where Marta Winters had just disappeared; imagining myself standing and striding after her, the set of my jaw and the glare of the sunlight as I went to warn her; imagining myself standing at her front door.

～

There's a story my mom likes to tell from my childhood, that I can't tell anymore if I actually remember myself or if I only remember her telling of it, about when I was seven years old, or thereabouts, and tried to let God decide whether I should go into the TV room or the kitchen. At that age, I had a particularly easy time understanding God as an immanent presence—my father had explained to me that God was everywhere and in everything, present even in the air we breathe—and when I looked at the two adjacent doorways, each about ten feet in front of me in the hallway, I felt Him implicitly close, surrounding me like an ocean around a fish, and it occurred to me that I could simply yield this decision over to Him. Looking at the parallel doorways of the kitchen and the TV room, at the finished brown floorboards of the kitchen shining yellow underneath the overhead lights and then the matte green of the carpet in the TV room where my father was watching cartoons, I felt the anxiety of this pending decision and then I felt that anxiety lift off, replaced by a tingling curiosity to see how being guided by God would feel. I closed my eyes and lowered my head until it was level to the ground, like a bull preparing to charge against a matador, and sprinted straight for the doors. I remember quite clearly (or my mother remembers quite clearly, in her telling) that the idea was to run until I was already in a room and then to slow down, open my eyes and see where I found myself—to see where God had decided that I should go. Instead, I ran headfirst into the sliver of wall between the doorways, cracking my head so hard against the wood that I split open a bloody gash in my scalp underneath my hair, all the way along the top surface of my skull.

My mother likes to bring this story up as a sort of origin story for my aggressive indecisiveness, as well as, I think, to shock our dinner guests into appreciating how terrifying I was to parent. But to me, the part that's always stood out is the belief, the mode of belief, that the story revolves around. My head continued to bleed for a long time after I collided with the wall and I eventually had to get stitches for the cut in my scalp, seven extremely painful stitches in the thin skin of my skullcap, and I cried for a long time while my dad held me in place by the shoulders and the nurse threaded the needle through and then snipped the cord at the end and he carried me back to the waiting room, still crying and crying, while my mother checked us out at the receptionist's desk. And yet even after all that, even after the stitches and the emergency room, even after the pounding headache and the blood and the strange electric horror of feeling a needle pierce my scalp, it never occurred to me to suspect that my reasoning had been flawed. I understood that God hadn't intervened, but I never doubted that He might have; and the story has an oddly tender quality now, whenever my mom tells it or whenever I remember it on my own, remembering what it felt like to know, without needing to believe, that God was something I breathed.

I stood with my mouth open on the doorstep for a long four seconds, blinking in the shadowed overhang of the veranda, after Marta Winters opened her front door. She was still wearing the same shapeless blue dress but the black messenger bag was gone, as was the straw hat and the nervous inattention, replaced now by a much steadier, wider-eyed alarm. I took a small step back and she stepped back also, one hand on the door.

"Mrs. Winters," I said finally, but the words seemed to catch at the back of my mouth. I cleared my throat and tried again. "Ms. Winters?"

She moved her head to the side, maybe in acknowledgment, and let the heavy door fall a couple inches closer to the jamb. "Can I help you?"

"Sorry to bother you," I said, feeling the light breeze on the hairs standing out on the back of my neck. I didn't think that she'd placed me as the bystander from the sidewalk earlier, but she seemed to recognize some part of my features, squinting with intent at my expression, my shirt and my shoes. I shifted back another half step, the porch boards creaking under my weight. "This is going to sound a little bit strange."

She glanced back up from my shoes and into my eyes. From some farther room inside, a dog let out a single bark.

"Could I have a glass of water, actually?" I asked.

Her brow lowered. Shifting her weight to the opposite side of her hip, she looked over her shoulder and then back at me, narrowing. "I'm sorry," she said, shaking her head. "Who are you, exactly?"

I licked my lips and she let the door fall another half foot shut and I jerked forward, thrusting a hand out to keep it from closing. "I work for a law firm," I blurted, blood rushing to my face and to my fingertips, "that's currently investigating you."

The door was only about twelve inches open as I said this to her, but it slowly opened wider as she relaxed her grip on the edge and allowed my arm to take more of the weight, and then all of the weight. Her face was blanched and her mouth open but she did not waver in her gaze except to glance down at my shirt again, and then my shoes again, and then back up to my face.

"I'm not here, for that, though. Or—on their behalf. I'm not here on the firm's behalf." I licked my lips again and then glanced over my shoulder, unable, in that moment, to return Marta's stare. "Could I come inside, actually, while we talk about this? I could just stand right inside the door, but I'd rather not talk out here, to be honest."

"You're," she said, her eyes wide and her chest heaving. "What are— that's—"

But she wasn't really standing in the doorway anymore and I was still the one holding the door open with my arm and so I stepped inside anyway, without her permission, and then let the door fall almost shut behind me. She shook her head very quickly, retreating. The room I found myself inside was surprisingly dim, given the time of day, with heavy blue hues from the curtains over the windows and none of the lights on indoors, and only the faintest glare of reflected sunlight in the surface of the walnut floorboards. At first I thought there was someone else there in the room with us, watching from around a corner or a door, until I saw the large Australian shepherd wagging its tail from behind a wooden gate in a nearby doorway. It barked.

"Sorry, I just," I said, keeping a foot wedged in the door so that I didn't feel like I'd entirely invaded, "I don't want to say too much outside. There are some detectives, potentially, and I just—"

"Get out."

I stopped, my palms raised at my sides, like I was trying to project calm toward a startled animal. But Marta Winters appeared only frozen, unwilling or unable to take in any gesture, hostile or otherwise.

"Okay," I said, slowly nodding. I pushed the door back open and backed a step out. "Sure, okay. I just—I just, wanted to say that—"

"I didn't say that you could come in." Previously diffused by the plain surprise of my declaration, her expression now refocused itself against me, her face thin with anger and her free hand clenched into a fist, the other gripping tight around the side of the front door. "I didn't say that you could come inside," she said again.

"No, I'm—sorry. I'm sorry." I was blushing all over my body now, and I almost tripped on the top step as I backed down, my foot slipping over the edge of the porch and then onto the front stair. I opened my mouth to say something more but couldn't overcome the surge of shame in my throat. "I'm sorry," I repeated instead.

"What the fuck do you mean?" She arrested my retreat just before I was able to turn to go. "Why is a law firm investigating me?"

I glanced down at the far sidewalk. I couldn't remember seeing the surveillance van parked on the street when I'd been walking up—the Garys were supposedly stopping by the city records office that afternoon to look up files on the property—but I also hadn't been looking very carefully before. "Here," I said, reaching into my pocket. I found a pen next to my phone and then found an old business card, and dropped to my haunches to jot my number and address across the top. I only noticed that it was a card for *Jessica Fortune and Apothecary* after I'd finished writing, and looked at it in my hand for a moment longer. I couldn't remember ever seeing a business card for the soothsayer, let alone taking one.

When I rose, Marta Winters seemed to rise slightly with me, lifting her neck and elevating upward on her toes, trying to maintain her tiny height advantage now that I was standing one step below her. Her blood seemed to have drained not only from her face but from her entire torso, her neck and her arms and her fingers as pale as her cheeks as she considered extending a forefinger and thumb to accept the proffered business card, and then reconsidered.

"I haven't done anything wrong," she said, glaring past me to the street below.

I nodded, slouching a little in my stance, trying to accommodate her anxiety by making myself even smaller. "All I was trying to say was, the firm I work for is going to be trying to make your life hard, soon. And I wanted to say that, if you just, go along, a little bit, you could maybe—"

"Fuck you." She slammed the door in my face.

I took a sharp breath and then held it, motionless, a perfectly still piece of the perfectly still surroundings. My chest felt tight but my eyes were clear, my shoulders hunched but my expression blank, the business card still held out in one hand.

After Marta's footsteps receded from hearing range, the dog finally started up again with its barking.

I pushed the pen back into my pocket, set the card down on the top step, and skittered back down the steps to the street.

～

I spoke to every neighbor on the block who answered, the rest of that afternoon. I stopped using the fake badge after the first couple of doors, after it seemed to raise more questions than I was really able to answer, but I managed to drink at least six separate glasses of water and learned far more about the neighborhood watch association than I'd ever expected to, and more times over than would have seemed possible, beforehand. While it's more than likely that there was just a strong correlation between the type of person who would talk to a stranger on the doorstep and the type of person who would join the watch, I couldn't help but form the impression that everyone on that street was an assiduous observer of the sidewalks and had all noticed that Robert and Marta Winters were profoundly irritating dog owners, inconsistently cleaning their Australian shepherd's massive shits and often smearing the pavement when they did deign to, and that everyone knew as well that the couple had never belonged to any church and weren't really the type to and were more likely to be reformist Jews, or Satanists, or some better-dressed version of New Age hippies. I nodded along and took notes or pretended to take notes on a little spiral notebook, studiously maintaining an even expression while I penciled geometric patterns in an Escher style, sketching intricate labyrinths out of short, straight lines. I had the strange sensation, all that afternoon, that I wasn't entirely real, or the afternoon wasn't entirely real around me; walls and ceilings moving closer, whenever I wasn't looking directly at them, on every side. Two of the older women offered me cookies and twice I nibbled at the edges of a Nabisco chocolate wafer, raising my eyebrows in lieu of a smile, before I stood to go. The Garys' van was already waiting at the sidewalk corner by the time I arrived.

"Anything good?" The high-pitched voice of the driver floated back to me through the open plastic panel between the cab and the van's rear, cheerful and bright, after thick-necked passenger-Gary slammed the rear doors shut behind me once more.

But I pretended not to hear, hunched over my knees on the bench along the right wall with my fingers threaded together, blinking back at the red and yellow and blue bulbs in the metal panels across from me, the soft white static on the miniature screens.

and it's not even clear that they don't feel it, either. Have you ever seen? Beyond the better-known, you know, walking barefoot across rows of burning coals, or sitting cross-legged on literal beds of nails--there are photographs, what look like real photographs, of fakirs with actual wounds, and the body itself--but not because they don't feel the pain. Or not necessarily.

INTERVIEWER: Well, sure. But that still doesn't mean that it's some-
                 thing that anyone could potentially do, all the same.
                 It's just a very American way of seeing it, to see this
                 and to see it as something that anyone could do, with
                 the right conditions and the right conditioning.

MARTA WINTERS: But they could feel just as much pain as we do. As I do,
                 I mean.

INTERVIEWER: Sure, but. Even if it's purely a matter of willpower,
                 to be able to walk barefoot over burning coals. Some
                 people might just be born with a superhuman amount
                 of willpower.

MARTA WINTERS: The point is that it's possible, though. That degree of
                 control. Have you seen these photographs? Sharp rods
                 of iron, heated or cold, inserted into the torso and it
                 doesn't even bleed, sometimes. Like the body itself, in
                 its fundamental, physical reaction--

INTERVIEWER: But it's still not possible for normal people. It's not
                 possible for you or me.

MARTA WINTERS: You don't really believe that, though.

She was seated on the couch when I came in, but this time not before the office opened, and also not alone: chatting easily with Willa behind the front desk, with her parted black hair lifted into a gleaming barrette at the back of her neck, Evelyn Forrester paused in her conversation and turned halfway to smile sarcastically in my direction, an elbow still resting lightly on the receptionist's desk behind her.

"I got here before the feds this time, it would seem," she said to me, but gazing through the window behind and to my left, in the direction of one of the closing storefronts across from our office. "Or so I hope."

I looked at her for a beat too long, heating, before I dropped my eyes down to the carpet. She was wearing different shoes this morning, I noticed, high-heeled black boots covered in buckles and straps, raising her almost to my own height as she listened to my mumbled pleasantry. She shifted a step into my path as I tried to shuffle past.

"Was it you?" she asked, holding a palm out low.

I looked back up at her, pulling my head back into my shoulders. The sequence of images constructed themselves instantly, in miniature, in the eye of my mind: Marta Winters standing furious in her own front room, after I departed; Marta Winters calling Evelyn Forrester as many times as it took for Evelyn to answer; Evelyn Forrester standing in front of me now, her neck extended and her eyes bright, shining with fury. I swallowed.

But the door opened behind me before I was forced to come up with a reply and John Zell stepped inside, apparently as overwhelmed as I was to find Evelyn Forrester waiting for him. She pivoted on a heel without approaching, maintaining her imperious distance.

"Zell," she said, her voice dripping. "You shit-eating worm. Do you know who called me last night? Asking me about things that only you and I should know?"

John Zell paled as he straightened, bracing himself for the blow. He wiped his palm on the side of his pant leg and then switched hands for his briefcase so that he could wipe the other. "Evelyn, it's good to see you," he muttered, blinking. "I'm not sure that I—"

"Fuck you it's good to see me. You leaked my private affairs to a fucking journalist, John."

I exhaled through my nose, unreasonably relieved. John lifted his head in the first half of a nod and then kept it raised, his eyes darting across different parts of the ceiling as he put the pieces together. He was avoiding looking at me, I knew, to keep from revealing anything in his glance.

"Mason Kantor. *Lake County Tribune.* Ring a bell? He called me to ask for an interview, to ask why I'd hired a law firm to look into my sister-in-law. What if he calls my mother next, John?" She took a step forward, towering, as John tried to keep himself tall and somehow failed. "What the *hell* is wrong with you?" she hissed through clenched teeth.

John held his stance but his skin continued to blanch as Evelyn closed in, his bottom lip curling in as he bit down on the corner with his upper teeth. "I assure you —"

"*Fuck* you. She's already withdrawn another two hundred grand. Did you even know that? While I'm already spending thousands of dollars trying to find my brother's body on the fucking *lake floor,* and you're out here spreading the word to the press?"

In this time, I'd taken advantage of Evelyn's advance across the office to withdraw myself against the end of Willa's desk, huddling in the corner with her as the confrontation unfolded; but I only realized that we'd formed into an audience when John glanced over, his skin white, and saw us both watching. Evelyn sniffed and stepped back, placed a hand on her barrette to check that it was still in place, and strode back over to the front entrance.

"One more week without results, and you're fired," she said, throwing the door open without looking over her shoulder. "And then I'll sue you to the fucking ground."

The door slammed shut behind her. Through the big front window, all three of us watched as she angled smoothly across the parking lot and then slid into her convertible, started the car, and pulled out.

"So fucking cool," Willa whispered.

The sounds of the office seemed to reemerge slowly from unconsciousness: the humming of the computer underneath Willa's desk, the intermittent ticks of the cooling vents, the distant rumblings and honks of the highway nearby. Willa rolled her chair back around to face her computer, humming very quietly to herself.

John straightened cautiously, touching his lip and then inspecting his fingers, as if expecting to see blood. I was surprised to notice how bad I felt for him.

"Well," he said, without meeting anyone's eye.

I turned and picked up a pen from a cup on Willa's desk, as though preparing to write something down, and then glanced about for a piece of paper. John stepped forward and then back, looking out at the parking lot and then back into the office, peering at the turn in the hallway. I kept waiting for his anger to arrive, for it to fall hurtling in my direction, but he only stayed pale, single hairs sticking out in haphazard directions from his carefully coiffed bangs.

"Well," he said again, and then cleared his throat. "That journalist is better at his job than I'd expected." He leaned down and picked his briefcase back up from where he'd placed it on the floor. "Peter, aren't there supposed to be coffees around here by now?"

I jumped slightly at the sound of my name, anticipating something quite different. But then I continued my forward motion anyhow, nodding quickly as I slid the pen into my breast pocket and snatched up my backpack and skipped over to the door.

～

That morning I'd slept through both my main alarm clock and the backup alarm on my cell phone, even though I hadn't stayed up especially late the night before. The sleeplessness of the night before last, it seemed, had finally caught up with me: despite the extra hour this morning, my eyelids felt leaden and my muscles didn't want to respond until I forced them to, up and out of bed and into my clothes and across the road and onto the bus, then off the bus and along the highway and into the office, and then back out of the office and across the highway and into the coffee shop, at the end of the impossibly long line. My body didn't want to move; and I didn't really see the point either, frankly. After the day before, even my constant anxiety about losing my job didn't seem as pressing, as though the dam had finally flooded over and now all my fears were strangely equalized, motionless under the same liquid dread. I was purposefully ignoring the idea of Marta Winters but it remained nonetheless, hovering above and underneath my consciousness like the inevitability of death, unthought and yet unforgettable, suffocating and vague. The night before I'd spent a long time standing in my tenement bedroom with all of the lights on and my cell phone in my hand, flipping it closed and back open, scrolling through all of the missed calls from my father and then flipping it closed again, running my hand through my hair and then sitting down at the desk I'd made from stacked cinder blocks and wooden boards and then standing, flipping my phone open again, running my hand again through my hair. When we were growing up, my brother and I had often invented private words for moods that we didn't know how to describe otherwise, and one of our go-tos had always been "squoogly"—a sort of nausea of anxiety, a restless squiggling in the stomach and in the legs that left you unable to move and unable to stop moving, unable to sit still and unable to lie down. In the years when we were still living in the small house, when we shared a bedroom next to the stairs and could always hear if our parents argued in the kitchen, I'd always felt profoundly squoogly listening to their raised voices through the floorboards, and Henry had always climbed into my bed, those years, after I asked him to, and fell asleep curled away from me on the side of my twin mattress, his breathing keeping time with mine as I gradually relaxed enough to sink into my pillow and close my eyes. By morning, he'd be back in his own bed and we'd be back to hating each other and trying to murder one another in various ways; but for the space of those nights, he stayed close by. In the months since he killed himself, the memory of his body weight on the mattress beside me always felt especially overwhelming, whenever I made the mistake of recalling it to mind. The line at the coffee shop finally reached its conclusion and I stared at the barista with my mouth open, exhaling, before I remembered John's usual coffee order and added my own and stepped back to wait. Then my phone vibrated in my pocket and I jumped, and walked quickly outside, my brother's sleep-breathing still loud in my mind as I prepared to seem too busy to talk to my father, to apologize briefly for missing his calls and then to apologize also for needing to get off the phone now, and I flipped the phone open and lifted it to my ear.

"Hey—"

"You never told me your name," the voice on the other end—very much not my father—said, cutting me off.

I closed my throat halfway through my inhale and then flipped the phone closed, as fast as that, and stumbled off the curb and into the road. There weren't any recognizable cars in the parking lot around me but I scanned them all the same with a sharp and profound unease, searching for the refurbished police van, certain that I was being watched and that the Garys were the ones watching, listening, tapping in. My phone began to buzz again in my hand and I shoved it into my pocket, but still held it enclosed in my palm, the vibrations tickling up my forearm as I stepped back up onto the sidewalk and then around the corner of the coffee shop, into a slightly shadier part of the complex, and pulled it back out. The number wasn't even from this state, judging by the area code.

Directly across from me, an old Ford pickup coughed to a start and then turned its lights on, despite the morning sunlight, and drifted forward, like an alligator floating closer through the surface scum.

~

One of my favorite essays in the art magazine that I'd almost published that past autumn, the *Movie Review Canoe*, was a piece by one of my former friends, Barry Theiss, about Lacan and the sense of the uncanny. Building off of the classic Freud essay on *unheimlich*, he began by discussing Lacan's assertion that one's sense of self was, in large part, to be understood as the literal definition of the word "I," and therefore the self was defined in the same way as all words were: as part of a web of differences, dissimilarities, contrasts. Uncanniness, in his telling, came precisely from encounters with things that were supposed to lack selfhood—things that we defined a "self" against, in terms of what a self was not—that nonetheless seemed to embody a will, and therefore indirectly weakened our own sense of what the word "I" meant by undermining its contrasts. Barry had developed the idea over a series of drunken conversations, always late at night, when the party was winding down but before the hosts had kicked out the last half-dozen or so lingering friends, the cigarettes burning down to the smokers' fingers, everyone drinking cups of the same peppermint schnapps because it was the only bottle with any liquor remaining; and Barry, an experimental sculptor who was always trying and failing to make the animated parts of his sculptures creepy and not kitsch, raised his voice to a fever pitch as he rolled up a sleeve and flapped an arm like a live fish along the table, asking us to imagine it chopped off and flopping on the surface on its own, a dismembered appendage with its own impulses, its own anxieties, panicking and blind.

But his words returned to me in a very different manner that morning outside the coffee shop, after I took that second phone call from Marta Winters and found myself listening to her fluctuating voice on the other end of the line, speaking softly and then loudly through the earpiece in my phone. Every object around me, every car and every parking spot, every window and every vacant storefront, seemed possibly conscious; and conversely, or by the same token, I felt strangely unreal among them, intensely aware of myself as a conjunction of mechanical tendons and blood vessels and bones, flexing my Achilles' heels as I lifted myself onto my toes and then stayed there, elevated, my calves tensed and straining as Marta Winters finally paused, waiting for me to respond. The cars crept past through the parking lot before me with their windows up and gleaming, my face reflected back in the glass.

But as it turned out, I hardly had any words to choose between, anyhow. Marta wanted me to clarify who I was and what the fuck I'd meant yesterday and that didn't appear to be entirely possible over the phone, for various reasons, and so we made plans to meet again that evening after work instead, to discuss in person. I hung up the phone and then looked for a long time at my hand, at the veins on the back of my hand and the hairs and the knuckles, the wrinkles along the surface of the knuckles and the small scar on the far side of my palm where I'd broken my hand once, the single freckle along the little flap of skin between my forefinger and my thumb. I returned to the coffee shop and picked up the steaming tray of coffees and carried them back across the highway, edged open the door to the office, placed them gingerly on the corner of Willa's desk, and lifted out John's favorite to hand-deliver. The atmosphere there was still bone-chilled from the encounter with Evelyn Forrester that morning, silent and rigid, John sitting motionless before his computer when I walked in. He jumped in his seat when he saw me, and then awkwardly reached out with both hands to accept the latte. He muttered a distracted thanks.

"I think she might like me," he said, practicing a small smile before he took his first sip. "Don't you think?"

I opened my mouth to reply and then thought better of it. The walls of his office seemed to be expanding inward, like an ear pressed to a screen door, listening.

"Like with kids, on the playground. You're always meanest to your crush."

I finally settled on a cautious nod, but this reaction was apparently either too timid or too slow in coming, and his small smile curved into a scowl. Earlier that morning, on my way out the door, he'd asked me directly if I'd insinuated anything about Evelyn to the journalist during our meeting, and had seemed to take my denial at face value; but I still felt certain that he'd seen right through the lie and was just biding his time, now, before flaying me alive. He waved a hand to dismiss me from the room and I returned to the lobby to fetch my own coffee and then set myself back up in my windowless office, took out my spiral notebook, and opened the computer program to type up my notes on yesterday's neighbor interviews and stared at the screen—and at the walls, and at the ceiling, and at the corners where the walls met the ceiling—for the following eight and a half hours straight, more or less unbroken, as the entire day slid smoothly by, leaning on my armrests to one side and then the other and then lowering my head to the surface of my desk with my eyes open before sitting back up upright, blinking, squinting, closing my eyes. I understood, instinctively, that the Garys already knew about my contact with Marta Winters and were going to intercept me that night, throw me into the back of their van and burn me alive, in the same way that I understood that there was another presence in my office with me and in the same way, also, that I couldn't stop imagining the moments after the heart stops beating but before the last electric impulses have left the brain, when the sparks of awareness are still routing the images and afterimages to the frontal lobe but there's only a fading consciousness there to meet them, unable to organize the impressions into objects, crumbling patterns in the sand. The hours when I could have left for lunch came and went and the day's hunger slowly spread and then hardened inside me, my body shriveling in every limb. Until six o'clock finally, suddenly arrived and I typed up twelve pages of notes in a headlong panic, my fingers flying over the keys, and I printed the pages to Willa's desk and lurched to my feet and out the door.

~

The restaurant was farther from Marta Winters's house than I would have expected, and harder to get to by bus than I'd made time for, even if I hadn't already left late. It was squirreled away between two huge brick apartment buildings on the south edge of the Loop and advertised only by a sandwich board along the sidewalk, and I walked straight past it in my rush from the bus stop before I turned around at the corner and rushed back. Sweat stood out at my temples as I skipped down the steps and pushed through the heavy wooden door with my shoulder and into the surprisingly deep, unevenly candlelit dining room, light flickering and flowing on every surface while I stopped and waited for my eyes to adjust. The illumination was weak but everywhere, hundreds of tiny flames guttering in glass cups on the tables and from myriad candle chandeliers above and complemented by gas lamps behind the bar that also seemed to quiver, adding even more motion and flutter to the room's yellow glow, tiny shadows dancing across the faces of every stranger in the room as they glanced over at me, it seemed, all at the same time, and then all glanced away. I took a short breath and held it. A maitre d' appeared from a dim corner to my right and cleared his throat.

Then a silhouette in the shape of Marta Winters appeared at the back of the room and I exhaled, my nostrils wide, and stepped straight past the maitre d' and toward her, mirroring her movements between the tables as she returned to her seat from the bathroom. I could tell the moment she saw me by the sharp straightening of her neck, her head pulled back and her shoulders square, looking slightly down her nose in my direction as she arrived at her chair and then stood behind to observe my approach. I pulled out the chair opposite and sat down. There was a little saucer of olive oil next to a small plate of focaccia fragments on the center of the tiny circular table and I realized that I was starving as soon as I saw it, and I pushed the bread into the oil and then shoved it into my mouth.

"So," she said, still standing. "Your name is Peter." In the inconstant firelight, her face seemed to be rapidly switching between many different expressions at once.

I swallowed a second piece of bread and reached for a third. She pulled out her chair and watched me chew for another moment before easing herself down onto the thin cushion, leaning her head back so as to keep looking down the bridge of her nose, despite her height disadvantage. A waiter floated past and I practically grabbed him by the tail of his coat to ask for another plateful of bread bites.

"You never told me what law firm it is, though, that you work for," she said, her voice low.

"Oh," I said, working hard to sop up as much oil as I could with the last remaining focaccia. "Masterson, Masterson & Zell. Out in Evanston. Not a big one, or anything."

Her eyes widened. "Oh," she said.

I registered my mistake only after I saw her expression. "I guess I probably shouldn't have told you that."

"No, that's." She blinked rapidly. "I appreciate your honesty."

"Please don't, like, contact them, though."

She nodded and then shook her head, considering. Her freckles weren't exactly invisible in the low light, but in the context of so many tiny shadows moving and re-moving over her skin they were impossible to distinguish from the general texture of her expression, her round cheeks and her careful frown. "Well," she said.

"Please, though." I stared at her, unblinking, ravenous, blood circulating warm under the surface of my skin.

She shook her head again. I saw the waiter approach and then watched him walk past with a lurch in my stomach, twisting around in my seat to try and catch his eye as he studiously gazed straight forward, plates of steaming rice and meat held high in either hand. Marta asked the obvious question and I gazed after him for another long moment, his hips shifting as he navigated between the tables and the barstools, feeling both the hesitation of my earlier anxiety and the urgency of my present hunger, my heartbeat in the soft part of my neck.

But the explanation took almost no time at all, once I finally began. There weren't even that many moving parts: the money, the murder, the Garys, the surveillance van. I addressed most of my comments to the crumbs on my plate as I pressed a fingertip to each individually and then lifted them, one by one, to my lips, savoring them for a particularly long time as I touched on the assertion that Marta had kicked her husband before he drowned and then the suspicious withdrawals from the family trust, the missing dead body, the variously considered strategies for blackmailing her into nonexistence. I tried to be coy about naming the particular individual who'd hired MM&Z, LLC, but realized only belatedly that the specific constellation of details and discontents pointed to exactly one possible culprit when Marta interrupted me to mutter—

"Evelyn, you bloodsucking *cunt.*"

—and I glanced up to see her pained expression, her forehead wrinkled and her skin pale with anger, and at the same moment noticed the waiter standing beside our table with his eyebrows as high as they would go, a saucer of olive oil and a little plate of bread in either palm. He leaned down to slip them onto the edge of the table and I mumbled a low "thank you," popping a piece of bread straight into my mouth and then moving the plates onto the center of the table, fitting neatly on top of the matching dirty dishes underneath. I could hear Marta audibly breathing, rapid inhales and exhales through her flared nostrils. I kept my eyes carefully lowered as I chewed. For the first time, sitting across from her in this ancient Italian restaurant with the candlelight hiding half of her features and distorting the other half, my gut slowly unclenching as the bread took the edge off my hunger and my eyes adjusted to the dim, it struck me that Marta Winters wasn't really that much older than me; she was only twenty-seven, twenty-eight at most. Just a few more years than I was out of college, and not even older than the oldest of my former classmates at art school. I could imagine her as one of my own friends, living in Manhattan for the first few years after graduating and then coming out to Chicago for law school, feeling her way blindly forward in the hopes that her life was actually moving in some straight direction, in the hopes that she was moving at all. Her eyes were bright and maybe moist with tears, glistening when the flickers illuminated the sides of her face, still sorting through the bewilderment of being told that she was so intently, so aggressively, so personally despised. She tucked a stray strand of hair behind her right ear and then crossed her arms over her chest, as if trying to control her breathing through sheer physical pressure.

"But who the fuck are you, though?" she said, her chest still heaving underneath her forearms. "Why come to my door? Why meet me here? Why tell me any of this at all?"

I lifted my glass of water and took a large swallow. "Mm," I said.

"Is this a move? Is this the part where you're the good cop, and you're threatening that I'll meet the bad cops, if I don't play along?"

I took another swallow and then set the glass back down on the table. A new waiter, different from before but wearing the exact same all-black shirt and pants and socks and shoes, appeared beside our table and asked if we'd decided on any drinks for the evening. Marta began to wave him away before I raised a finger and ordered a double gin and tonic.

"No, but," I said, keeping my head turned to observe the bar along the right wall beside us, the handful of older Italians drinking glasses of wine or bourbon on the stools, "I can see how you'd think that."

An elderly gentleman at the far corner of the bar raised his wineglass and the bartender uncorked a fresh bottle of red with a flourish, the sound of the cork echoing in a sudden coincidence of silence throughout the dining room, and then the splash of wine eddying in the glass.

"My brother died recently," I said, watching.

The elderly gentleman raised his glass to the bartender, thanking him, before taking a long sip, the red wine staining the top of his lip after he lowered the glass. Marta shifted in her chair. The new waiter—or maybe the first one, in the same clothes as before—slid my double gin and tonic onto the corner of the table almost without my noticing, disappearing just as I returned my attention to the table. I downed half of the drink in a quick succession of tiny sips. Marta opened her mouth to say something in the same moment that the waiter reappeared with a pitcher of ice water, pouring it thickly to fill my water glass back to the top.

"Are you ready to order?" he asked, looking away.

"Oh," Marta said, shaking her head. "We're just—"

"Yes, actually. Could we get the oysters?" I asked, noticing the menu in front of me for the first time and skimming my finger along the lines, speed-reading the appetizers and then the entrees. "A half dozen? And this, what is this? Shrimp scampi. And another plate of bread and olive oil, if that's all right."

The waiter nodded and took my menu and then we both turned to look at Marta, staring levelly back at me, shadows dancing along the ridges of her furrowed brow.

～

Marta stood to leave the restaurant twice over the twenty minutes or so that followed, but never managed to make it more than three steps before she turned around and sat back down. The extra plate of focaccia and olive oil arrived and then the plate of oysters, arrayed in a half circle on a bed of crushed ice around three little metal cups of different sauces, and I devoured them all almost as soon as they came, each of the pieces of bread and the full saucer of oil and every oyster but one, which Marta picked up and set on her plate and then completely forgot about, apparently, with all the focused absent-mindedness of a mathematician losing their glasses on the top of their head. I glanced at it often, with waning longing and increasing concern, as the meat shimmered and warmed in its complex shell.

But Marta was plainly too overwhelmed, in many senses, to be entirely present in the dining room at all times. Before the food arrived, she listened to the initial details of my brother's passing with a fairly insulting impatience, rolling her eyes when I told her that he was a suicide and offering blunt suggestions for more convincing alternatives — "what about falling from an airplane? or hit by a falling airplane's debris" — until I lapsed into silence and she flushed red, finally ashamed, and stood abruptly to go. But the same guilt that compelled her to escape seemed to compel her, equally, to stay, and she sat back down and began to offer her own explanation by way of apology; although what it was exactly that she was explaining, neither of us quite seemed to know.

"I'm sorry," she said, smoothing her sleeves underneath her palms, or maybe just rubbing her upper arms. "I just don't get it, I guess."

I looked at her and she looked away, and then smiled thinly at the waiter as he arrived with the third round of bread and oil. She moved back in her seat as he set the new plates down and then took the old, dirty plates away with him.

"It just doesn't really make any sense," she continued, her expression creasing. "What's so special about you, you know?"

I paused, a teardrop of olive oil forming at the edge of the bread segment in my fingers. Both she and I watched as it slid in a zigzag along the side of my palm. I lifted my hand to my lips and licked off the droplet, and put the rest of the piece of bread in my mouth.

"My husband," she said. "Robert, he—"

She rubbed her upper arms again and then lifted her palms higher, smoothing her hair back underneath her hands, with a twist in her mouth like she had decided against saying something but was still choosing what to say next, instead.

"—in the first few days after he drowned, I didn't believe that he was actually gone," she went on, leaning back and then forward onto an elbow as the plate of oysters arrived. She looked at the closest oyster for a long time before lifting it by the shell from the bed of ice and setting it down in the exact center of her plate. "I didn't believe it, I mean. It didn't make any sense to me. The idea that he was down there, in that water, more or less all of what he'd always been—but there wasn't anything left of him, supposedly, in existence. Like there wasn't anything at all. Even with almost all of him still there, still all there, at the bottom of the lake. Exactly the same, only at the bottom of all that freezing cold water."

I grimaced as I swallowed my first oyster, feeling the slickness as it wormed its way down along my tongue. But Marta was looking away, furrowing her brow instead up at the coffered ceiling. Listening to her go on, I was beginning to feel somewhat preoccupied with her in ways that I wasn't quite able to understand, but that I didn't really feel the need to understand just yet. Despite the bizarre picture she was painting of her husband's refrigerated corpse at the bottom of the lake—or maybe because of it—she was beginning to seem strangely familiar, not like we'd met before but like I'd actually known her before, like I'd known her name and heard her story, like we'd gone to college or high school together or played the same sport; like I might have met her parents once in passing, at some game or graduation; like there might be some photo, in some lost corner of the internet, of us all standing in the same group together, smiling at the same flash.

"People kept using the phrase 'like waiting to wake up from a dream,' I remember, in the first few days. And I used it, too, for a little while. But that wasn't, it wasn't really." She put a fingertip in her mouth and bit down on one of the edges, on the end of a hangnail, and pulled off a small strip of skin between her teeth. "Did you find it hard to believe that your brother was really dead, after he hung himself?"

A droplet of blood quickly formed against her cuticle where she'd bitten it, liquid crimson filling the flickering crevice between her fingernail and fingertip. There were similar patches of red alongside her other fingernails, I noticed for the first time, as well. I told her that I didn't really know how to answer for myself, but that my mother still didn't believe that my brother had truly departed—and I described, in broad strokes, my mom's obsession with Henry's afterlife, her increasingly strident attempts to contact his spirit, her engagements with psychics and mediums and the Lady Jessica, the missed phone calls from my dad. My second gin disappeared along with the last of my oysters and the waiter came and cleared the plates while Marta's expression slowly smoothed, listening, into a perfectly blank neutrality, except for a single vertical crease between her eyebrows that deepened particularly as I described the rabbit's guts on the breadboard, the flickering of the lights. She motioned to the waiter just before he left and asked for a glass of white wine, also. It took me longer than it should have to notice that her chest was heaving.

"You spoke to him. Your brother," she said, with some difficulty, blinking as though something had flown into her eye. "He heard."

It was the same rapid breathing as before, only shallower, and almost silent—like a deer in a clearing, I thought, who's just realized that she's being watched.

"No," I said.

But she barely seemed to hear me. Without ceasing her blinking or her rapid inhales and exhales, she stood, gathered her jacket from the back of her chair and into her arms, took one step toward the door and then pivoted on a heel and sat back down. Her skin was flushed all over, her frizzy hair wild over her ears and her eyes bright, gleaming in the candlelight. The suddenness of the shift was almost as unsettling as the shift itself. The waiter arrived with her glass of wine and she held it in her hand for a moment, her mouth open as if already midsentence, and then tipped it back and chugged a third of the glass in one gulp.

"Robert," she said, breathless, before taking another, smaller sip from the edge of her glass. "I haven't been able to, I mean—nothing like that. But he, it seemed like he—I wouldn't have called you this morning. I wouldn't be here at all." She shook her head.

"It wasn't real, though." Watching her abrupt fluster, I was reminded painfully of my mother's reaction to the Lady Jessica, once my brother's suicide had been approximately described. I wanted to reach out and grab her, to catch her before she fell too hard. "My brother is dead, Marta."

"The only reason I came, I mean. After you came to the door, and—it wasn't anything like you just described. That's—beyond." She made a dismissive gesture with her hand, twisting her neck in one direction and then the other, taking another sip of her wine. "Robert wanted me to contact you. To reach out to you, to call your number from the card. I could feel it. I could tell. As soon as I saw your card on the step, I could tell that Robert wanted me to. But I didn't understand why. At first I thought it was just that he wanted to warn me, I guess, that his sister had hired a bunch of nincompoops to stalk me."

She closed her eyes and then opened them, staring wide-eyed across the table at me and then wide-eyed at the plate of shrimp scampi, steaming, floating over the table between us as the waiter cleared room to set it down.

"Could we, actually," she said, composing her face into a careful smile. "Could we actually get this to go, instead?"

the Cartesian subject here, "who appears at the moment when doubt is recognized as certainty"—so this "subject" is synonymous with the pronoun "I" as commonly understood in, for example, the clauses "I think" or "I am." Therefore, if "the sum of the effects of speech" is to be understood as the all-encompassing division of the world into differences as the mind learns language—as it learns to differentiate the phenomena of experience according to the lines of language—then the "I" is thereby a sign within that structure; a remainder of what is left over after all the non-self of the world has been demarcated. It is a word defined by association and by what it has not been defined as not. And, therefore, a word that has as much malleability—and vulnerability—as any other in the web of a living language.

Freud's essay on the uncanny touches on a similar aspect of selfhood, albeit from a different direction, and not nearly so directly. The essay lists a number of different horror tropes that inspire that *unheimlich* feeling in readers and then declares that the connecting thread through all of them is the threatened return of the repressed, such as, in his guiding example, the return of the "repressed savage" that lurks within all "civilized" men. The descriptive passages, however, are rather more suggestive of an alternative thesis: when Freud tries to connect the thread between the uncanniness of injuries to the eyes, of twins, of automata, and of the return of severed limbs, what strikes the modern reader is not so much "the return of the repressed" as that which undermines aspects of the definition of the word "I." The eyes are the windows to the self; twins threaten our own naive equation of uniqueness as identity; automata undermine our understanding of "will" and animation as qualifications for selfhood; and the return of severed limbs calls into question the arbitrary boundaries of what parts of our bodies constitute "ourselves." Even his purported fears of savagery, for Freud represented by the return of animism and thereby the supposition that all objects have selves, clearly threaten selfhood by threatening its contrast to the inanimate. While not in contradiction to his original idea, his own examples more directly advance the thesis that the feeling of "uncanniness" is instead predicated on a repressed anxiety about selfhood, and especially an anxiety about the unreliable and imprecise contrasts that together bound the word "I."

The uncanny, then, is precisely the feeling of one's own definition slipping. Freud already put forward the idea of psychological phenomena as made up of signs, but by locating psychological experience within language, Lacan allows us to take the analysis another step further still. The idea that trees have selfhood is threatening to us because it suggests, within the relational structure of language, that we have as much selfhood as a tree does. And far worse, then—because it overlaps with far more of our definition—are animated

In the back of the taxicab, Marta talked constantly, quietly, in a steady and unceasing rhythm, of a piece with her regular inhales and exhales. She was explaining something—many things—as though searching for the right question by answering, and answering.

Evelyn had always hated her, she began, from the very first time that they'd met. During their first dinner together, she and Robert and Evelyn had gathered at a tiny Mediterranean restaurant right next to the University of Chicago and Evelyn had insisted on ordering three carafes of wine for just the three of them over less than two hours, with no food except for pita and hummus and these little stuffed eggplants with tahini, appetizer after appetizer always putting off the main course, until Marta was so drunk that she couldn't remember anything of what she'd told her and Robert refused to explain why he was so angry the next morning; and from then on, at every Forrester family holiday, Evelyn made it a habit to knock Marta off-balance with hints and details from her own overshared stories, repeated anew to her now in the presence of Robert's mother, his friends from college, the whole table at Thanksgiving. *Didn't you lose your virginity to a man in his fifties, I thought?* Evelyn didn't even seem to mind that the awkwardness redounded right back upon her, inevitably—she just cared that Marta was so intensely bothered by it, and that Robert was so intensely bothered in turn. There was a story, apparently, of one time that Robert had humiliated one of her boyfriends at the dinner table, that she'd never forgotten and wanted to make sure that Robert never forgot, either; but then there was also a story of a time that Evelyn had dated the ex-boyfriend of one of Robert's girlfriends, and brought him to Easter when the girlfriend was also there; and so on. Marta often found herself disliking them both equally, whenever they were all compelled to gather together in one place. They were just one of those wealthy families, she explained, slipping a finger between her seat belt and her chest and then pulling it away from her, rearranging the strap so that there wouldn't be so much pressure on the side of her neck.

But she and Robert also, admittedly, had a fairly unequal relationship at that point in their dating, and she could never quite find a way to point out to him what she saw so clearly, that he was an equal participant in this toxic pattern—that his whole family was, really, in each their own way. Marta and he had started dating right after she first moved to Chicago, after a fairly disastrous set of years for her in New York, and she'd soon found herself both precipitously in love with him and almost entirely enclosed within his world, with almost no friends who weren't also his friends, who hadn't originally been just his friends, who weren't still more his friends than hers. Which was part of Robert's perfection, really, in how she'd wanted to reinvent herself and had been able to re-invent herself so completely inside his Chicago, in his apartment and in his eyes. But it was also a little terrifying, sometimes, to turn around and realize that she'd couldn't really see anymore where it was she'd started from. It made her feel painfully anxious whenever they argued, that they might split up and she'd find herself, finally, nowhere, and with no one to turn to for help. Back in Manhattan, she'd often struggled with a feeling that she could only describe as a sort of restlessness, but far more sinister than that particular word implied—a sort of teetering boredom that consumed her for entire stretches of days, it felt like, with the hours expanding around her and no way to escape the decisions she'd already made, the chances she'd already missed, the doors she'd already closed and the couch she'd already spent so many hours lying upon. Dat-ing Robert, for all his faults, had always held the promise of a way out of herself, if only by way of an ego that was large enough to swallow them both. Not that she didn't also love him, of course, and more powerfully than she really had words to express.

"Really," she said, turning her gaze from the taxi window and straight-ening, as though only then remembering that I was there.

For a moment, I expected her to look over at me and I stared straight forward also, carefully preparing to seem like I hadn't noticed. I had started to imagine her in the moment after she came back up out of the water, after she'd left him down below, and I was exceedingly anxious that she'd be able to see this thought plain on my features if I wasn't careful to look away; and then both of us stayed frozen, blushing forward in parallel, as the silence stiffened between us in the cab's back seat, broken only by the thumping of the wheels over the potholes in the road beneath. I opened my mouth to say something and then stopped, and cleared my throat instead.

But staying quiet seemed even louder than speaking, and I cleared my throat a second time and tried again, talking in a surprisingly loud voice before I even really knew what I was talking about, raising my eyebrows high at the dirty plexiglass partition between the back seat and the front of the cab, at the front windshield beyond.

The first time that my mother tried to communicate with Henry after his suicide, I said to Marta, tracking the cars with my gaze as they approached and then flashed past in the opposite lane, was at his funeral. She'd begun by humming. Sitting in the front pew at the funeral service between me and my father, her face streaked with tears and her shoulders and arms wrapped together underneath a sheer black shawl, she had started by vibrating her larynx at the very bottom of her register, too quiet for anyone but her and me and possibly my father to hear. She could feel Henry's vibration inside her own, she explained to us afterward: she could feel his spirit, humming with her and through her, as she sang. Over the weeks that followed she purchased six different tuning forks, two portable amp-and-microphone sets, and a fifteen-piece kit for making music by running a wet finger around the tops of wineglasses and spent hours making elaborate arrangements with them in my brother's childhood bedroom, setting up the cords and the amps and the acoustic glasses around the tuning forks and then laying herself down on the bed or on the carpet and crying, usually for about an hour or so, until she fell asleep on the floor or curled on the mattress. She could hear him, she called out to me any time that she noticed me walking past in the hallway, whenever my footsteps creaked on the other side of the open door.

He died because there was something that he needed to say but that he hadn't had the words for, she repeated often, over and over, usually once to both my father and me and then once more to just me, after my father abruptly stood from the table and left the room. *We need to listen,* she said.

But her obsession became much harder to navigate after she began to involve other living people. At first it was just our neighbors, gathered tightly together in an extremely uncomfortable circle in our living room while my mom hummed and sometimes chanted, substituting in meditative *ums* and *ahms* and *ohms* whenever the rhythm of the language suited her; but then our neighbors learned to avoid her, and she began instead to visit professionals downtown. She liked to take me with her because I'd always loved psychics, starting from when I was little and continuing through high school and college, and because it felt important for both of us to be physically close as much as possible at that time, to be together in the same car or together in the same basement room, her hand on my arm as we sat next to one another on the mystic's couch. But it was extremely painful, all the same. And after she started to invite these professionals back to our house, to conduct sessions in our front room or in Henry's childhood bedroom or even, one time, in the garage in his former duplex where Dad had found him—where Dad had cut Henry down himself and then held him in his arms—it became such an overwhelming tension that Dad moved out of the house and into a hotel just outside the city, into a fourth-floor room beside the national forest with a bay window that looked straight out over the ocean of trees, for four nights and five days.

Marta opened her mouth as if to say something, that single vertical crease visible again between her eyebrows, and I paused, waiting, watching the streetlights slowly approach and then zip past the cab window. My heart wasn't beating any louder or faster than before but I felt strangely aware, in that moment, of its beating. I'd been trying to explain why I couldn't help her, I finally realized. Marta rapped on the taxi partition with her knuckle and pointed to the side of the road.

The cab pulled to a sharp stop at the corner, leaning us both forward in our seats and then pushing us back. I opened the door and stepped out while Marta paid. The night air had gotten much colder—"crisper," my dad would have called it—in the hour or so since darkness had fallen, the evening wind loud in the trees. For the first time since climbing into the cab with her, I began to feel the strange gravity of my own presence here, of my own steps on the street we were about to walk down. Marta climbed out from the door behind me and I stepped away from her. She took my wrist in her hand.

"Marta," I said, yanking my arm free. "I'm sorry, but I can't—"

"No. You can. You have to." She glanced over her shoulder, unable to hold my gaze for more than half a second, peering down the dark sidewalk toward her home. "I'm—please." In the shadows, it was hard to see exactly the look on her face, but I imagined that I could feel her embarrassment radiating out like so much heat, hearing herself out loud. "Robert brought you to me—he brought you to me, I mean—because he wanted me to show you. He wanted you to help me. And you came, you came to the door, because you wanted to help me. Didn't you? From Masterson, and Masterson, and Evelyn?"

But the law firm's name only sent me another step back farther, the hairs on my forearms standing on end. I craned my neck to look again into the dark road beyond her shoulder. "It's just," I said, shaking my head faster now, "it's not—"

She caught my right hand in her left and then stepped sharply toward me, her warmth suddenly very close to my skin.

"Please," she said.

∼

We ended up approaching the house through the backyard, by way of the neighbor's backyard on a parallel street, to avoid stepping foot on Marta's front walk. Approached from this angle, the house seemed to loom even larger than before, rising straight out of the ground with no mediation of the stone stairway along the front; crunching our feet on the sticks and dead leaves along the side of the neighbor's house and then launching over the low fence like two teenagers, we looked up at the old colonial with the same shrinking feeling, it seemed to me, neither of us speaking or even audibly breathing as we crept along the grass and then into the basement entrance, the thick walls dark around us and tight on every side. Marta led the way through the gloom without turning on any lights, up the creaking steps and then into the first floor, where her dog scared both of us straight out of our skins with a bark like a loud shout, as soon as we stepped foot into the brightly lit kitchen.

"Archie, shut *up*," Marta said, rushing over to the big Australian shepherd and taking him by the ears, giving him deep scratches around his collar as he continued to bark, barely any quieter than before. "Shut *up*, shut *up*, shut *up*, shut *up*."

The kitchen was beautiful, spotless and huge, with gleaming chrome countertops and gleaming chrome appliances beside a gleaming chrome fridge and all arranged around a gleaming marble island counter in the middle, with a textured white slab for the surface and identically textured white slabs for the sides. It was a magazine kitchen, in so many words, the type of room that appliance makers use to sell you their microwaves, in the same way that bikini designers use supermodels to sell their swimsuits. But despite all its size and capacity, it still didn't seem to contain anywhere to stand. The ocher wooden floorboards captured and reflected the soft ceiling light in miniature orbs of luminescence within the smooth finish, focal points of reflection that I followed with my eyes as I edged forward into the space, tiptoeing away from the encroaching darkness of the basement and blinking while my pupils adjusted from the night. Even the dog was too perfect: long shags of black and off-white and off-brown and exuberant, overjoyed and overfriendly in exactly the way that dogs are supposed to be, lapsing from his loud barks only to lick Marta's hands and face and then trotting over to me to lick my hands, pushing his nose and then the top of his head into my hip. Marta followed after him to my side, holding on to his collar as she tried and failed to pull him off.

"Sorry," she said, grimacing. "He likes people."

I smiled and bent down, allowing her to release his collar as I took his head in my hands and scratched him. "That's all right," I said, uncomfortable. "I like people, too."

But the normalcy of the dog's enthusiasm only seemed to heighten our awareness of our own abnormality, the bizarre fact that I was here at all, crouched in the far corner of my surveillance target's expensive kitchen while I scratched behind her dog's ears with my fingernails. She found a leash from among the coats hanging on the wall and pulled Archie away in order to attach it to his collar, explaining that he was usually better behaved with it on, her cheeks burning for no clear reason. I nodded and stepped back.

"Thank you, also," she said, her blush deepening, "again. It's been—hard. Doing this alone. Trying to get it all to work, I mean."

I looked at her and then looked away, my heart rate increasing. It felt strange, and undoubtedly creepy, to focus in this moment on how pretty she looked with her cheeks so flushed. "Sure," I said.

"When you said, when you described the"—she made a gesture with her free hand, tugging Archie off me with the other—"it was like a lightbulb, really. It's just so obvious, thinking about it now, what I was doing wrong. But it shouldn't take more than a few minutes, I don't think. I'm really, really excited to try."

She looked at me, the corners of her eyes glistening but her smile wavering, and I returned her smile in kind. But I was grateful when she turned and began leading the way forward, and I could listen to the long description of her discoveries—the websites she first encountered, the books they'd led her toward, the materials she'd been stockpiling and the attempts that had failed so far—without worrying about what expression I wore on my face.

The rest of the first floor was more familiar than the kitchen, more of the deeper blues that I'd noticed earlier when I'd stood just inside the front door, but there still didn't seem to be very much room for humans. It was like a version of those mythical cities built for giants, I thought, only for rich people in Chicago. We stepped through two darkened rooms of dustless bookshelves and couches and expensive rugs, the dog's leash dragging loudly on the floorboards and then conspicuously quiet on the fabrics as he panted after Marta, before we emerged into the front hallway, where we finally encountered the first evidence of people actually living inside: a disordered heap of mail, boxes and letters piled almost waist-high across a good three-foot square next to the door, flowing over the little sideboard and up from the floor and surrounded by scatterings of trash, empty envelopes, and opened packages, along with a little pile of dog toys and paraphernalia on the farther side by the door. Marta apologized in passing, waving an arm at the pile, but as we rose the residue of daily life only increased on every side. I could see so clearly the straitened flow of her recent mornings and afternoons and evenings—isolated and alone, every day, in this gleaming home—that I began to feel something of that combination of intense discomfort and intimate closeness that I'd become used to experiencing when reading stolen private documents at my desk, hearing words in my head that no one was supposed to have ever read aloud. Worn sweaters and sweatshirts and dirty pajama bottoms and discarded socks littered the sides of the steps and the corners of the center landing, mixed with the dried leaves of the dying plants hanging along the banisters and the shrunken cores of used candles, the wax melted into stubs and small sculptures, like statues of tiny monsters, and at least one crumpled paper bag of take-out fast food. Then in the skinny upstairs hallway, a narrow five-foot lane between parallel walls of doors, the floors were cluttered with more clothes as well as crumpled books and papers and a laptop glowing, half-open, on the threshold of a bedroom door; forgotten glasses of water still half-full with liquid and other glasses with tea candles inside; many more crumpled paper bags and paper boxes of takeout, not a few of which still had some French fries poking out from beneath the lid; and an actual candelabra, strikingly old and mottled and apparently genuine silver and with tall candles stuck in each of the cups, that Marta stooped down to pick up from the floor beside the final doorway in the upstairs hall. Archie briefly stopped his loud panting between us to let out a sharp bark.

". . . and this piece, almost a hundred years old, which was actually so expensive that—stop it, Archie," Marta scolded, but without looking down, as he barked a second time. She produced a small lighter and then proceeded to light the candlewicks, one by one, until each of the nine flames were burning bright before her eyes. Her face glowed.

"Here," she said, opening the door.

∼

At this point, I'd relented to Marta's desire to walk me through her ritual but only, internally, on the condition that I find the earliest possible opportunity to exit and take it: to leave after ten minutes, fifteen at most, as soon as I'd helped her feel slightly more stable in this low moment and could move on without abandoning her, essentially. Her tone and her expressions were all too painfully mimicked from my mother to ignore without hearing them both in my head, I felt sure, if I didn't at least try to help her—and I felt bad, too, knowing what she was about to endure from the Garys and from John Zell, and was still holding out hope that I might be able to convince her to give them what they wanted and move on. I liked her, in so many words. She seemed like she was falling apart.

After she pushed open the last door in her upstairs hallway, however, and then led me inside, the candelabra flickering beside and above her, I realized that this could all be true and at the same time wrong: that she could be a real person, a person like me, needing and deserving of help, and yet I could still be wrong to provide it because I didn't, in fact, know her. I had no idea who this woman was. I should not have come. I should not have knocked on her door and I should not have given her my number, I should not have met her for dinner and I should not have climbed into her taxicab and I should not have entered through the basement door, should not have followed her up the stairs and should not have crossed the threshold to the kitchen, should not have followed her into the main house and should not have entered into this candlelit room and seen the chalk diagrams on the otherwise empty wooden floor, the bright-white patterns smeared in parts with a glossy red-brown and glimmering with the reflected radiance of seven small gemstones, refracting the candelabra's glow in equidistant halos, shimmering from the centers of the osculant circles drawn around. It had once been a bedroom, I understood, seeing the bed frame propped up and leaning vertically against the far wall, with the large boudoir and desk and leather chair pushed and piled up roughly alongside; and as I withdrew a half step back toward the threshold, toward the barking Australian shepherd who hadn't made the same mistake of crossing into the room, I couldn't help but imagine the tortured sequence of days that had transformed this room from a place of everyday sleeping and waking into this intricate geometry of desperation. Marta Winters was a complete stranger to me, I repeated aloud to the inside of my mind.

The diagram was far more complex than I could make out in the poor lighting. There was a single large circle around almost the circumference of the room, with two satellite circles on opposite diagonals and then five adjacent circles arranged inside and each of them marked by a thick symbol, a seemingly arbitrary mix of directional symbols—a larger triangle with a reversed triangle inside, an arrow pointing north—and Greek-ish letters, along with more wavelike drawings that seemed more like musical notation than anything else. Smaller circles with concomitantly smaller symbols interspersed the largest circle and some of the crevices between the central five, crowding the space with a density of meaning that seemed poorly designed, frankly, like a sentence stuffed with too many verbs. Only the five circles in the middle and the two satellite circles outside had the glimmering gemstones set in the centers, but all of the symbols were smeared over or under with that same red-brown. Marta took care not to touch any of the chalked lines with her shoes as she stepped inside and placed the candelabra in the very center, and then came back to the door and tugged Archie inside. I shuffled, with severe reluctance, only a little farther into the room to give her space to drag him forward. It was hard to tell if the room was unnaturally cold or if this was just an effect of the beads of sweat that now dotted the exposed skin on my arms and my elbows, my neck and the backs of my ears.

"For the first few days," Marta said, wrapping the leash around her hand to yank the reluctant Archie into the room, "when I was in the hospital and I knew, inside, that Robert couldn't have gone, but everything around me said that he'd stopped existing, the hardest part—the hardest part—was the minutes." She finally succeeded in pulling Archie inside enough that she could close the door behind him and then tied his leash tightly to the inner doorknob. He backed into the wooden frame, mixing his barking now with whimpering, his voice like a squeaky hinge in the back of his maw. "The minutes and the seconds, I mean. The time.

I couldn't fathom what I was supposed to do, now or ever, with all this time. Do you know what I mean? All those minutes, and seconds, that add up into each day. I used to say 'boredom,' but that's not really what it was. But it was the easiest way to get people at least close to the general idea: how fundamentally, fatally *boring* it seemed. For that day, and for every day after. Imagining myself wading through every moment, living through every day, every minute and every second, from now until eternity. Like that restlessness that I mentioned earlier, only." She stepped carefully back across the diagram and removed the two candles on either end of the candelabra and then placed them into single candle holders beside the two outer circles. "And so it was such an extraordinary relief, such an extraordinary relief, to feel him again, afterward. To feel his presence near me. Not gone. Not at all gone. The first night that I got back from the hospital and I slept in this room and I could feel that he was back here, that he was back here with me, and I just. I just felt."

She made a gesture like fireworks with her hands and I took a sharp breath through my nostrils, preparing to say something, and she held up a palm. I felt a foreboding like a nausea, like the internal flexion of muscle in the gut that pushes the half-digested food and stomach acid back up the esophagus and into the mouth.

"I'm just so grateful to you for being here, I have to tell you," she continued, her chest rising and falling. "It was beginning to feel, I mean — since that first night back, and since feeling his presence, but then trying to get closer to him and not being able to, and not being able to really speak to him, or to really hear him, and then feeling him beginning to fade, his presence beginning to fade, and none of these things" — she gestured at the chalk outlines, at the gems — "none of it working like it was supposed to, and I knew it was because I needed another person, that's what all the books said, because I needed a medium, a tether to the other side but I didn't have anyone, anyone at all. And I didn't know what to do, who to talk to. I didn't have anyone to talk to about it. Except, now."

There were tears in her eyes but they didn't seem like tears to me, anymore. Most of me wanted to leave immediately, to turn and open the door and run from this chilly and cursed room and down the stairs and out the front door and out of Marta's life forever, back into my apartment and into my bed—but there was another part, a smaller but firmer part, that continued to insist that I knew her, that persisted in feeling that I'd known her for as long as I'd known myself, and that I should help her. This woman had drowned her husband, I understood; she had been one hundred feet underwater with him and then left him there to suffocate; and now she was twisted into the tightest of knots, clinging with bloody fingertips to this possibility that he might not have died at all. In the soft candlelight, her face open and her eyes glistening, her thick freckles fading in and out of the luminescence as she breathed, some small voice thought that she might need me.

"Here," she said, leading me to the center of the largest circle, in between the five internal circles, and then handing me a short knife. "You can just prick your thumb, if you'd like."

I looked wide-eyed at the glinting metal in my palm and then I looked wide-eyed at her, breathing through my open mouth, as she rolled up her sleeve and slashed horizontally across her scarred wrist with her own knife, a curtain of blood falling quickly, efficiently down her forearm toward her elbow. She dropped down to her knees and smeared the blood onto each of the nearest five symbols in turn, a fresh layer of the glossy red-brown.

This is not my body, she intoned quietly, almost a hum. *This is not my blood.*

The chalk seemed to smear a little bit underneath the forceful dragging of her wet wrist over the inscriptions, but she either didn't notice or didn't care. My heart pounded.

This is not my ankle, she continued, coming back to the center to take another candlestick from the candelabra, nodding in gentle reminder at the knife in my hand. Then she stepped over to one of the outside circles, holding the flickering candle in both hands before her. *This is not my thumb.*

They must be tears of excitement, I realized, now sliding down one of her cheeks in a thin trickle. I looked down at the knife in my hand

and then wrapped my fingers around the handle, taking an even deeper breath than before, and pushed the point into the end of my thumb. But it was exceedingly difficult to apply any real pressure. I twisted the point into the skin, but there was too much instinctive caution in the muscles themselves, it seemed, to easily draw blood. It hurt powerfully, but no cut formed. I felt ludicrous, insane.

"I don't—" I started, almost in the same moment that Archie suddenly let out one of his shouting barks and I jerked, pushing the point of the knife deep into my thumb and I cried out and dropped it onto the ground, pain arcing through my hand and up my arm. I clutched my forearm with my opposite hand.

"Thank you," Marta exhaled.

I darted a bewildered, terrified glance at the dog and then at Marta. Pain lanced from my thumb and through my whole arm, all the way to my shoulder.

"You remember the words?" she asked.

I stared at her, and then down at the patterns on the floor around me. Even my own actions in this space had begun to seem entirely unreal, fundamentally impossible. I stepped over to the nearest symbol, an hourglass drawn out of straight lines, and squeezed a few drops from the cut in my thumb into the residue of Marta's blood.

"This is not my body," I heard myself say through clenched teeth, before walking over to the next symbol. "This is not my blood." I felt like I was watching myself from a distance, from at least ten or fifteen feet above. "This is not my, ankle, and this is. Not my thumb."

"Thank you." Even though I didn't look up I could still feel her energy radiating out from her, could hear her chest heaving as she watched me take a candle and then retreat to the outside circle diagonal from hers. The nape of my neck tingled as the sweat dried against the cold air. I closed my eyes and tried to steady my breathing, to slow my pulse, to focus on the smell of the hot wax candle in my hands. I was going to be gone from here very soon, after just a minute or so more, I reminded myself. The floorboards creaked.

When I opened my eyes, Marta was crouched in the center of the biggest circle, next to the candelabra, with Archie loudly whining, cradled in her arms.

~

In all the endless discomfort and heinous cruelty of that visit with my mother to Jessica Fortune and Apothecary, I'd never once thought to appreciate the dispatch with which the Lady had executed her craft. It had never occurred to me to admire the efficiency and speed of her movements, the seamless strapping of the rabbit to the breadboard and then the precise incision, unhesitating and complete, one single stroke and then finished. Not that it had spared the rabbit from any pain—it was genuine torture, to keep it alive during its disemboweling—but, frankly, because it spared me from any feeling like I was ever there at all for the murder; that there was ever any moment when I could've made a move, and was thereby complicit for having not moved in that moment.

When Marta Winters gathered her Australian shepherd into her arms in the center of the chalk drawings, on the other hand, I was there the whole time. I was standing motionless, frozen with shock and disbelief, as I thought only that I'd misinterpreted her tears completely— inversely, almost—and she kissed his muzzle and petted his ears back and explained aloud how I'd shown her another mistake, too, that she'd been making beforehand: the books had all insisted that the ritual required a sacrifice to open the connection to the other side, but she hadn't registered that the meaning of the word "sacrifice" was meant in an older sense, a more original sense, until I described the rabbit in the apothecary's shop. *A sacrifice commensurate of loss to the lost,* she recited aloud. She was weeping freely but without sobs, tears trickling in steady streams along either cheek as Archie began to struggle and I opened my mouth as if to speak and she locked her elbows around him, and then she wrapped her legs around his for good measure; but her anxiety was too palpable, too strong of a smell for his sensitive dog's nose and Archie yelped and began to struggle, wriggling his whole dog body and then finally clawing and scratching at her arms and she sank the knife into the side of his throat almost without meaning to, it seemed, and I stumbled backward as they both stiffened as one creature, their bodies clenched tight together and spasming like two dancers choking on a howl, gargling on the blood in his throat, and I made to take a step forward and she thrust her knife again into the same spot, into the side of Archie's neck and his eyes gleamed and panicked, his universe crumbling, and she gasped out a sob and he sank his teeth into the meat of her forearm, and she yelped and elbowed him onto his side but he held on to her, pulling her with his teeth down with him, and she tumbled sideways and plunged the knife over and again into his neck and his chest and the candelabra was knocked over and the room's lighting seemed to reverse itself, shadows disappearing and reappearing on opposite walls, until a part of the dog's fur caught and flamed up and Archie let out a last, deafening howl, high-pitched and squeaking, the light spreading sickly across the lower half of the room and Marta cried out and yanked her arm free of his jaws and covered the fire with her sweater, suffocating the flame and soaking the cloth in his spreading blood in one motion, resuming the near-darkness as the candles flickered out against the floorboards and Archie finally stopped jerking, and I breathed.

In the light of the only remaining lit candles, the pair of wicks flickering from the outer two circles, Marta's face was outlined only on the edges, either side illuminated but the center obscured, the shape of a human being without any of the details. My legs were tingling but I was still too shocked to move, or even to unlock my knees. I stared, my eyes drying.

Marta found the lighter on the floor beside her and then set the candelabra back upright, exhaling loudly as she arranged it on the ground and then inserted the candlesticks, one by one, back into the cups. She appeared to be concentrating very hard on her breathing: her mouth open around each inhale and blinking, holding the air in her lungs, before she exhaled. She sparked the lighter and then moved the flame down the row of candlewicks, relighting them in order, one after the next.

The dull pain where I'd cut my thumb began to sharpen again, arcing back up my elbow and my triceps. My chest heaved.

"Robert," she said, in a quiet voice that nonetheless seemed to boom, bouncing throughout the room. Her face was streaked with tears but her eyes were bright: that same plain determination that I'd earlier mistaken for excitement, that I now mistook for grief. She sniffed. "Robert Daniel Forrester." She lit the last candle and then sat back, her hands on the ground only inches from the spreading pool of blood underneath Archie's corpse. Her forearm was pockmarked where the dog had sunk his teeth into her flesh, bleeding in trickles and flows. "This is your body."

The tingling extended up from my legs and into my torso, the tops of my arms. "Marta," I tried to say, but found my voice caught somewhere in the middle of my throat. My whole body was hot, and rapidly getting hotter—the room seemed to have become much warmer in just the last few moments, more quickly than should have been possible. My heart raced inside the ache in my arm.

"This is your blood." The spreading pool on the floor reached her fingertip and she twitched her hand back, bumping the candelabra with her elbow, and only just caught it in time before it tipped over again. "This is your ankle." She pushed herself up to an unsteady standing position and sniffed again, her skin pale and wet with sweat and her dog's spatter, her hands shaking.

My body had already begun to sweat all over, all along my armpits and my fingers, the little flaps of skin between. "Marta—"

"This is your thumb."

Then she stepped into the outside circle opposite mine, and I cleared my throat to keep speaking but stalled as the warmth increased again: the whole room suddenly suffused with an impossible humidity, a heavy heat that spread through the air and settled on every part of my skin, on the goose bumps rising along the backs of my hands. A swamp heat. Marta let out a little choked gasp of surprise, barely able to breathe through her own astonishment.

"This is your body," she whispered, ecstatic, terrified.

And the light, too, was increasing—not the flames themselves, but the refracted candlelight from the gemstones began to swell brighter, radiating wider and more powerful halos that colored the walls with white and yellow and violet, rotating in kaleidoscopic patterns on the walls, the white chalk outlines shining as if from a direct light above. I opened my mouth to shout, to cry out at the top of my lungs, but I couldn't seem to create any vibration in my larynx; I tried to take a step forward, and then a step back, but both of my legs seemed to be asleep. My heart thudded with adrenaline and fear but I simply could not bring my limbs to move. In the increased light, the spreading pool around the dead dog seemed to glimmer in its own way, a strange motion of illumination around his inert head and limbs, multicolored in the roving reflections.

"Return to your body!" Marta yelled out, her voice amplified in the thick humidity and filling the room at the same moment that one of the candles next to Archie's body tipped out of its cup and onto his limp tail, and his fur smoldered back into flame.

～

Marta and I could never agree, the one time we broached the subject afterward, on when exactly the warmth began to pass from the room. In her telling, it lingered for at least some minutes while she chanted and sang the various lines from the ritual, sustaining the energy in the space, maintaining her brief moment of closeness to Robert—and only after the smoke from Archie's fur began to truly thicken and the stench choked her off in her incantations did that tension slacken and the heavy heat recede. She spent a long time right next to Robert's presence, in her version; standing with him, standing near him; feeling his breath in her chest. It was the only way that she was able to figure out, she insisted later on, what to do next.

On my end of the room, however, the change was immediate. The humidity seeped out of the room like a bucket with a leak, receding in a level plane from the ceiling down to the floor as the air thinned and chilled and the gemstones dimmed, returning to their previous uneven flickering reflections. Marta's voice began to break as she started to repeat her words from earlier, her voice louder and higher, glancing around the room as though looking for where the energy had disappeared to. My tongue swollen, overlarge in the back of my mouth. My legs were tingling all over and my clothes were soaked in sweat but mostly I just felt suddenly exhausted—like I'd been exhausted for days, for weeks—completely and in every muscle, my feet finally too tired to keep standing at all. I sank down to my haunches on the floor, then eased myself down into a sitting position on the wooden boards.

"This is your body," Marta repeated, her voice breaking, gripping her arms over her chest. "Robert Daniel Forrester. This is your blood."

I wrapped my knees around with both arms, my breath still hot and heavy in the rapidly cooling atmosphere, and hugged my legs against my torso. The smell of burnt fur was beginning to fill the room, rising in the thin smoke from the smoldering dead animal. The flame spread gradually, in fits and starts, over the remaining dry areas.

"Fuck." Marta released her arms and pushed her hands into her hair, gripping it back from her face. "*Fuck.*"

I coughed and covered my mouth and nose in the crook of my elbow, shielding myself from the rising stink. Marta glanced at me, wide-eyed, and then back at Archie's corpse.

"It was just the fire. Wasn't it? It was just Archie, wasn't supposed to catch fire. He was just, he was too close to the—candles. Because that's, that's when it—before he caught, from the candle—it was working. It was going to work." She shook her head very quickly and then abruptly launched herself forward, striding carelessly over the chalk markings and slamming the door open and then thundering down the hall, slamming another door open at the opposite end of the house. In the distance, I heard a faucet beginning to run.

The fire spread to another patch of untouched fur and briefly flared, sending up a chuff of thicker smoke that already had me throwing up, it felt like, in the back of my throat, even with my mouth and nose covered. I coughed again and forced myself back to my feet.

But I was just so intensely, so head-to-toe tired at that point, I could barely move at more than a snail's crawl. I stumbled through the open door and into the upstairs hallway, into the narrow passage with the discarded books and clothes and the half-eaten take-out food and the glowing half-closed laptop, the water glasses with used candles inside and the water glasses with water inside and the floorboards groaning beneath my weight as I trudged to the stairwell and shuffled down. My legs felt impossibly heavy, my shoulders hunched under their own weight and my throat almost closed up to keep from vomiting, locked around my nausea and the increasing pressure in my lungs. All I wanted to do was stop and lie down, to close my eyes and never open them, even though all I really wanted to do was get out. On more than one stair I let my eyelids fall briefly shut and then I had to catch myself against the railing, holding back my rising dizziness, as I blinked myself back half-awake. It felt like I was in a dream, but like a waking dream where I'd lost control over my limbs and fingers, like I was alert on the inside but couldn't get my muscles to respond to my impulses, couldn't get myself to run in time before the dream collapsed on every side and I woke up in my real-world bedroom and then still couldn't twitch from underneath my blanket, paralyzed.

In the end, I only made it as far as the first room of perfect bookshelves and perfect couches, to the old Turkish-style divan closest to the stairs on the ground floor, before I crawled onto the cushion and buried my eyes beneath the side of a pillow, yielding myself to unconsciousness.

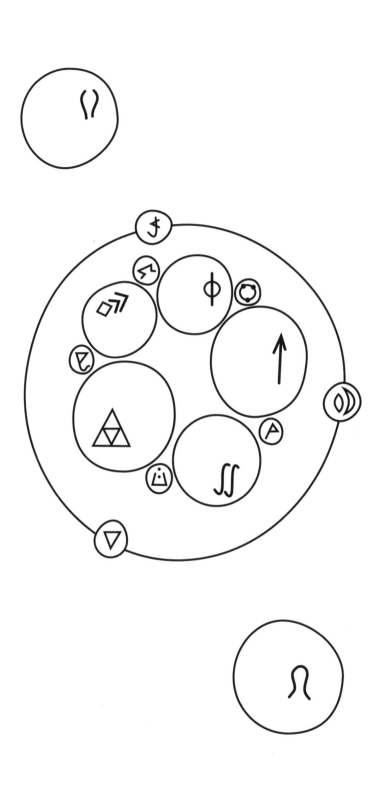

ROBERT

~ ~ ~

In my dream, the knocking belonged to a uniformed police officer, cracking on the wooden panel of my tenement room with the bottom of his nightstick, the cuffs already jingling in his hand to take me down. At first, he was there to arrest me for a crime I didn't commit; then he was there to arrest me for a crime that I had committed, but that hadn't been my fault; and then finally for a crime that I had committed and was to blame for, but would rather die than admit to; the blood dripping from my hands. I lurched to my feet before I'd quite opened my eyes. The doorbell rang, clear and deafening, two tones like hammer strokes against my ears, and I stumbled the rest of the way to the front door and threw it open, blinking my eyes open in the harsh sunlight.

In the first few seconds, before my pupils contracted enough to see more than a silhouette of a person on the front step, I was mostly confused by the sunlight itself: my front door was supposed to open into a hallway. Then the silhouette resolved into a well-dressed older woman, with her gray-blond hair perfectly coiffed into a stylized bun above her head and squinting, her mouth open and moving like she was speaking to me. Because she was speaking to me, I realized.

". . . Marta home?" she asked, her voice wavering at the upper end of a polite tone.

I stepped back, my heart shrinking, as I remembered. The after-smell of burnt fur seemed to reach the both of us at exactly the same time, drifting down the main stairwell and over the threshold, the older woman wrinkling her nose as the blood drained from my skin.

"Um," I said. That same feeling of unreality that I'd encountered yesterday, when I'd first heard back from Marta, seeped into the edges of my perception: the sense that all of my impressions were merely electric impulses along neural pathways, images on a distant screen. "Sorry, I'm—"

"Is someone at the door?" a voice called out from upstairs, floating down the steps after the burnt-dog stench. The stairs creaked behind me. "Peter, you didn't—did you, open the—is there someone there for me?"

"Marta?" the older woman called out, stepping to one side to raise her voice over my shoulder. I stepped to the other side to move around her, pushing abruptly past to make my way outside. "Oh," she said, pulling back.

But I was already rushing down the front stairway to the sidewalk, almost tripping over my feet as I bounded over the steps and then broke into a sprint.

～

I couldn't tell what time it was because my phone was dead in my pocket, but I had a fair idea from the angle and the weight of the sunlight that I was much later than usual when I finally arrived at the bus stop next to MM&Z, LLC. The air was uncomfortably thick, sweat forming on my skin as soon as I stepped off the bus and summoning a profoundly unpleasant memory of the night before, and by the time that I managed to make it to the office—darting across the highway and then loping through the strip mall parking lot, weaving between the parked and moving cars—my shirt was stained around the collar and underneath my arms, droplets of sweat stinging at the corners of my eyes. I shouldered open the double door of the office and made straight for the bathroom. When I emerged, my face damp now with both sweat and splashes of water, I found Willa standing so close outside the bathroom door that I almost walked straight into her, droplets flicking from my fingertips as I raised my hands in surrender.

"Peter," she said, her eyes wide.

I stared at her and she stared at me, but we still didn't quite seem to be making eye contact; I felt instead more like an observed animal, like a dog or a lizard, whose interiority was being actively imagined but not, in fact, accepted as given by the human staring down. Like she wanted to know something, in other words, but didn't know how to ask.

"Are you—"

"John wants you in his office." Her eyes narrowed as she stepped back.

I moved to walk past her and then jumped as she suddenly wrapped me into a tight hug.

"He's an asshole," she said quietly, patting my back.

I accepted the hug belatedly, lifting my arms right as she turned and strode off. I watched her round the corner and then listened to the receding sounds of her footsteps, the squeaking of the little wheels of her desk chair as they rolled on the carpet. The air conditioning began to dry both the water on my face and the sweat along my sides, my body newly cold as the moisture evaporated, and I involuntarily remembered how the temperature had shifted in the upstairs room the night before at Marta's, the heat draining into cold so slowly that for a few seconds I had been freezing on my face while still sweltering around my lower half, humid around my thighs. I lifted the bottom of my shirt to dry my face against the cloth before walking down the hallway to John's office.

I knocked lightly, three taps with a single knuckle, on the frame of the open door.

At that point, I had a fairly good premonition of what was going to happen next, but it seemed there was nowhere else to fall but down. John was sitting in his office flanked by the Garys, both the muscular-necked younger Gary and the hunched and wrinkled one, seated facing away from the door in leather chairs on either side of John's mahogany desk. The older Gary's high-pitched voice was in the middle of a joke when I stepped inside and he broke off just before the punch line, reluctantly trailing off, as I approached and then stopped on top of the pile of Persian rugs.

"Ha," the younger Gary huffed once, without smiling.

John cleared his throat and stared at me, his eyes small. I stared back.

There were large prints of photographs on his desk, I could see, sticking out of the kind of manila folder that the Garys always used for case materials.

"You know, I have to hand it to you, Peter," he said finally, his eyes still narrow. "If I didn't know better, I might think that you were just incredibly good at your job."

He flipped open the folder and held up the first printed photograph, of Marta and me struggling over the fence in her backyard last night, and then a second photograph of the gray-blond older woman and me, standing in Marta's front doorway this morning. I couldn't see the photos especially clearly, standing in the middle of that long room, but I remembered the events well enough that I could guess the details.

"Unfortunately for you, I do know better," he said.

I crossed my arms over my chest. I wanted to care that he was about to fire me, and in an abstract sense I did care—after so many weeks of built-up stress and tension, after all those hours of dread and fear at this specific possibility, it was undeniable that I cared intently about keeping this job. But more concretely, the dusty smell of the Persian rugs underneath my feet was beginning to seem vaguely redolent of the stench from that morning, of that whiff of burnt dog floating down the central stairs, and it was hard to feel anything else over my increasing impatience to get this over with and be allowed to leave this room, this building, this air. I stepped to the side but the smell lingered, and I had to fight to suppress the images that were already rising behind my eyes.

"What the fuck were you doing, exactly, may I ask?"

I swallowed and then cleared my throat, my breath held tight underneath my crossed arms. The way the flame had burned through the fur and then drew bubbles, it looked like, from beneath the exposed skin. "Does it matter?" I asked.

"Well." John shifted in his seat to pull his shoulders back, his chest puffed out. "You are fired, obviously, but—"

"Great." I turned to go.

"—but if you don't want to be sued for fucking negligence, I *strongly* suggest that you—"

I raised a hand in goodbye as I made it to the office door and John slammed his hands on the table, standing. I paused with extreme reluctance. The Garys sat back and looked from one of us to the other, the older one chewing on a grin.

"Tell us what you said to her, Peter," John barked. "You're not leaving here until you tell us what you talked about. If you make this easy, I could be convinced to give you a sort of, severance package, say — two thousand dollars, maybe. If it's good."

I shook my head, stepping out the open door and into the hallway.

"If you make this *hard*, though," John yelled after me, but his voice was already receding as I turned the corner and then he was barely audible at all in the front lobby, a stranger shouting to another stranger in a passing car.

~

But the whole morning seemed to be missing something essential, something elemental, even after I stepped outside. Like a word repeated over and over until it was slowly, entirely drained of its sense and became merely sound, there was something about the sunlight and the highway and the cars flying by, the wind whipping past as I waited for my return bus to arrive, that seemed strangely thinned, like I'd leaned too close to the pixels and now could only see circles of red and blue and green. Some basic neural talent of synthesis seemed to have been suspended, internally, broken down or shocked into inoperability, overloaded or undercharged and discarded, not working, junked. The trucks thumped past in the right lane and the sedans zipped by in the opposite lane and the sunlight collected into a painful glare on the shop windows behind me but it was only light and sound, only sheens and movements and broken colors, different degrees of vibrations, the smell of exhaust. It made me feel tired again, all over again, just to witness. The reality of Marta's ritual, that increasing heat and the glowing lights and the nearness, that palpable proximity, had made my whole being feel newly uncertain; and I found myself intensely anxious standing by the side of the highway, not because my life was collapsing but because I was worried that my body might do something abrupt and arbitrary without my entirely willing it to, might step into the road on an impulse and I'd be hit by a rushing truck and fly into the sky, my field of vision inverting and then inverting again as my body lifted and then stalled, turned, twisted, fell.

I stepped back from the road and huddled near the bushes beside the strip mall entrance until the bus finally arrived and I climbed inside.

Back at my apartment, I plugged my phone into the outlet and then sat down on the floor beside the charger, waiting with my head tipped back against the wall until it had enough juice to turn on. I was planning to make a call to Naphtha, to see if it'd be all right if I came over and hung out on her couch for a while, to hear her voice and to ask if she wanted to fuck and to feel the grounding weight of her insults, the familiar friction of her disdain. I didn't know if she would actually be free on a late week-day morning—I didn't entirely know what she did during the day, these days—but I figured I could at least send her a text and tell her that I was coming over before showing up at her door. I was beginning to feel a little fundamentally undermined, in the fashion of that teetering feeling that Marta had described: something of those minutes and seconds extending, unending, curling like light over the horizon of the day, leaving the ground underneath me feeling uneven and massive, rotating slowly on its axis. For a brief moment, I wondered if Marta was doing okay.

Then my phone lit with a signal that it was two percent charged and I held the power button to wake it up and it started vibrating with incoming text and voice messages, and then kept vibrating, over and over, for almost two minutes straight. I knew the time exactly because I was looking at the little window-screen on the outside as it buzzed, 11:39 into 11:40 and then 11:41, the grainy thumbnail of the Andes rising underneath. At first I wondered if my old friends, my former roommates and larger friend group from art school, might not have reached out to contact me. But they were only from Dad—sixty-five text messages and thirteen voicemails over the last day or so, in addition to the seven voicemails he'd already left in the days preceding. An alert popped up on my screen that he'd completely filled my voicemail inbox.

I scrolled through to his number and dialed without reading or listening to a single one of his messages. He didn't answer. My lower back was beginning to ache after sitting on the hardwood floor for so long and I laid myself down as I listened to the ring and then his recorded voicemail prompt, arranging a dirty shirt underneath my head to form a pillow from the floor. I was in the middle of leaving a monotone apology, acknowledging that I'd been hard to reach without explaining why, when his cell number began to beep into my phone, returning my call in that moment. I looked at his name on the screen, chewing on the inside of my cheek, before I pressed the button to switch lines.

"So!" he began.

I restarted my apology in the same routine manner, a manner that I knew he loathed but that I was helpless, it seemed, after so long of being a habitually insolent son, to avoid taking on. I imagined that I could hear him breathing through his flared nostrils as he listened, his teeth clenched beneath a thin smile.

"You didn't read any of my messages," he said, cutting me off. "None of them. Not one."

I bit down on the corner of my lip. "I mean," I said.

"Are you with your mother right now?"

"Mom?"

He exhaled an awkward, angry laugh, insane with impatience. "You've got to be fucking kidding me, Peter. You didn't read a single one."

I blinked, taken aback by his swearing. "Sorry, I—"

"I just got back from the police station, from filing a missing-person report for your mother. You're lucky I decided not to file one for you, too. Do you have any idea of how *fucking* frustrating it is, to hear that you didn't read even one of my texts? How *angry* that makes me feel?"

I sat up straight, the floorboards cool underneath my palm. "For Mom? Sorry, you—a missing-person report for Mom?"

"She never came back after that day when you called me. I never even knew if she made it to Chicago after she disappeared, other than from your phone call. It's been four *days*, Peter. You never even told me if she landed, or if you ever saw her at all. Not in four *days* of calling you, and texting you, and leaving you voicemail messages, and texting you over and over again." He took an audible breath, loud static against the receiver on his end of the line. He was crying, possibly. "I'm sorry, I am just. This just makes me so *incredibly* angry to hear."

I was hunched over my legs, now, curled almost into a ball. "I think just three days, actually," I said in a small voice, my eyebrows high.

"Sorry?"

I cleared my throat. "It's, um. Sorry. I'm sorry, that I didn't call you back earlier."

"It's been four days. You're seriously arguing with me about that? You're seriously choosing to argue with me, about this, right now."

"No, I'm—" I took a long breath through my nostrils. My apartment was filthy, I realized, dust visible in the air, dirty clothes all over the floor. "She came on Sunday, and today is Wednesday, is all I meant. You filed a missing-person report?"

"Sunday. Monday. Tuesday. Wednesday. Four days."

I rose to my feet and started picking up clothes, throwing them over the elbow of my phone arm. "Well. Seventy-two hours, I guess."

"But you did see her on Sunday? She actually did arrive there, in Chicago."

I dumped my first load of clothes onto the top of my overflowing laundry hamper and then bent down to collect more, gathering the smaller pieces onto my arm, the socks and the underwear and the random winter beanies. In as few words as I could manage, I explained to him Mom's visit of three days before, the trip to the soothsayer and the misbegotten séance, the hardware store I'd dropped her off at afterward, while he ground his teeth on the other end of the line.

"I'd like you to come home," he said, cutting in a few words before I was quite finished. "I can buy you a ticket for this afternoon. All right?"

"This afternoon, as in—today?" I placed the socks and underwear and winter hats on top of the teetering pile of laundry and then watched as they rolled directly off and back onto the floor, avalanching a pair of dirty pants from the hamper along with them. "It's the middle of the week, Dad."

"Take a couple of days off. Your mother is fucking missing, Peter. I don't want to do this alone."

I chewed on the inside of my cheek again, my face tightening, staring at the closest sock on the ground.

~

In the first few months after Henry died, my mother had disappeared from the house a handful of times without warning, but only once for more than a single twenty-four-hour period. The first few trips, it turned out that she'd only gone to Joshua Tree or Sequoia without telling us and without taking her phone, and always with the same of the grief groups that she'd started attending—an outdoor hiking group, she told us, specifically for the parents of children who'd died. They weren't supposed to take phones, she explained. Dad always hated it, staring small-eyed at the wall for as long as she was speaking, but he didn't seem to have the wherewithal to actually argue back at that time, still only a few months since.

Until one weekend, around the beginning of December, close to the end of my two months home—after I'd already bought my plane ticket back, but before I'd told my parents that I was leaving—when he and I woke up on Saturday morning and found that Mom was gone again, absent from the floor of Henry's room and absent from the living room couch where she sometimes slept, with no coffee in the pot and with her car missing from the garage, her phone snugly plugged into its charger on the kitchen countertop. It was clear enough what had happened, but Dad still insisted on going through the motions of confusion. He made the coffee and poured her a mug and left it on the countertop, walked over to the neighbors to ask if Mom had stopped by their house at all that morning, called her old work to see if they'd seen her around. I couldn't tell if it was a committed form of passive-aggression or simply willful ignorance, but in any case I just stayed out of his way. He asked me two times that day, once in the morning and once before sunset, if I wouldn't mind mowing the goddamn lawn, and I reminded him on both occasions that I already had, just the day before. He gave me the same look each time, like he was trying to cross his eyes but he didn't know how to. That night I drove into town for dinner and bought myself a sandwich and a coffee at the family restaurant next to the highway off-ramp, and then when I returned home all the windows were dark except for his. I walked through the house without flipping any of the lights on, until I'd creaked up the steps and down the hallway and into my bedroom.

Then Sunday arrived and my mother still hadn't reappeared and both of us were newly unsettled, but since we didn't really have the language to speak about it, we mostly went through the same sequence as the day before. Dad dumped out Mom's untouched mug of coffee from the morning prior and poured her a new one, knocked at the neighbors' again to ask if they'd seen her around, and then settled into the living room couch to watch the football pregame shows while I read a book in the easy chair and glanced at the screen when the commercials came on. He shot to his feet every once in a while, seemingly at random, whenever he thought that he'd heard the telephone ringing—rushing into the kitchen and then pulling the phone off the hook, pressing the receiver to his ear—before he returned to the couch and stared again at the TV screen. The first game started and he snorted and shook his head at the dropped passes, the sacks. Then the phone actually rang and he and I both stiffened, listening to the grating chime from the kitchen, before he pushed himself up and ran to answer.

She'd been picked up by the police outside of Twentynine Palms. Standing barefoot by the side of the highway, shivering in the thin light of predawn, she'd flagged down a cruiser and then babbled a long stream of gibberish as soon as the cop slowed down, syllables and urgent sounds that she seemed to earnestly believe was language, with her pupils so heavily dilated that the cop couldn't see her irises at all. Eventually, he managed to convince her to take a ride back to the police station for a nap and then a hot coffee; and after she finished the coffee, finally speaking English again, she'd asked for a phone call.

The "outdoor hiking group," as it turned out, had really been an ayahuasca-based healing group. Led by a locally trained shaman and an area real estate agent, they took small groups of grieving parents into the woods or the desert and guided them on hallucinogenic journeys to help them to connect and move on. Mom hadn't explained all this, obviously, because she knew how furious my dad would be at just the idea; which was also why she'd been so clandestine about when and how long she went off for. On this particular trip, though, she'd been granted permission to take a larger dose than she'd previously tried and then had vomited almost immediately on one of the other participants, throwing up on the woman's arm while they were all holding hands in a circle, and this other mom had started screaming that my mother was an alien creature from deep underground, yowling at the very top of her lungs in the middle of the desert and Mom was so ashamed that she simply ran, sprinting through the scrub and weeping, the sky collapsing above her and the cracked soil crumbling underneath her feet. She'd apparently gone so fast that the guides hadn't been able to keep up with her, either — this was before she'd taken off and subsequently lost her shoes — and then she'd found herself at the interstate, now convinced that she was indeed an alien from deep underground and trying to explain the emergency of her collapsing planet, using her native tongue, to the policeman.

Dad's eyes were bright at the corners as he listened, driving in clenched silence, his knuckles white around the steering wheel. But if Mom noticed, her eyes still rimmed with red in the passenger seat, she only spoke faster and faster, giggling nervously as she described the strange noises that she'd believed corresponded to certain words in her head, the way the ground had felt like an ocean underneath her bare heels. Dad flinched at every laugh and then slowly, possibly without realizing, lifted his foot off the gas pedal. The car gradually eased down from sixty-five miles an hour to forty, and then thirty, twenty, ten. Mom stopped talking and looked over at him. The other cars on the highway honked as they navigated around.

"Please stop laughing," he said.

Mom looked at him, and started to reply. "Charles, I just—"

"You could have been raped." He spoke over her, blinking through his tears.

Mom blushed. "That's—"

But he was already shouting at that point, still facing forward toward the windshield but screaming her down, narrating the awful eventualities that he'd imagined and that he was still imagining, apparently, with his shoulders high around his ears and all the cords of muscle along his neck pulled taut and visible, his skin reddening on his face and around his collarbone. He'd always been prone to occasional outbursts of rage when I was growing up, but in the months since finding Henry he hadn't seemed able to maintain any real lasting anger; only now, all those weeks of postponed wrath were finally bursting their dam. My mom sat back with her neck tucked into her chest as she absorbed this sudden onslaught, her eyes small. From my angle, sitting behind the driver's seat, it was hard to tell what exact expression she wore on her face. After the first minute or so of Dad's diatribe, she turned to look out her window and I turned to look out mine, at the outrage of the other drivers as they yelled and honked and detoured around our stopped car in the right lane of the highway.

Eventually Dad ran out of steam and started the car moving again, accelerating slowly to merge back into the flowing traffic and precipitating a whole new flurry of honks and irritated glares from the other drivers, and then he drove us the rest of the way home in silence. Mom didn't say a word. After we pulled into our driveway Dad got out quickly, pushing his car door open and then storming up the walk and into the house, while Mom and I eased out of our seats and watched him go.

Without looking over, I asked if she was doing all right. She shook her head very slightly, almost imperceptibly. I walked over to wrap her into a hug but she held me at bay with her fingers out in an open fan.

"Sorry," she said, staring intently at the pavement around my sneakers. "It's just. A very delicate place, after a bad trip on hallucinogens."

I stepped back and she stepped past me, her head down.

Over the following few days she and my father spoke only once in my hearing, and only then because each seemed to believe the other had said something: walking past one another in the hall, she asked him *What?* and he asked her *Excuse me?* and then they realized, and passed on. She ate in Henry's bedroom and he slept on the couch, watching the TV long into the early morning. Neither of them actually went anywhere near their own bed, as far as I could tell. I told them two days before my flight—telling each of them separately, in their different parts of the house—that I was leaving at the end of the week, and each of them asked, in their own way, for me to stay. I replied to Dad that I was leaving, but that he could still call me on the phone if he wanted to talk. I told Mom that I'd sleep on it before I made up my mind.

⁓

He was waiting for me in the arrivals terminal of Fresno Yosemite airport with a piece of paper in both hands, my name scrawled in black marker across the center. I glared at the sign and then glared at him, my suitcase rolling to a stop behind my heel. He frowned.

"Seriously, Dad?"

"In case we didn't recognize each other, I thought."

"Can't I be here for maybe, two minutes, before you pick an argument."

"Me? I'm picking the argument?"

I suppressed a sigh and rolled my suitcase past him, my jaw clenched around my reply. He crumpled the piece of paper and told me that I was going in the wrong direction, and then led me toward the cell phone parking lot on the opposite side. The dry August air flew into my eyes like a gust as soon as the terminal's doors slid open. I squinted, coughing into an elbow.

"There's a fire," Dad said, fumbling with his keys. My suitcase wheels clacked loudly on the blacktop as we strode onto the road and across the lanes of parked cars. "Inside the park, right now. Lot of smoke."

I coughed in agreement, duly taking note of the grayed-out sky in a different way than before. Even though I'd agreed on the phone to come here and had then come, ostensibly of my own free will, I couldn't help feeling continually surprised that I'd actually done so. Internally, I reminded myself that it was only two days till my return ticket.

"Thank you, also," Dad said as he heaved my suitcase into the bed of his brand-new pickup, apparently hearing my thought. "It's been really awful, these past few days. Being in the house alone."

I climbed into the truck's cab, my stomach sinking. I hadn't actually thought about the house yet, or what it would feel like to go back there. He climbed into the driver's side and slammed the door shut.

"I keep thinking that everyone's going to die," he said, as if in answer to a question. "I can't stop watching these, documentaries—History Channel shows, I don't know what you call them—about the San Andreas Fault, or the San Francisco earthquake." He reached out without looking and grabbed my shoulder, pushing his thumb into the hollow of my clavicle. "I'm really grateful that you're here, Peter."

I nodded, holding my breath without quite understanding why. "Sure," I said.

He turned on the engine without acknowledging my response, backed up hard into the bumper of a parked car and then swore, lurched forward into drive, and shot the truck toward the exit.

That afternoon, just before boarding the plane to Fresno, I'd received a call from Marta on my cell phone. It had taken me a moment to recognize the number. Standing in line to show the gateway attendant my ticket and my passport, shuffling forward as another boarding group was called and more people flocked to gather behind us in line, I held my phone in my palm and tried to recall why the area code looked so familiar. A number from New York. The woman behind me cleared her throat and I realized that an empty space had opened up before me and I stumbled forward, the back of my neck prickling, and showed the ticket-taker my bar code to scan. I stood to the side of the entrance to the plane's jet bridge and flipped the phone open just after it stopped buzzing in my palm and then listened, without saying hello, to the dead silence of the disconnected line.

After I landed, though, I found myself taking out my phone roughly once every ten minutes to see if she'd called again and I'd missed it, or if she'd texted and I hadn't felt the vibration against my thigh. I scrolled through my missed calls and highlighted her number twice in the first five minutes of riding in the passenger seat of my dad's new pickup, nodding along while he described the leasing process at the dealership and I wondered if I should call her back, if only just to see if she'd answer, to hear the tone of her voice and if the Garys had started to attack her, if John had begun to intimidate her, to ask her why she'd called. Dad turned on the radio and then turned it off and told me where he'd already checked that day for Mom and where he'd been planning to check on the way home, if that was all right with me, and I said sure and he kept us driving straight on the interstate after our normal exit, coasting a little under the speed limit in the right lane, the paint lines radiating bright underneath his headlights. By that point the police had established, in the time since the missing-person report had been filed, that my mother had indeed flown back from Chicago on the last leg of her round trip on Monday, according to the flight logs from the airline. Which meant that she was in California, as like as not. It was a little like learning that the pain in your stomach is coming from a tumor in your intestine, Dad said, leaning forward to scan the berm past my shoulder: the kind of certainty that only made you feel anxious in a different direction, knowing exactly where to worry about. I smiled, shifting awkwardly under his indirect gaze.

"You know, I got," I started, pausing for a moment to chew on my bottom lip. "I actually got fired from my job, this morning. Before you called."

He glanced up at my face. "Shit, kid."

"I mean, it's fine. Or. It isn't, but—"

"You loved that job, though."

I widened my eyes, withdrawing my head against the headrest. "Um."

He gripped my shoulder once more and shook me, forward and back. I bared my teeth in a polite grimace.

"You'll be all right," he said, glancing back to the road while holding fast with his fingers. "It'll all work out, Peter."

I took a breath with a surprising amount of difficulty. In his last few months, Henry had become increasingly frustrated with the fact that we only ever had other people's words to speak with, that we only ever had this inherited vocabulary and grammar from our surrounding society and the resulting unbridgeable distance in our conversations because he could never share his own language, his complete meanings, except at the agreed-upon meeting points of English. It was like he needed other people's permission to be heard, he felt.

No one fucking listens when I'm fucking speaking to them, he said often, over and over, whenever he managed to get me on the phone.

"You need money?" Dad asked, squinting at a shape along the side of the highway.

I lowered my brow, exhaled through my nose, and said no; and then, shaking my head, maybe. He released my shoulder to take the steering wheel with both hands, holding it steady as he slowed the car down to thirty-five miles an hour and peered at an approaching billboard, and then at the next billboard after. My chest felt sore, constricted. Along the side of the highway, the trunks of the trees seemed to rise to the surface of the liquid dark before sinking back down as the headlights passed, the bark glinting like skin.

and there's only so many times you can fucking say it, before you just have to start bashing your head into a fucking wall. Nothing's THERE if you don't see it. Things EXIST because they're EXPE-RIENCED and people SEE what they EXPECT TO which means if you're not fucking expected then you're not even fucking there at all. You don't fucking exist. The entire universe could be a fucking hologram but it's meaningless because no one can ever see it, it's just a theory on a black-board, a way of writing equations out in chalk so that they all work out when you plug them into other equations. It's like if everyone wrote ∂ instead of 2. All that matters is that you add up to fucking four. I've never fucking existed. It's taken me my whole life to fucking see it but I've never actually existed for anyone else, there's never been one single fucking living breathing eye-to-eye actual moment when one single other person looked me STRAIGHT ON and saw what was actually there, and not just what they fuck-ing thought might already be there. I'm a fucking BLOT. No one ever fucking sees anyone else. Peo-ple just agree to play the same fucking game so that they can pretend together that it's not a game and these words aren't just pieces that they're pushing around on a fucking board. Judging each other's moves, waiting for their turn. Being an actual fucking HUMAN BEING isn't part of the fucking rules. There's no rule for LOOKING UP from the fucking chessboard. There's no rule for trying to SEE the person on the other side of

The phone was ringing when I came downstairs for breakfast, and by the time I came into the kitchen Dad was already standing in the corner next to the landline receiver, twirling the spiral cord around his forefinger and then twisting it tight, cutting off the blood flow to his fingertip while he nodded and said, "Uh-huh." I pulled a bowl down from the cupboard and poured myself some cereal. It was only a few minutes after sunrise outside, I realized, squinting at the gray light leaking through the windows. With the time difference, I seemed to have woken up just a little after five.

Dad hung up the phone and my teeth crunched into the dry cereal, the sound of my own chewing cacophonous against my inner ear as he started to speak.

"The cops tracked her down, with her credit card," he said, his brow creasing and then uncreasing, glancing at me and then out the kitchen window, at the backyard outside. "She's just at a motel, in town. That old place across from the strip mall. Next to the 43."

I rubbed my left eye with the back of my wrist and squinted at him with my right, feeling my depth perception briefly shift into cyclops vision. Dad finally settled on a deep frown. I let my arm down and took another bite of cereal.

"They were," he continued, as though he hadn't just paused for a good ten seconds. "They went to see her, already, to check in with her, and make sure it was okay that they gave me her address."

I looked at him, looking out the window. He'd been balding for about as long as I could remember but he'd only recently begun shaving his head completely, buzzing all the hair on every side so that his head was almost evenly naked except for the five-o'clock shadow where his comb-over had once begun. It came off better this way, for the most part, except that the wrinkles on his forehead now seemed much wider than before, longer and more lasting, remaining in persistent thin lines above his brow even after his expression had otherwise cleared. I couldn't tell if he seemed smaller, also, or if he'd always been this small.

"That's weird," I said, nodding.

"It is weird," he agreed.

He made himself another cup of coffee and then chugged it down as I finished my cereal, and then we both rose in the same moment, our gazes trained on different spots on the floor, and walked in single file to put our shoes on.

~

After we pulled off the road and into the parking lot, I realized that I did actually know this particular motel by sight. About two minutes before the on-ramp to the highway, with two stories in the shape of a square horseshoe encircling the large gravel lot, it was one of those buildings that I'd driven past for at least ten years without once really thinking about, the neon sign for NO/VACANCY always noticed without being seen, like a stranger's face on the subway. The gravel crunched underneath our tires as Dad swerved into the spot closest to the entrance, hopped out, and slammed the door behind. I stayed in shotgun and chewed on my tongue. The way the motel was set up, the rooms all seemed to gaze down on the cars parked in the middle, and I had the strange sense that Mom might already be standing somewhere on the walkway on the second floor, leaning over the banister or looking out from inside her room. Dad had tried to call her cell phone multiple times on the ride over, but still only got sent straight to voicemail. I climbed out of the passenger seat at the same time that he strode out of the front office, and then I followed him in a straight diagonal across the parking lot.

The door was propped open on the catch of the chain lock, shuddering slightly as Dad pounded on the top with the bottom of his fist, calling out Mom's name and then pushing it open with his forearm. From over his shoulder, I could see her sitting cross-legged on the end of the motel bed with her eyes closed and her mouth pinched, her nostrils flared. She'd been meditating in front of the Weather Channel, it appeared, with the sound off on the TV. The disembodied arms of a weatherman gestured broadly at a spill of bright yellow, spreading over a map of bright blue.

"Beatrice," Dad said again, stepping inside. I held an arm out to keep the door from closing.

She took a deep breath before opening her eyes, then stared straight forward at the television. "Hi, Charles."

He ran his palm over his bald head. She turned and raised her eyebrows.

"Peter!" she said, in a very different tone. "You're in California!"

I gritted my teeth into a grimace, propping the door open with my shoulder. "Dad thought you were dead, Mom."

"Yes, I'm—the police were here, earlier. I'm sorry that you had to come all this way, just for. But." She glanced above me and then below me, everywhere except returning my gaze. "I am very glad to see you. It's really good to see you, honey."

I stared at her. I wanted to get angry but I realized that this would be synonymous, in this situation, with taking Dad's side, and I felt urgently the need to not take either side. I shouldn't be here at all, I was finally realizing.

Both Mom and I turned to look at Dad, girding ourselves for the coming eruption. But he only seemed to be shrinking smaller, even smaller than after the phone call this morning, his arms crossed over his chest and leaning far forward, so far that he'd almost dropped to his haunches. He looked like he was trying to give himself the Heimlich maneuver, or like he was trying to find a position in which he could comfortably breathe.

"I'm sorry, Charles," Mom said, but in the untouched tone of a stranger who's accidentally seen something private, comforting someone they barely know.

Dad shook his head, his torso parallel to the carpet, the top of his head slightly pink underneath the mix of indoor fluorescence and sunlight through the door. "I can't," he started. "I, just."

"I know," Mom said.

He twisted his head to the side to look at her and I looked away, blood rushing to my face. There was no space for me in that room but it felt equally too much to leave, at this point, especially with the door slamming behind me if I left. Dad lowered his eyes to the ground and curved his back, his arms still crossed but more like he was just freezing cold, huddling into himself for warmth.

"Why didn't you just tell me?" he said.

Mom took a breath and looked at the Weather Channel, at the bright red now spreading over the map.

"I was going to," she replied, very quietly. "I was getting ready to, I mean."

He shook his head, his whole torso, side to side.

"These things," Mom said, glancing to the opposite side of the room, toward the open door to the bathroom, "they test you, as a couple, you know? They either, they bring you together, or. They drive you apart."

Dad shook his head in longer swings, swaying back and forth with his arms crossed, his torso still parallel to the floor. "No," he said.

I was breathing very shallowly, at the very top of my lungs, the quietest inhales that I could manage through my open mouth. I was small also, I realized.

"I'm sorry, Charles," Mom said.

He bent his knees and laced his fingers over his bald head, rocking, forward and back. His knees cracked under his weight.

"No," he said.

Lying on my back in my bed beside the stairway, listening to my parents argue in the kitchen on the first floor.

⁓

Dad felt too unsteady in his body, in his breathing and in his hands, to drive on the way back, so he handed me the keys and laid himself down instead in the bed of the pickup, his elbows over his eyes. I tried to drive slowly but still felt sharp pangs of guilt every time the truck bumped over a crack in the pavement or turned a little faster than I meant it to, the rear swinging around as I angled through town back toward our house. When I pulled into the driveway and got out to see how he'd borne the ride, I found that he'd already covered himself, like a corpse underneath a shroud, with his bright blue tarp. Even the outline of his body was barely visible under the normal crags and valleys of the plasticky material. I opened my mouth to say something, to announce that we'd arrived, but my voice didn't seem to be in my throat in that moment. I went inside.

There wasn't anything changed in the house since that morning, the front doormat still askew from where I'd nudged it on my way out and the same dirty cereal bowl in the kitchen sink, but this now bothered me inexpressibly and I rinsed the bowl with soap and water and then returned to the front room, turning on every overhead light and every lamp as I went. I spent a long time arranging the mat so that it was perfectly flush again with the threshold. For some reason I couldn't stop thinking about when we'd first moved to this house, when I was around nine years old or so and Henry was twelve, and I'd spent all day running around in my sock feet and sliding as far as I could on the wooden floorboards while Henry marched through and announced which of the rooms he hated the most. I rose from fixing the doormat, squinting at the sliver of space between the threshold and the edge of the cloth, and had to fight the impulse—more like a need or a craving than a desire—to slip off my shoes and do it again, to gather a running start and launch myself to slide as far as I could along the naked wood.

I sensed my mom calling me just before my phone began to vibrate in my pocket, and I took out my cell and briskly flipped it open and closed. There were more lights to turn on, I noticed, in other rooms in the house, and I strode through and began turning on the overheads and twisting the switches on the lamps as my mom called me again, and again I hung up on her, and then I rounded back to the kitchen and padded upstairs while she called a third time and I hung up faster, catching her in rhythm now, and she called back even faster still. The fifth and the sixth times I just let it ring, holding my cell phone in my right palm as I went through the bedrooms and turned on the bedside lamps and the little bulbs around the bathroom mirrors. Then I wedged my phone into the very center of my sock drawer and slid it shut, sat down at my desk, and opened my laptop.

I hadn't actually gotten a chance, I realized, to sit down and try to figure out what had happened to me at Marta Winters's two nights before. In all of the upheavals since leaving her house, with Dad's call and then the subsequent sinkhole of family that I'd fallen down, I'd had to set aside her muggy bedroom and my memories of the murdered dog, moving past the radiant gemstones and the chalk diagram and the gray-blond woman at the door as though there was nothing more to think about; but there was plainly much more to think about. Something had happened to me there, in that heat and then that exhaustion, in the increasing glow and then the cold afterward; something could be happening to me still. I sat down at my desk feeling almost grateful to have such a powerfully absorbing task in this moment when I wanted so powerfully to be absorbed.

But it was frustratingly difficult to come across anything even remotely related to what I'd gone through. There were plenty of historical articles about entirely different rituals and plenty of how-tos on other methods to bring your late husband back from the dead, but nothing at all about the particular steps and particular words that Marta had used. I looked up voodoo and I looked up tarot, I looked up mysticism and I looked up Kabbalistic traditions and I looked up Catholic miracles and I looked up acupuncture, shrunken heads, the Stone Age settlement of the Polynesian island chains, the travels of Captain Cook, his death on Hawaii; I googled obscure diseases and I researched the *DSM* definitions of various forms of hallucination and I paged through witness accounts of UFO abductions and experimentation, theories on the U.S. government origins of Lyme disease, clicked through to a Satanist website that I took far too long to realize was porn; I scrolled through old custom websites that unfurled in one unending page of text and images and I checked through a number of occultist message boards, eventually looking through Google Books images of old texts that the users popularly referenced; but nothing linked to anything remotely similar to the diagram that Marta had drawn, or anything like the words she'd intoned that night. I tried searching the phrases *I am not my body/I am not my blood/I am not my ankle* but only found myself led to Walt Whitman poems and articles on ankle sprains.

I began to feel anxious, annoyed, clicking harder than I needed to and grinding my teeth as I waited for the advertisements to load so that I could X out of them. I was looking for a greater absorption than this, a better project, something large enough to fully swallow my focus from this morning and this day. I wheeled my chair back and pushed my fingers into my hair, feeling the stretch in my scalp as the ends pulled on the roots. I wondered if I could just ask Marta directly; I wondered if she would answer if I called her on her cell phone. I leaned down and pulled open my sock drawer, located my cell in the center of the clothes, and navigated to Marta's number in my missed calls, bit down on a fingernail and then swallowed, feeling the keratin scratch on the inside of my esophagus.

Then my phone began to buzz again with another call from my mother. My expression condensed as I looked at her name flashing on the little window. I flipped the phone open and lifted it to my ear.

⁓

She walked into the coffee shop with an expression of wilting sadness that set my teeth on edge even before I'd outwardly acknowledged that I'd seen her, while my expression was still otherwise set in a squinting frown, as though focused on something exceptionally irritating on the other side of the plate-glass window. Her shoes shuffled loudly on the tile floor and her bag's buckle clanked against the overlarge buttons of her shirt and I realized, finally, that she hadn't spotted me, or at least she was acting as if she hadn't. I lifted my head and turned as though absent-mindedly toward her, my eyes glazed.

"Oh," Mom said with an exhale of relief, or something like relief, noticing me. She shuffled over and clinked her bag to the floor, scraped the opposite chair out from under the table, and settled herself into the hard seat.

I rubbed my eyes, pushing my fingertips into my eye sockets. When I finally opened them, my vision of my mother's face across from me was pockmarked by blind spots, a patchwork of blurs that slowly resolved into an expression of intent concern. She reached out and took my hand in hers.

"You shouldn't have had to be there, for that," she said, choosing each word carefully before pronouncing the next. "I'm sorry that you were there for that, I mean."

I pulled my hand away, glaring at her and then glaring past her, my face furrowed. The barista called out my name from behind the counter.

My mother continued her apology as I stood and strode over to fetch my drink, her voice lifting and then trailing off as I fitted a lid to the cup. I carried it back to the table and sat down.

"Why are you doing this, Mom?" I said, looking at my own reflection in the front window.

She crossed her arms. "Well," she said. "I wanted to apologize, to you, firstly. And also—"

"No. Why are you doing this, I mean." I took a tiny sip of coffee and returned the stare of a little girl walking past on the sidewalk outside, her button nose only inches from the window. "Couldn't you just wait? A little bit longer? At least, longer than nine months?"

She drew her head back, genuinely surprised. "I—" she started. "I didn't expect this from you, Peter."

I watched the little girl disappear at the end of the window's pane and then reappear a moment later, crossing the street and twisting her head around to keep looking at me. I deepened my frown.

"This isn't something that I'm 'doing,'" Mom said, measuring her words out with a wrinkled nose. "It's not fair to call it that. You know that's not fair, Peter." She was genuinely angry, I realized. Underneath my hardened expression, I felt a soft bloom of shame. "How dare you."

I folded my arms over my chest. "Fine. Sorry."

"How dare you, Peter. As if this is something that I—something that I *wanted* to happen, as if—"

"All right." I took a breath, looking through the window glass for a new stranger to walk past. "I'm sorry."

She glared at me over a thin frown while the barista called out another

133

customer's name. There were tears in her eyes, but they didn't fall down her cheeks and she didn't wipe them. She took out a small notebook and set it down on the table.

"I've been thinking a lot," she said, "about when I was your and Henry's age. Back when I had just graduated from university, and I was still living at my parents', at their old fixer-upper near Erie." Her expression was still angry but there was another emotion visible through it, an ocean wave with the sand and seashells clear underneath. "Before I met your father, I mean, or had any idea that I would ever marry and settle down."

She opened her notebook and flipped past a series of thickly scribbled notes, all the way to the end. Then she flipped it back over and started at the beginning again. I took another sip of coffee.

"There was this sort of, openness, back then, in how I thought about myself—about who I was, I mean. A different set of assumptions. There was this feeling like, I remember—this feeling that I could still decide on myself. That I could decide to be this way, or that way, and that I just had to be careful which I chose."

"Honestly, Mom," I said, suppressing a heavy sigh in my chest. "I'm sorry, but—right now, this—" I made a gesture with my fingers without unfolding my arms. "I wanted to ask you about something. Something else."

She glanced up at me, her expression drawn. She was hurt, I could tell. I looked down into the black liquid in my tiny coffee mug.

"How did you find the Lady Jessica, when you were looking for mediums?"

She blinked, her face relaxing into a rather plain relief. I felt myself tense, anticipating her excitement.

"Oh," she said, beginning to smile.

"Just, when you were looking for someone to help you take advantage of the, alignment. How did you know where to start looking. In so many words."

"No, but that's—that's a lovely coincidence, really. Or not a coincidence at all, I should say. I've been thinking about that a lot, too, Peter. A *lot* about it. I can't stop thinking about it, it feels like, some days."

I clenched my hand into fist, gripping my biceps opposite. "Right. Sure. But I really did just want to know—"

"No, I mean it, though. We got too—or, I got too—wrapped up in the immediate, the bad feelings, of Henry not wanting to share. But it was really, if you think about it—it was really incredibly successful. *Incredibly* successful. The Lady Jessica, you know, she was able to really make contact with Henry's spirit and then learn all the real details of his passing, and that means that his spirit has to be, in fact, still—"

"—but, that's not—Mom. Stop. That's not what I'm—"

"—he's *out there*, Peter. And not even that far off. Henry is *near*. And I mean, in retrospect—obviously he doesn't want to talk to me. He's never wanted to talk to me. If anything, that's maybe the best proof that she, that Lady Jessica, really found our son. Our Henry, I mean. It's honestly embarrassing, thinking back on it, that I'd even expected—that I'd never thought through that that—wasn't really what he needed. But I've been researching astral projection, recently, and I've learned that you can actually visit it yourself, the astral plane, while you're still living, as long as you're careful to go only for a short period of time and I realized that *that's*—"

I stood up so quickly that my chair screeched, its feet scraping loudly on the wooden floor and then accidentally tipping over backward, crashing with a sudden clap of thunder against the parquet.

～

When I was in my last year at art school, it took me a dangerously long time to decide on a topic for a senior thesis. I was a painting major, technically speaking, but I'd done a lot of projects incorporating other media and I felt certain that I wanted to make something as technically complicated as I could manage: a canvas with at least one part of the frame mechanized, I envisioned, with a motor and ideally some sort of liquid flowing down a track, along with a projected image overlaid on top and music playing, or at least some arrangement of sounds, coming out of a number of speakers placed around the room and with the volume rotating smoothly in a circle, as though the noise were slowly gathering as you stood and looked. But I had no idea, beyond that, what the painting was to be about. The pieces that had tended to win prizes at SAIC during my time there, the ones that I'd envied and resented for the amount of attention they'd received, had all featured subjects and materials that were painfully autobiographical, usually showcasing some particularly meaningful and bloody trauma from the artist's personal history: one girl had included her own hair in a plastic bag, recovered from the crime scene by the police after she was beaten, assaulted, and mugged, while another of my acquaintances/almost-friends had centered his work on his own missing teeth — two bottom front teeth and an upper canine, specifically — that he'd actually saved in a jar since childhood after they were knocked out during one of his father's regular outbursts. The teeth, in particular, haunted me. Both in the fact of their existence and in the unbelievable foresight, frankly, of holding on to them so long, as if he'd known already as a nine-year-old how fucking gold these teeth would be in a senior thesis twelve-odd years later. I felt decades behind just think-ing about it, and decades too normal as well. I didn't have any authentic splinter of trauma lodged in my psyche; I didn't have any truth to tell. But I still wanted, needed to be a truth-teller, and I needed something to center my mechanized canvas and my double-layered projection and my stereo sound around.

I called Naphtha's number from my cell phone about six times, or thereabouts, over the four hours that followed that brief coffee with my mom. After leaving the shop I wandered briskly in the direction of my old high school, and then past my old high school to the 99, and then back from the 99 and all the way to the 180 and then I pulled my phone out of my pocket, the afternoon August heat shimmering around me and pushing down into my skin, and dialed Naphtha three times in quick suc-cession. I didn't have anything to say to her, really, but it still bothered me that she didn't answer. I walked another half mile in the general di-rection of the state university and then called her two more times again. I wanted to have someone to call, to have someone who would answer. I breathed for a moment into her voicemail, considering saying something, before I hung up and waited for a gap in the traffic to dart through.

When Henry died, about five months after I graduated—after I'd turned in a thoroughly mediocre self-portrait, a naked man with the head and hands and feet outside the range of the canvas, with less of a mechanized frame than a wind-up toy loosely attached to the top-right corner—there was a part of me that wondered, very quietly, if his suicide was enough for me to become a real artist now. It wasn't a voice that I heard very often, or very many times at all in the first month or so; but in the later weeks, and especially after I came back to Chicago and found myself desperate for any sort of foothold, I spent a long time discussing the details with myself, trying to work out the math. Having a brother who'd killed himself probably wasn't enough on its own, I decided, but combined with something technically interesting—and I spent a number of weekends taking sketches of birds, pigeons and sparrows, imagining something mobile and frightening, something that would swoop down and terrify you the moment you stepped into the room. I never ended up going anywhere with it, or even putting any colors to canvas, but it was a strangely comforting fantasy of control while it lasted: the fantasy of intimacy with an audience, of a crowd of faces accepting my authenticity as paid-for and earned without any further need of convincing, strangers ready and willing to take me on faith.

My parents' front yard was piled high with cardboard boxes by the time I made it back, quadruple-stacked almost eight feet into the air, from the edge of the walkway all the way to the edge of the lawn and surrounded on every side by a cacophony of furniture, chairs and end tables and at least one of the living room couches, its cushions loose or leaning against the backrest. It looked like a sort of homemade play structure in the yellow late-afternoon sunlight, a pyramid of cardboard surrounded by pillows, pushed together and teetering from various angles, casting long shadows over the pavement and the grass as I stepped around and toward the open front door. But I stopped on the threshold, my toes on the edge of going in. I couldn't see my dad inside but I could hear the loud crackling of tape being unscrolled and snapped off somewhere upstairs, somewhere beyond the half-disheveled, half-untouched front hallway, with the rug rolled up and leaning by the far corner like a bystander hunched over its folded arms and the side table exactly as it was that morning, the same unopened envelopes tipping the same two inches over the edge and drooping toward the floor. My stomach knotted. I turned around and called Naphtha a sixth time and then hung up on the first ring, my jaw clenched. I navigated to Marta Winters's number in my missed calls.

In my head, there was already a set of phrases that I'd prepared to share with Naphtha as soon as she answered. I was going to tell her the bare details of the day and then I was going to tell her about my idea for a series of paintings to craft around it, walk her through the shapes and the references and the materials that I'd need, the way the paintings would relate and build off each other and ask her opinion on the whole concept. I was going to ask her if I could stay at the warehouse for a bit while I worked on it, if I could use their strange basement as a studio space; I was going to describe my increasing dread at the idea of going back to my own apartment, the actual fear that seemed to be climbing inside me — like insects crawling on the wrong side of my skin — when I pictured myself back there alone, when I imagined myself in my studio bedroom with no one to talk to and nowhere to go. And I was working on a possible remark about loneliness, too, about how loneliness sometimes feels like the house is burning while you're locked inside and sometimes it feels like a justified humiliation, like you're despised because you deserve to be despised.

Marta answered on the fifth ring and then waited for a moment, perfect silence on the other side of the line, as though listening. I took a step back from my dad's threshold, my Adam's apple withdrawn high into my throat.

"Hello?" she said.

~

On my flight back the following morning, I spent a long time imagining that my body had been possessed by Marta's husband, Robert, during that ritual in her second-floor bedroom. At first I felt this as a rather severe anxiety, thinking back on the details and remembering the words, the incantation and the stench; but by the time I settled into my seat, buckled my seat belt and lifted the cover on the window, I found myself mainly just curious instead. I'd changed my ticket to the earliest departing flight from California to Chicago and so I was on a plane that took off only a little after dawn, boarding in the near-dark of four forty-five and then rising into the clouds just as the horizon was beginning to color, blue spreading across the sky framed by my tiny window and I imagined what it would be like to access, directly, all of Robert's earliest memories of meeting Marta for the first time: his memory of catching her eye during the cocktail hour at their mutual friends' wedding, but failing to find the courage to walk up and tell her my name until we happened to be sitting only two seats away from each other during the dinner, angling to overhear each other's conversations and laughing, as if together, at the better wedding toasts, before the dancing started and I stood and introduced myself on the way to the floor. She was wearing a tight black dress, I imagined, slinky and sequined and accidentally emphasizing her freckles, like she was trying to be a different kind of girl than she usually was, like she was almost pulling it off. I was hot in my tuxedo as we danced in a group circle together. I wanted to pull her aside and I imagined that she wanted me to pull her aside and at the end of the night I pretended to smoke cigarettes so that I could catch a moment outdoors in a smaller group and she joined me, and I asked for her number. She typed it in my phone with a shy look. We went out for drinks the following weekend and I fingered her for a long time on her couch afterward, pushing my fingertip back and forth and down and around her clitoris until her chest was heaving, sparkling with sweat, and she pushed me off and made me leave before we had sex and I tried to kiss her longer in the doorway and she shoved me off, flushed, and told me to call her another time, and then the next night I came back over and fucked her hard against the head of her bed frame, pushing and writhing on all fours and my dick so hard in the airplane that it began to hurt, pulsing with too much blood against the leg of my jeans, the sky outside the little square window now evenly blue, flat and cloudless. I crossed my legs, trying to constrain or least to hide my erection; but then I began to imagine the later stages of our relationship, the knots of rope around her wrists and mine, her thighs tight around my sides.

After the plane landed I was determined to get home and masturbate as quickly as humanly possible, or at least as fast as possible when riding public transportation. I felt somewhat distantly grotesque, sharing communal space while so horny, but I didn't seem able to think about anything else at that point and I closed my eyes on the train and then on the bus and let the fantasies roll and expand according to their own logic, wishing with all the longing in my chest that I could feel her naked skin against mine. An older gentleman took the seat beside me on the bus and I curled myself into a ball away from him and against the window, my eyes wide and unseeing, until my stop finally arrived and I carefully stood and then bounded off and onto the sidewalk, my bags slung loose around my shoulders, and strode toward home.

I recognized the long white van immediately, parked on the street across from my tenement building. But I was confused enough by its presence there that I didn't stop or even slow down very much, stepping with only a little more hesitation toward the lobby's decrepit double door, idly hoping that I could slip inside before anyone noticed me. Then I saw the Garys, already standing outside the van and leaning, respectively, on the hood and against the passenger-side door. The older Gary gave me a black-gloved wave. My body deflated.

"New guy!" the older Gary called out.

They were about sixty feet off, I calculated; as good a head start as any, it seemed. Only I didn't actually have anywhere to run to, nowhere in the city I could hide where they weren't already staked outside. The Garys tossed their cigarettes on the ground and started walking toward me. I hitched my bags back onto my shoulders and continued toward my apartment.

"New guy, new guy, new guy, new guy," the older Gary said as we drew closer, shaking his head. "Where've you been, man?"

I swallowed. The younger, thicker Gary was wearing a new brown-leather jacket and what appeared to be brass knuckles, glinting on his fingers as he circled around and then past me, covering my retreat. They stopped on either side of me and I stopped also. I'd gone to see my parents, I muttered.

"That's nice. They're doing well?"

I looked to the side, to the old warehouse with every first-floor window broken across the street from my apartment building. I knew that there was probably someone, or a number of people, inside, but I sincerely doubted that any of them would care if I began to shout. "They're getting divorced," I said.

The older Gary barked out a laugh. "Wow," he said, incredulous. "Really having the worst day of sixth grade today, huh?"

The other Gary chuckled. I twitched one side of my mouth.

"Listen, new guy." He folded his arms and the other Gary stepped closer behind me, herding me into a tighter space between them. "I like you. But John fucking hates you now. He wants to know what you told the target, and frankly, so do we. But he told us to beat the shit out of you either way." He spat on the ground and the younger Gary seized my shoulders, gripping me in place. I kicked out my legs and he wrapped an elbow around in a choke hold, tightening until I went limp. The older Gary moved another step closer, took out his pack of cigarettes, and shook out three into his hand.

"So," he said, placing one cigarette in his lips, handing one to the other Gary, and then holding the third out to me. As much as I was able with my head wrapped in the thick Gary's elbow, I shook my head, *no thanks.* He shrugged. "Here's what I'm thinking. Yes, we're going to beat the shit out of you either way. But." He lit his cigarette and then handed the lighter to the other Gary, who sparked the flame terrifyingly close to my hair. "We'll beat you up a little bit less, I promise, if you talk to us first."

I started to choke out a response and he nodded to the other Gary, who loosened, slightly, his grip around my neck. I gasped a full breath into my chest, and then another, feeling my blood racing through my neck and into my brain.

"First and foremost. Did you tell her what firm you worked for?" Gary asked, the end of his cigarette crackling as he puffed, inches from my nose. "John's name?" He exhaled as if only incidentally blowing smoke into my eyes. "Is the firm, itself, exposed?"

I blinked rapidly, my chest trying hard to heave underneath the thick Gary's constriction.

"You're killing me here, new guy."

"I wasn't—" I began to whimper, but broke off as the elbow was released from around my throat and then rammed, instead, with a full body's weight into the side of my skull.

~

My head pounded for a long time, flat on the pavement, after they finally stepped away and left me lying on the sidewalk. Like an echo of the blows that it had just received, reverberating, from the inside and the out: that throbbing of flesh against bone. After I lifted myself up, pushing onto all fours and then stumbling to my feet, and dragged my bags the rest of the way to the apartment; after I heaved everything up the stairs and into my bedroom and then heaved my body into the shower, into the scalding, searing heat and then the scalding, searing soap; after I gingerly inspected and probed my yellowing bruises, the cuts on my cheek and the dark splotch beside my right eye; after I dressed myself, as best as I was able, and then went back outside and to the bus stop again; after I hopped off next to Marta's, then walked the long way around to her house. My heartbeat hammering against my skull from the inside, pulsing with ache. There was no white van parked on the road parallel to hers, but I still felt watched as I crawled and then fell over the fence in her neighbors' backyard, struggled to my feet and across the unkempt lawn and then pounded the bottom of my fist on her basement door.

The door swung open on the third knock and I jerked back, surprised. Marta must have been in the basement already, doing something else or just waiting for me by the door, it seemed. She flushed. Standing in the dim basement in a hoodie and loose pajama pants, she seemed much smaller than I remembered, but otherwise just as strangely familiar, and just as strangely pretty.

"Jesus Christ," she said, her face creasing with concern.

I raised a hand to my temple and then flinched, remembering the bruise only after my fingertips grazed the bump and the pain traced again through the veins of my cheek.

"I got fired," I explained.

As if on cue, my head resumed its pounding, the return of my attention summoning the throb of headache back into rhythm. Marta craned her neck to look over my shoulder.

"I've been thinking a lot about you," I said.

Marta drew her head back, blinking. The basement was much better-lit than before, white sunlight leaking in through casement windows behind her, but it still felt hard to see her face very clearly. I cleared my throat and accidentally set off a brief fit of coughing, my voice catching on a purl of liquid in my throat.

"I can't stop thinking about you, I mean," I went on.

Her eyes, I realized, were the prettiest part about her: shining and brown and terrified, it seemed like, but determined not to look away. She stared evenly into my right eye and then into my left. Her blush deepened.

"That's, actually—" she said, pausing to clear her throat. "That's actually very encouraging to hear."

I started to smile and then stopped, my eyes squinted, as I tried to decipher this.

"Here," she said, stepping back and pulling the door open wider behind her. "Why don't you come inside? And I'll see if I can find some Band-Aids, for those cuts."

but any actor worth their salt will tell you the answer, already: the objective. The desire, the goal. Every human soul is trapped inside its own system of internal rhythms and references, impenetrable to the outsider and thereby meaningless, facts and associations floating without expression and hence utterly unconvincing, to our solipsist, as to the authentic existence of any alternative consciousness. But the point at which that interiority is forced to come into contact with the outside world—the point at which that interiority is subject to/focused on/obsessed with the objects of the world that we share with others—the experience of **desire**—that forms a point of entry, so to speak. I cannot easily access or understand another person's daydreams about an apple, but I can immediately believe that other person when they tell me that they are hungry, and I know what that feels like on the inside for them without further explanation; and I can begin to imagine, from there, what their daydreams about an apple might be. Desire gives us a way *in*. The monomaniac who perforce requires convincing that their interlocutor is in fact a real, authentic human being—that is to say, an audience—requires presentations of personality that are focused around such contact points between private experience and the shared world because this gives the presentation a common referent, a legible vanishing point upon which to stabilize, fundamentally, the viewer's perspective. And here, again, we encounter the same assumptions in the practice of art as in the practice of

The tea began to sing in its kettle while Marta was still in the other room, so I stood from the kitchen table and stepped over to the stove to turn it off. In my peripheral vision, I saw Marta reappearing in the doorway just as I was clicking the knob, rising onto her toes as though on the verge of saying something; but when I turned, there were only footsteps receding back down the hall. The back of my neck burned. I sat down at the table and adjusted the cloth placemat with my fingertips, tugging it so that it was flush with the edge and then sliding it forward and twirling it beneath my forefinger, watching the straight lines of the geometric pattern blur into curves as they spun. Then I stood and checked on the tea again, lifting the cover on the spout so that the steam rose out and over my palm, the moisture and the painful heat. I heard Marta's barefoot padding in the hallway and then I heard her stop just before the threshold. I glanced up and smiled.

There were only a few times in my life that I'd experienced the electric atmosphere of sharing a room with someone I'd just confessed my attraction to. It was always excruciatingly thrilling: the air emulsified, in equal measure, with hope and humiliation, both of them suspended and sustained in every look and gesture, in Marta's subtly rearranged hair from the bathroom and in her particular smile as she showed me the box of Band-Aids and then handed them over; in my own heavy-breathed smile as I thanked her.

"Would you—" she asked, tentative. I looked almost up at her, my gaze stalling on her shoulder. "Would you like to use the bathroom mirror?"

"Oh," I said. I stood abruptly, scraping the chair on the floor. "Right. Yes."

"First door on the left. In the hall."

"Right." I stepped past her, our bodies almost touching as she withdrew to give me room. "Thank you."

But I couldn't remember a single time, in any of those prior instances, that the ambiguity had lasted this long—at least three minutes and counting since Marta had let me in and led me up to the kitchen from the basement. I'd been rejected often enough but always quite briskly, in word or in gesture, after I made myself clear, and similarly for the rarer instances when my attraction was reciprocated. The only experience that I could recall that felt at all like this was what happened on the opposite side of a relationship, when I was in the process of being dumped by my junior-year girlfriend and we kept meeting to talk only to end up fucking on her couch, in her dormitory bathroom, on the library stairs. Even though she and I no longer even liked each other at that point, there was just too much heat between our bodies to ignore. I peeled open a Band-Aid and placed it gingerly over the yellow-brown mishmash of colors beside my right eye, and then added another alongside for good measure. There were also a number of cuts along my lip, but I couldn't figure out a way to place a Band-Aid along them that didn't look ugly, it seemed to me, and so I left them open and gently bleeding at the corners of my mouth. I spent another minute arranging my hair, and then another minute after that trying to make my hair look like it hadn't just been arranged, before I exited the bathroom and carried the box of Band-Aids back.

Marta was sitting at the kitchen table with her feet propped on my chair from a moment before, her back half-turned and steam rising from the mug in her palms. She looked up when she heard me, smiled, and lifted her chin at another mug on the countertop.

"I didn't know what tea you wanted," she said. "There's chamomile, green, and Earl Grey. In the long boxes."

I glanced down at the cardboard containers, lined with individual paper rectangles of tea bags, and then at the large bottle of Jack Daniel's beside. I picked it up by the neck, raising an eyebrow. She laughed and told me to go ahead. For a moment I wondered what it was that was so different about the kitchen this time around—whether the appliances were slightly less gleaming, or whether the handful of loose items on the island countertop made it seem a little more human-scale—until I remembered, in a brief moment of rapid blinking, the dog. I poured two fingers of whiskey into the mug and then dunked two bags of Earl Grey in after.

"I'm glad that you came back here," Marta said, watching me with her face hidden behind the edge of her sip. "I didn't think that you would, honestly. But. I'm glad."

I licked my lips, tasting the hot aftertang of the whiskey in the back of my throat after I swallowed.

"When you left," she went on, gesturing minutely with the ends of her fingers, "the day before yesterday, after Tricia arrived, I thought that I was screwed. That you were going to screw me over, I mean. Whatever you'd been looking for, I thought, whatever your law firm had wanted to find when they sent you over to me—there couldn't be anything worse than that."

I exhaled through my nostrils, just shy of a laugh, feeling the alcohol in the back of my palate as the air moved through. I was leaning a hip against the island countertop but I couldn't figure out what to do with my arms in this position; I wanted to cup my mug but I felt too intentional about mirroring her pose and so I held the cup loose in one hand and let the other lie flat on the marble, as though preparing to drum my fingertips in impatience. Then I folded that free hand under my elbow and wedged it against my side, took another sip.

"There was a girl I knew, in New York, in my first year after graduating," Marta continued, flicking her gaze to the sunny window to watch a breeze flutter through the plants out back. "She used to say, all the time. *All the fucking men are working together.* Whenever some guy stood her up and it felt like the waiter had already sensed, a full hour before she realized, that her date wasn't going to come, or whenever she crossed the road and a driver honked and the traffic cop took the driver's side, or whenever she wanted to hook up with some guy who turned out to be best friends, already, with one of her ex-boyfriends. She'd declare that all the fucking men were on the same team against her—but in this funny voice, always, so that we all started to imitate her, too. All of us in our friend group. Whenever some asshole got away with something because some other asshole wouldn't do his job, or whenever we just felt like we were being squashed. 'There is hope, but not for us.'" She set the mug down on the table before her and ran her fingers through her hair, briefly flattening her wide curls against the sides of her head. "That feeling like the whole world is organizing itself against you, the walls closing in."

I took another scorching sip of Earl Grey and swallowed, smiling, tracing the heat as it burned through the back of my throat and then spread beneath my sternum. The adrenaline of confessing my attraction to Marta was beginning to deteriorate into a sudden, lurching anxiety—a collapsing suspicion that I might, in fact, be the only person feeling the sexual tension in the room. I knew that what I'd said was unambiguous, but I began to worry that she was choosing, now, to interpret it ambiguously, her hands relaxed around her mug and her face turned toward the window, furrowed around her recollection as though she'd momentarily forgotten that I was there. I was curious to learn about this other part of her life, unrelated to her husband and to everything else that we'd talked about previously, but I wanted her to be looking at me while she described it.

"Anyway," she said, shaking her head. "It came to mind, after you left. You and your law firm poised, like an owl over a field, to ruin my life."

I stared at her, waiting for her to notice the weight of my gaze. The inside of my body felt boiling hot. If I was forced to think about my life outside this moment with Marta Winters, outside her kitchen and this mug of spiked tea, it would open out endless underneath me like a bottomless falling, I knew: the free fall of no one to talk to, nowhere to go. I noticed again the pounding of my headache, the intricate throbbing beneath the bruises on my face. Marta lifted her mug to her lips.

"Can I ask you a question," I said.

She kept her mug cupped in front of her mouth as she took a series of very small sips. "Mm."

"How did you know, when you first fell in love—how did you know that you were really in love?"

She withdrew her head again, in that small, surprised way she had, finally catching my stare for half a moment before looking down at the floorboards. But her cheeks rose with a private smile, I thought. "That's a funny question," she said.

"Well." I breathed heavy, the mug warm beneath my fingers, struggling to keep my balance as I leaned against the countertop. "I was going to ask if I could kiss you, but it seemed a little direct."

Her eyes went wide. She darted a glance up and looked hard into my right eye and then into my left, and then at the bottle of whiskey on the countertop behind me. I could barely breathe. She straightened in her chair.

"Robert died less than four weeks ago, Peter," she said, staring intently at the polished floorboards between us.

I set my tea down and swallowed a mouthful of air, a large bubble entering my stomach. I began to stutter out an apology and she lifted her gaze again to my eyes, her mouth open. I broke off. The wind outside the window died and I heard the sound that the trees in the yard had been making in retrospect, outlining the present silence.

"Do you know, I haven't been able to feel him," she said, "at all, since that ritual in our old bedroom. I haven't been able to feel his presence. Robert's." She looked in each of my eyes in turn again. "It's been fucking awful," she said.

I wanted to look away but I understood that I couldn't, my body twisted in an awkward facsimile of ease against the countertop and Marta ramrod straight in her chair, one hand wrapped around the top of the chair back, her legs crossed in my direction. She was as lonely as I was, I thought.

"At first, I wondered if maybe I just couldn't sense him anymore. That he was still here, that is, and I just couldn't feel it. But that didn't really feel any less terrible. Imagining that he and I were nearby but separated, permanently. It didn't seem like I was any less to blame, or that it was any less my fault." She leaned forward in her chair, allowing only the smallest slouch at the top of her posture. "But then I started to wonder if, instead, something had happened in that bedroom—because it did, didn't it? Something did happen there. You felt it, as much as I did."

She paused, waiting for a reaction, an affirmation, but I was only able to blink. I could feel the bubble of air that I'd swallowed beginning to form into a burp, ascending back up my esophagus.

"And I started to wonder if it actually had worked, only not in the way that I'd thought."

The kitchen hadn't seemed as large when I'd first walked in but in that moment it began to expand again, resuming its oversmoothness again, the marble countertop and the clean table and the wooden floor seeming to gleam brighter as I looked at them, but painfully, as if someone had just switched on an overhead fluorescent. There was too much distance between us, it seemed, for me to make out Marta's expression.

"Have you been able to feel Robert's presence at all?" she asked.

I carefully exhaled the burp through my nostrils, as silently as I could, with a fist over my mouth.

"I'm not sure," I lied.

She lengthened her neck again, turning to look at me at an angle, as though trying to catch my eye in a crowded party. Her profile was beautiful, I thought. Elegantly shadowed, even in the bright daylight of the kitchen.

"Are you—" she started, her cheeks flushing.

I stood up straighter, sensing the return of the tension in the air.

"—I guess, I started to wonder," she began again, "if there wasn't something that had happened with you. To you, I mean. During what happened."

We both understood perfectly well what she was implying but neither of us had the words to either offer or accept the proposition that she was gently floating, like a boat from shore, into the conversation between us. I poured a little more whiskey into my mug of tea and she made a face and I lifted the bottle. She put on a thin smile. I carried the Jack Daniel's over to the dinner table, feeling the full weight of my body as I moved it across the room, step by step.

She watched me pour for a long two seconds before she raised a finger. I pulled the bottle back.

"How would—" she said, not just her cheeks flushed now but her neck also, the tips of her ears. "How would you kiss me? If I said that you could."

I took a breath and held it, set the bottle of whiskey down on the

150

kitchen table, turned back toward the counter to fetch my own mug again, changed my mind and completed the turn into a full circle and then pulled out the chair beside Marta and slowly, cautiously, sat down. My heart thumped just underneath the surface of my wrists, my fingertips. I reached out a hand toward hers.

"Mnn." Marta shook her head, pulling her hand away. "Robert hates holding hands."

"Right."

"He takes my cheek in his hand, or wraps his arm around my waist, usually, when he kisses me."

"Right. Sure." I licked my lips and lifted my hand to her cheek, pushing her hair back with my knuckle, and leaned in. I closed my eyes.

But she stopped me, hard, with a hand pressed on my diaphragm, before I could touch my lips to hers.

"No," she said, shaking her head. "That's not."

I opened my eyes very close to her face and she pushed me back farther.

"That's not right," she said.

"Right." I wanted to stop for a glass of water but I didn't want to back off in this pivotal moment, to let the balance fall any further away from me than it already had. She was so pretty that my skin hurt, aching to reach out and touch her. "Here," I said, taking her wrist in my hand as I stood, tugging her gently up with me. "Maybe, let's try this standing."

She didn't exactly nod but she rose nonetheless, taking a quick gulp of her drink and then pushing herself from her chair. The sunlight in the kitchen began to seem vaguely absurd, shining so brightly on us in this moment, as we drank hot toddies and I tried to learn how to kiss like a dead husband in the broad light of day, the refrigerator humming and the central air conditioning clicking from somewhere above us or somewhere deep inside the walls. But I was determined not to turn back. I wanted her more than anyone, anything I could remember wanting before. I put an arm around her waist and pulled her close to me and then ducked my head down and kissed her quickly, my lips parted over hers.

"*Mnn*," she protested, surprised. But she didn't shove me back again until a second or two later, after our tongues had already touched. *"No."* She stepped away and caught herself with a hand behind her back on the island counter, shaking her head very quickly, very slightly side to side. My heart dropped into my stomach. "You're not doing it right," she said.

I raised my hands in surrender, stepping back.

"Just, everything," she said, gesturing broadly at my torso. "It's wrong, Peter. That's not how he holds me. You're not listening to what I'm saying." Her voice was pitched with emotion and there were tears in the corners of her eyes, her hands fluttering in front of her and then fluttering through her hair as she pushed her fingers into her bangs and then back, pressing against the sides of her head. The dread in my gut began to change phase, seeing her.

"Can I—" I started quietly, as though afraid that she might scare if I talked too loud.

But then she did, immediately: as soon as I began speaking she gave a sudden start and then withdrew, striding around the countertop and directly out of the kitchen, into the first of the adjoining rooms and then the next and then, footsteps creaking on the boards, straight up the front staircase. At the end of the second-floor hallway, a door closed.

I stared at the doorway to the library, at the last place her silhouette had been visible. My hands seemed to be moving of their own accord from my pockets to the buttons of my button-down to the sides of my thighs, rubbing the fabric along the seam, and then the mug of tea on the countertop. I carried it to the table and sat down.

~

Marta's front door opened two hours and fifteen minutes after she left me alone in the kitchen, or thereabouts, judging from the time on the oven clock. I'd only started tracking the time after about fifteen minutes had passed already, and then spent a long while trying to decide if it was really closer to fifteen or ten minutes in total, if I hadn't noted the minute until after five minutes had already passed; and I still hadn't made up my mind by the time the doorbell rang and then a key fit the lock, the mechanism turning and the hinges squeaking as they swung open and two booted footsteps rang out in the front hall, followed by an older woman's voice calling for Marta. I lifted my head from the table's surface slowly, as though waking up from a nap, the texture of the tablecloth imprinted into my left cheek.

"Marta?" the older woman called again. The front staircase creaked under her hard footsteps. "Marta, are you and Archie on a walk?"

The steps receded and then deepened above the kitchen ceiling. A door opened and I tried to take a sip of my mug and found it empty, and stood. I could hear voices through the floorboards now, Marta and the older woman's. In a vague sense, I understood that I wasn't supposed to be there, that I had failed my moment with Marta and humiliated myself and should never dare to show my face in that kitchen again; but my thirst was still more specific, and I stepped over to the sink to fill the cup. Until the footsteps suddenly thundered much closer and I turned around to see Marta and the same older woman who'd woken me up the last time I was here, before I'd shoved past her to get to the road, now standing not ten feet away in a doorway that I'd thought was a closet.

". . . but he'll probably be just at the back door, is my bet, as soon as you . . ." the older woman continued and then trailed off, glancing with a strange slowness in my direction. ". . . oh!"

"Oh!" Marta said behind her, with a complicated expression. They looked about as surprised as I was to find myself there.

I turned off the kitchen faucet and took a gulp of warm water.

"Wait," the older woman said, her face condensing into comprehension. "Hold on. We almost met, the other day, I believe." She approached a smile from a great distance, her pupils focused intently on the glass in my hand. "You're Marta's former classmate. Her friend from Brown. Only now you've got a few more bruises, it looks like. Ouch."

"Oh—"

"It's Peter, yes? Do I have that right?"

I felt pinned to a dartboard, skewered into place with a bull's-eye on my chest. I said "Yes" at the same time that Marta said "No," and then she said "Yes" at the same time that I said "Sorry," and I took another sip of water. The older woman ticked her head to the side, glancing at Marta, with the smile still somewhat far-off from her face.

"This is Peter," Marta said, stepping gingerly between us. "He's been in town, and he was nice enough to come over for breakfast this morning, after—falling off his bike. Peter, this is my mother-in-law, Tricia."

"Hi," I said, abject, offering a small wave in lieu of walking over for a handshake. Tricia lifted her fingers in return. "Sorry about—" I started, at the same time that Marta asked Tricia if she wanted a bottle of sparkling water and Tricia said sure, and Marta stepped around the island countertop to the gleaming silver fridge. I tried to catch her eye as she stepped past me but she stared resolutely forward, a bulb of muscle clenched around her jaw.

"Sorry about the other day," I finally finished, pressing my lips together beneath my heated cheeks. "I was late for work. Very late."

Tricia shook her head to say *no problem*. The smile had almost arrived. "Apology accepted. Just ask me to dance first, next time, before you whirl me around."

"You're Marta's mother-in-law?"

She shuffled to the far side of the island countertop and then pulled a stool out of thin air, a small circular seat with a tripod of metal legs underneath, and perched herself on the very edge. She was inspecting me still, I understood, but she'd acquiesced to sharing a room. I knew that I should return the attention, that I should seem the guest who's only interested in making friends and eating breakfast, but I couldn't help glancing over again at Marta as she leaned into the fridge and then returned with two miniature green bottles of mineral water—putting her hand on Tricia's arm as she passed one over—even as I knew that my observations were being intently observed.

"I'm Bobby's mother," Tricia said, squeezing Marta's hand back. "Did you know Bobby?"

"Peter just got to town," Marta explained. She drew herself to a height to unscrew her own mineral water. "I don't remember—did you ever meet Robert?"

I looked at her. "No," I said.

"I've been telling Peter about you," Marta continued without looking at either of us. "How important it's been, everyone's support this month. Our afternoon coffees. He just got in recently, I would've mentioned, but it was unexpected."

Tricia nodded, smiling at me. She was much older than my own parents, closer to my grandmother who'd passed a few years before, but in her jeweled shawl and overcoat she looked more like a child playing old woman, her eyes bright. She ticked her head to the opposite side.

"But you work around here?" she asked me. "In Chicago, I mean."

"Oh. Yes." I noticed that my water glass was empty, and I turned to set it down in the sink basin. "Well." I picked up a cloth napkin from the oven handle and wiped my fingers. I hadn't felt this specific type of awful since high school, I felt fairly certain. "I just got fired, actually," I admitted.

Tricia moved her head backward. "Oh no," she said.

Marta looked like she was trying to fade like an iguana.

Tricia worked through a few different expressions of concern before she settled on the long-awaited smile. "Well. It's good that you're here, though, because we need bodies to help look for their Archie—have you seen the dog downstairs at all, while you've been here? I was asking Marta where he was, because he's usually so loud, and it turns out that she hasn't seen him at all in the last hour. We've been calling his name, but he hasn't come."

"Archie?"

"Their Australian shepherd. We just adore him—you must've only seen him since his accident, though? The other day, Marta had to take him to the vet hospital, awful accident with a burning candle, but he was back this morning. Was it this morning, Marta?"

I cleared my throat and Marta set her mineral water down and began agreeing very quickly, rapidly confirming that she'd picked Archie up actually yesterday morning and then expressing her own increasing concern and guiding Tricia by the elbow down from the stool and out of the kitchen, toward the front room where Marta could put her shoes on, flipping the light switches in each room as they walked through. I waited for a space of two breaths before following. Marta seemed less unconvincing than too convincing, seeming to drum up Tricia's own anxieties with her never-ending list of things that could've gone wrong.

". . . and the cars don't even slow down, sometimes," Marta went on, pulling her boots out from the shoe rack. "I've heard of them sometimes dragging animals along underneath, for miles sometimes, and then even the bodies are gone, and the families never even know what happened."

"I'm a private detective, actually," I blurted out, too loudly, as I stepped after them into the front hallway. "I was, I mean."

"I hope not," Tricia said to Marta, and then turned to me. "A detective?"

I found my right sneaker and pushed my foot into it, then cast about for my left. "A private detective. Just a paralegal, technically, for a law firm that does private detective stuff."

"I really hope that's not true, Marta." Tricia was nodding along, as though listening to me, but without breaking her stare from the side of Marta's face. "That gives me the chills, just thinking about it."

Marta finished lacing up her boots and threw the front door open, the sunlight and the sounds of the street entering with a gust of warm air, the humidity of August in Illinois. I stepped back, remembering the white van with a fresh twist in my stomach.

"Although, you know," I said, breathing shallowly, "the first mistake, usually, is that everyone goes out looking. And if the person who's lost comes back to where they thought everyone was, and then no one's there, they go off again."

Tricia raised an eyebrow, opening her mouth as if to say something.

"That's fine," Marta said, still speaking almost too fast to comprehend. "That's good. That's good, Tricia. Peter can stay here and you and I can go look for Archie and I'll bet we'll probably find him, like you said, before we even know it, but we should go, yes? And Peter can keep an eye out here while we look. All right"—she snatched her broad straw sun hat from the coat rack before she stepped out the door—"are you coming, Trish? I'm worried that he's gotten too far, but I think if we start looking we'll probably find him, I hope, although I think you're probably right, Tricia, he's probably not even too far. I hope he hasn't gotten himself too far." Her skin was completely white, but otherwise I was impressed by how equably she was able to hold herself, leading the two of them out onto the landing with something almost like a rueful smile.

"I'll check the backyard," I called out after them, watching Tricia murmur in Marta's ear as they walked down the steps. "I'll just be in the backyard, then, in case he comes back there." I was only realizing then that Marta hadn't looked at me once since she'd come downstairs, since she'd first taken me in with that shocked glance upon entering the kitchen. I stared after her, at the receding oval of her big straw sun hat and at Tricia's gray-blond hair, waiting anxiously for a surreptitious glance in my direction, for a confirmation that we were on the same team. But she only strode forward, arm in arm with Robert's mother, calling the dead dog's name louder and louder as they progressed down the sidewalk.

~

In many ways, I felt consummately strange, sitting cross-legged in the grass in Marta's backyard to wait for her and her mother-in-law to come back from pretending to search and searching, respectively. I had goose bumps on my skin despite the humidity and I felt weirdly tall, or elongated, as though this patch of yard had been built for someone with roughly two-thirds of my proportions and there was no way for my leg to fully extend without shoving a foot into a flower bed or a bush branch. But I didn't feel nearly strange enough, still, for the circumstances: I didn't feel any pulsing anxiety, no more sweat on the back of my neck and no tightness in my stomach, my lower back. I mostly just felt numb. There had been so many actions over the last few days that I seemed to have finally run out of reactions, jostled into a groove and now just rolling forward, regardless. I imagined Marta and Tricia variously dawdling and darting around corners as they traced Tetris shapes through the neighborhood and their shouts grew weaker and stronger,

Marta's voice beginning to break as she got caught up in the moment and began to feel genuine emotion; I imagined if I had done something different in the kitchen earlier and Marta hadn't scared and gone upstairs, and instead we'd stood in silence for a time and just shared a space together, our hearts beating in the same room; I imagined if she'd kissed me on her own. The wind picked back up and shuffled the humidity slightly above and to the left and I leaned back onto my elbows, careful not to lean so far that a bush scratched my neck. I mostly just felt afraid that Marta might ask me to leave, now that dusk was beginning to fall.

I heard their voices as they rounded the corner of the block and then nothing over the rest of the neighborhood noises until the front door opened and closed. A car pulled into a neighbor's driveway and a man stood from the driver's side, his face a shadow under a hat. An outdoor light buzzed on directly above me. Marta's back door opened behind and I craned my neck to see her, alone, invisible underneath the glare of the bright bulb.

"She thinks we're fucking," she said, a little louder than I thought she needed to.

"Ah."

Marta stepped out of the light and onto a bench that had apparently been there the whole time, ensconced slightly in the thin hedge beside the stone footpath. "I'm honestly more surprised that you're still here," she said. "You can't stay here, you know."

I sat up straighter. "Could I, actually, though?"

She crossed her legs and glared above me, at the hydrangea flowers over my head. "Tricia's just gone to print out flyers," she said. "She's coming back in twenty minutes, half an hour. I'm supposed to be making phone calls right now, technically. Knocking on the neighbors' doors."

I began idly pulling the grass from the ground in clumps between my fingers, nodding obediently. I wasn't close to giving up yet but I didn't want to seem difficult, and I tried my best to look like I was quietly processing her refusal, adapting myself to her concerns. I did note, with some keen interest, that there didn't seem to be any lingering stiffness on Marta's part after my mistakes earlier that afternoon;

she looked exhausted, arching her back upward to stare with parted lips at the sky, but hardly seemed bothered by my presence for the moment. The sunlight was weaker than before but it was still in that stage of early dusk when it seemed to be bringing out the colors only more strongly, more vividly contrasting the green grass and the drooping red and yellow flowers and the blooming purple bushes, the oak tree and its lengthening shadow. One street over, a car drove past and another neighbor's front door slammed shut. Marta lifted her hands to cover her face and then very slowly doubled over, flattening her torso until her head was between her knees, her hair falling around and concealing her face completely.

I realized that she was crying only when she sniffed, her fingers linked behind the back of her head, her elbows cinched over her ears.

"I can't do this anymore," she said, but so muffled that I could barely hear her over the rustling leaves.

I let the torn blades of grass filter between my fingers and back down to the surface of the lawn. Marta's hands roved through her hair. Then she abruptly threw her head back, her eyes clear except for the thin streams of tears along her cheeks. She was the only other person in existence.

"Do you know," she said, her voice still quiet as she shook her head, "what the worst thing I'd ever done used to be, a month ago? I used to think about it sometimes, and feel embarrassed about it specifically, with those exact words—as the worst thing that I'd ever done in my life. In high school one of my friends had a chronic illness, something with her stomach that none of the doctors could figure out, and I got really frustrated with her always canceling on our plans and didn't understand what was the matter, didn't really have the patience to understand, and I convinced our whole friend group to stop including her. They all followed my lead, and froze her out. And when she finally called me to ask about it, to ask if I could help her out, I came over to her house with a bottle of Tums, and her mother greeted me at the door and we got to talking about how it was almost certainly psychosomatic, how it was all in my friend's head, and then that same week her mother pulled her out of school to send her to a monthlong psychiatric retreat." She pushed the heel of her hand into her cheek, smearing the residue of tears. "A few years later, long after we'd stopped talking to each other, I learned that she'd been diagnosed with some rare stomach disorder. After however long of losing all of her friends and trying to will herself into not-feeling the pain that she was feeling every morning, every afternoon, every night." She arched her back again, closing her eyes against the fading sunlight, her mouth crumpled. "I used to make myself feel awful, right in the pit of my gut, anytime I remembered that. I still feel awful about it, honestly." She covered her face with her hands. "I'm such a fucking awful human being."

I rose from my sitting position slowly, pushing myself off my knuckles and then approaching the bench in a slight hunch, carefully refraining from my full height, before I took a seat on the farthest corner of the bench from Marta. She doubled forward, her fingertips pressed into her eyelids.

"I miss my dog," she said.

I reached out a hand and placed it gingerly, barely, on the edge of her shoulder, and then let it rest more heavily after she didn't pull away. She shook minutely but violently, a hurricane in a glass jar. The sunlight gradually dimmed and the neighbors' cars returned to their driveways all around us, the car doors slamming and the front doors opening, the momentary greetings between passersby on the sidewalks. But I could've stayed there for an hour longer, or more, if she hadn't finally wiped her face with her fingertips and then squeezed my hand, thanking me. I drew my arm away.

"I don't know if I can keep pretending with Tricia like this," she said, but in a more even voice than she'd been able to manage for some time. "She's not dumb, you know? And with Evelyn, too, just waiting in the wings."

I nodded, rubbing my hands together between my joggling knees. "She doesn't seem like she suspects anything," I ventured, my voice rather higher than I'd intended. "About Archie, I mean. For what it's worth."

Marta exhaled through her nose, something like a breathy snort, not quite agreeing. Then she stood from the bench and laid herself down on the grass of the lawn, flat on her back and with her hands flat beside her, staring with open eyes at the darkening branches of the hydrangea and the tree farther above her, her mind rising miles from our proximity in the garden. I stayed on the bench, my clothes rustling as I constantly adjusted and readjusted my posture, shifting my arms and my legs, uncrossing my ankles and fixing my shirt where it had bunched around my armpits.

After a while, a car finally turned and pulled into Marta's driveway, and then a door slammed and bootsteps rang on the stones of the front stairway. Only slightly muted by the walls, we could hear Marta's doorbell ring out, harsh and loud, two times in fairly short succession, and then a third time after another minute's wait. Neither Marta nor I visibly tensed but we remained perfectly motionless, her eyes staring unblinking up at the evening blue and my arms folded, uncrossed. The doorbell chimed a fourth time and then Marta's phone buzzed in her pocket, stopped buzzing and then buzzed again, the light of the screen glowing through the denim of her jeans. The doorbell rang a fifth time.

Overhead, a red light blinked across the evening sky.

The bootsteps rang again on the stone stairway, possibly louder than the first time, and then the car door slammed once more. The sedan's wheels crunched as they receded up the driveway and then onto the road.

The yard was almost fully night, at that point. The lines between the tree's shadow and the darker dirt of the flower beds had just about converged, outside the outdoor lamp's spotlight. Bugs had crept out from the leaves and the branches and were buzzing idly at the flowers, at my hands. Marta dragged herself a little bit backward as she pushed herself upright, rustling the bushes against her back and then snapping a twig when she stood, stumbling once to the side before straightening. She told me again that I couldn't stay there and I asked her if I could just sleep on the couch, possibly, please. She looked at me for a long time with her arms folded over her chest. Then she turned with an ambiguous gesture, fluttering one of her hands above her shoulder, and began to walk back toward the basement door. My body surged with anxiety and longing, watching her leave. She was how I became new, I felt certain: I could remake myself completely for her, and I wanted to, almost as badly as I wanted her to fall in love with me.

She reemerged about forty seconds later, carrying a nylon bag with a two-person tent inside it, another nylon bag with tent stakes, and a rolled-up sleeping bag.

HAVE YOU SEEN THIS DOG?

"Archibald" responds to "Archie"
Call Trish 872-212-3782

$1000 REWARD!

At the bottom of the ocean, lungs move regardless of breathing. Flowing water lifts and falls through the outlines of space as given, as received, filling and coursing and rising lightless or clear as the currents circle, as the chest expands. I opened my eyes from the dream without entirely believing it was air entering my lungs and I shot up coughing and gasping, my hand on my Adam's apple and my forehead scraping against the tent door's zipper, the world dark. I rubbed my chest with my palm as I waited for my heartbeat to steady. I understood that I wasn't underwater but I also understood that I might be, and I emerged from the tent with my breath held and my eyes narrow. There wasn't any sun on the horizon but there was a gray smudge on the side of some stars, and a bright light shining from the kitchen windows. My heart skipped a beat, remembering. I found a handful of pebbles on the ground and began throwing them at the glass panes.

Marta showed up in the basement doorway about two minutes later with what looked like a sack of coal under one arm. She shut the door and locked it behind her after she came out.

"Good morning," she said. "I was thinking that I probably shouldn't let you into the house."

I yawned at her. "Hunh," I said.

"You're a complete stranger, you know? And the only thing I know about you is that you were hired by my real, actual enemies." She set the sack of coal down beside the tent and then jogged back around the corner of the house, and reappeared with a tripod barbecue and steel chimney. "I feel bad that you got fired, and I appreciate that you need to hide, but I think we should maintain a boundary. No more indoors."

I moved out of the way of the barbecue and took a seat on the bench, then laid myself down on the long planks. "Should I pee out here?"

"Please don't."

A packet of hot dogs and a packet of hot dog buns appeared to have already been placed on the end of the bench where I was trying to lay my head, along with a fistful of individual ketchup packets. I sat up onto an elbow and handed them over to Marta, who stashed them inside the door of the tent. The briquettes clanged in the chimney as Marta poured them in.

"I'm in love with you, though," I said.

Marta rolled her eyes. She squeezed a heavy dollop of lighter fluid over the charcoal and then lit a match, flames bursting back at her fingertips as soon as she dropped it on top.

"You really think the firm sent me here to seduce you?" I grinned around the edges of another yawn. "You think I'm their seductive paralegal on call."

She squinted at me skeptically. I wondered where the bottle of lighter fluid had come from—if that, too, had been underneath my head a moment before. The coals crackled.

"One hot dog or two," she asked.

I yawned a third time. The yard had seemed larger in my dream, when it had been filled with water. The only problem was that I really did have to pee. Marta picked up the chimney after it began billowing smoke and then dumped the coals, a shower of sparks, into the barbecue's basin.

~

We were going to Evelyn's that morning, I learned over breakfast, as soon as the sun was at a more normal part of its arc. Marta knew from Tricia that Evelyn was coming back from her pied-à-terre on a red-eye that night and was bound to be at her Loop apartment until at least noon, more than enough time for Marta to intercept her, with me in tow, and threaten to countersue using my testimony unless she backed off. Marta had spent a long time the night before staring at the ceiling in her bedroom and imagining vividly all of the plans that Evelyn was drafting against her, and she'd only been able to fall asleep after she'd come up with a plan of her own, to preemptively counterattack and free us both from MM&Z in one fell swoop. I opened a ketchup packet with considerable difficulty and then drew a line of sauce along the length of my hot dog, not exactly nodding along. After we finished eating and put the lid on the barbecue to suffocate the coals, Marta brought out her laptop and a large, plastic-covered pillow for herself and we watched old Batman cartoons from the 1990s, sitting almost close to one another on the dewy grass, until the light was strong enough that it was hard to see the screen.

I only realized that my phone's battery had survived the night when it buzzed with a text message, and then another text message immediately afterward, after we rose to go to Marta's car.

hey hi hello, Naphtha had sent me, followed shortly by, *sry for etc etc! instead of being mad tho come to my party tn, special 4 u. come come plz come*

I glared down at the screen for what felt like a long moment, feeling a brief return to another recent version of myself, and that recent version's flare of intense resentment. I considered scrolling through the phone to see how long she'd taken, this time, to text me back, but in the end decided to power it off instead, to pretend that the battery had died while I was sleeping. Marta came back from putting away her laptop and charcoal and I raised a hand to wave to her for no particular reason. She gave me an alarmed look as she opened the driver's-side door and then climbed inside. I climbed in after her, swallowing a blush.

"We should go to the bank, also," she said, mostly to herself, as she backed up and into the road. "What time do banks usually open?"

The clock in the center console read 6:17, but by the time I started to reply Marta had already begun to talk to someone named Cathy on her cell phone—either an incoming call or someone who'd answered almost immediately, just about as soon as Marta pressed the button—and then she casually asked this Cathy to arrange an extraordinarily large transfer of money into her checking account. I stared forward, feeling like a kid in a doctor's office while the physician spoke with my mother. Marta put on a small frown after she hung up, signaling clearly that she was in no mood to explain, and then abruptly accerated onto Fullerton, her seat belt still dangling free over her shoulder as she wove expertly through the traffic on the way to Lake Shore Drive.

I'd never been to the Loop so early on a weekend morning before and I was surprised to see how crowded it was even on a Saturday, the sidewalks already clogged with overtime financiers and the street parking spots mostly filled, as if there'd been an earlier wave of weekend commuters while it was still dark and we were only in time to pick up their leavings, having arrived after dawn. The archvillain towers gleamed a little less evilly in the early-morning sunshine and one or two of the street hawkers were still setting up their carts but otherwise the city was in full churn, it seemed to me, with only a slightly higher contrast than usual between the extremely expensive black and near-black suits and the fully gray, browned, and gray-brown clothes of the departing night shifters, the incoming janitorial and restaurant staff. For a moment I remembered the bank bailouts and the stimulus bill, but only in the manner that I sometimes remembered the landline phone number for the home where I'd first grown up; digits that read themselves aloud to me automatically, like a fingertip over braille, whenever my attention happened to graze past a familiar sequence. Marta turned on her blinker and swung the car into a parking garage so close to a pedestrian that he was able to reach out and slam his fist on the trunk as we drove past, screaming at us to slow the fuck down.

I only noted what building we were inside after we entered the lobby, and I could stare out the huge plate-glass windows to the sidewalk beyond. Back when my friends and I were living in SAIC's freshman dorms, in our first year of art school—right at the center of the Loop, only a few blocks from the Art Institute—we used to call this tower the Obelisk, because of its off-white color and its windowless appearance, all of the glass specially tinted to reflect with that same off-white on the outside so that just those in the building could look down on those without and no one on the ground could see them looking. It had always felt more like a monument than a building, and not in a good sense. I was surprised to learn that there were any residential units at all.

"Please don't," Marta said, gazing intently at her own reflection in the gold double doors of the elevator, "talk."

I looked at the glimmering quartz flooring and then at the massive chandeliers hanging from the far-off lobby ceiling, trying to guess the distance in my head. I could feel that Marta was intensely anxious beside me but it seemed best, under the circumstances, to project calm instead. The elevator doors dinged open and she took me by the arm, escorting me brusquely onto the platform and then holding on tightly after a crush of businesspeople pushed in after us, curling her body to mine. I controlled my breathing carefully, intentionally, inhaling and then holding the breath in my chest before exhaling, more than once closing my eyes.

～

The hallway between the elevator and Evelyn's apartment door was only about ten feet long and five across, with clean wooden paneling and absolutely massive potted plants on either wall, huge leaning ferns and what may have been an entire young palm tree, before ending in a robust front door with a little third-eye of glass in the center. Marta stepped up and knocked on the door loudly, purposefully, with the knuckle of her forefinger.

"Evelyn!" she called out, almost a shout. "Evelyn, it's Marta!"

We could hear the heeled footsteps on the wooden floorboards inside the penthouse as they approached and then stopped, and then the heavy silence afterward. Marta kept her expression of self-righteous indignation perfectly even, as though entirely unaware of being observed. I rotated around in a slow circle, glancing at every corner of the hallway in turn.

The inside footsteps resumed, this time receding from the door. Marta snorted and started to pound on the door with the bottom of her fist.

"Evelyn!" she shouted louder. "You can't fucking hide from me, Evelyn. Peter's told me everything! I know about you, and I know about the fucking law firm, and I know about the—"

The heavy door swung open so swiftly and so silently that Marta almost pounded her fist straight into Evelyn, who stepped neatly aside just in time, withdrawing a half foot back into her apartment. Marta jerked herself backward with a stuttered apology and Evelyn pulled the door wider, slipping a tiny wedge under the bottom with her foot to keep it from falling closed again.

"What the fuck," Evelyn said, glaring. Then she noticed me, with a double take so smooth as to be almost invisible. "What the fuck?"

She looked stunning in a much different way than I'd expected, a cloth belt cinched tight around a kimono and a crown of what appeared to be flowers intertwined around her forehead. Her eyes were heavily made up with a scare of red and black eye shadow and her lips were colored using a tone that exactly matched the surrounding skin, creating the uncanny impression that she had no lips at all. I had a brief experience of seeing my feelings from the outside, looking between her and Marta—I knew that Evelyn was the most attractive woman I'd ever seen, and especially so in that alien makeup, but Marta just seemed so much more real beside her, flattening her hair against the sides of her head with her palms and fighting off a visible wave of panic as she gathered her resolve and began to speak.

"Aren't you the intern, from my law firm?" Evelyn raised her voice over Marta's, pointing at me with one hand while she reached down for a pack of cigarettes with the other. "You are, aren't you? What the *fuck*."

"This is Peter. He's told me everything, Evelyn. You hired a law firm to dig up blackmail on me?"

"I'm sorry, one second. You are fucking the intern. From my law firm. You and him." She lit her cigarette, her eyes saucers. "Is *he* the guy that Mom was talking about?"

I only noticed that the ceilings were mirrors when the spark of her lighter seemed to fly ten feet above her and I hissed a breath into my teeth, my hair standing on end. "I was fired," I said.

Evelyn barked out a laugh, genuinely surprised. "No shit," she said.

Marta clenched her jaw. "He knocked on my door because he felt bad about what he'd been hired to do to me, Evelyn. What you hired him to do to me." She pressed her eyes shut and then opened them. "Also, we're not having sex."

But Evelyn was staring at me, her eyes narrowing in the reflection of the ceiling's mirror. The ember of her cigarette crackled as she inhaled. "He felt bad for you," she said.

"He did, Evelyn. Because I apparently belong to a family that hires lawyers to *investigate* each other, and scare the shit out of each other. But it has to fucking stop, Evelyn." Marta crossed her arms, wrinkling her nose against the cloud of smoke that Evelyn blew in her direction. "The jig is up. I'll sue you back, if your lawyers keep harassing me like this. Peter will testify that you asked them to do illegal things."

Evelyn snorted, smoke flowing from her nostrils like a painted dragon. "This is some fucking gall," she said. "You think it's illegal to hire a law firm to investigate another person? You think *I'm* in the wrong here."

Marta drew herself up as tall as she was able, but I could tell that she regretted not wearing higher heels. "You have to stop, Evelyn," she began. "Or I'll call your mother, and——"

Evelyn cut her off with a sharp step forward into the hallway, ashing her cigarette directly at Marta as she spoke. "Fucking call her, then. Maybe you can explain to her why my investigators found my brother's Australian shepherd in a zipped-up trash bag in your garbage bin, dead as a board and riddled with fucking *knife wounds.*"

I raised my eyebrows as high as I was able. Marta stumbled backward, as if hit by a blow.

"That's," Marta started, blinking rapidly.

"You're a complete fucking maniac. You came here to *threaten* me? You weren't even happy just murdering my brother, you had to fucking carve up his dog, too. And then you threw his body out in the *trash*, with a bunch of bottles and cans. What was it, Marta? Was Archie making you feel guilty, looking at you? Or did you just want to kill his dog, too, to round it out."

"I didn't," Marta said, her voice quiet, her skin white. "Archie is missing."

Evelyn ran the tip of her tongue over her bottom lip. "So someone else stabbed him with a kitchen knife and then stuffed him into your garbage can. Using your brand of garbage bags." She took another drag and exhaled twin streams of smoke through her nostrils again. "You're a fucking psychopath."

"Archie. Is missing," Marta repeated, her voice almost too small to make out.

Evelyn curled her lip in disgust. "I can't believe that you came here to threaten me." She ground the cigarette out into a tin plate just inside the door. "You do know that she murdered her last lover, right?" she said to me without glancing in my direction. "You worked her case, you must know. Elbow to the throat? Drowned him, underwater? My brother. His body still hasn't been found."

"No," Marta said, slowly shaking her head back and forth. "We're going to sue you, Evelyn. You and your law firm. If you don't leave us alone."

"She kicked him in the chest. Knocked his head against a wall, at the bottom of Lake Michigan, and then left. And then *told* me."

Marta's shoulders were shaking, I noticed, unsteady above her ragged breaths. I wanted to wrap her into a hug and then lift and carry her back into the elevator, to remove her from this hallway and this penthouse floor, to ride back down to the ground level and then get her some hot soup at the Potbelly nearby. I wanted to kiss her on the side of her neck.

"Here's what's going to happen," Evelyn said, advancing a single step into the hallway. "You're going to give back all of the money, Marta. All of it. And then you're going to disappear, never to speak to me or my mother again, never to look either of us in the fucking eye if you ever walk past us in the street. Or." Doubled in the glass mirror of the ceiling, her red-and-black eye makeup and shining dark kimono looked like a bird of prey and its shadow, cornering Marta from the sky and from the ground. "I'm going to send Archie's body to my fucking mother and she's going to cut you off, completely. And then I'm going to keep my investigators on retainer to follow you and fuck with you for the rest of your miserable life. I'll make a million-dollar donation to your law school on the express condition that they fail you out. I'll have my men send flyers to your neighbors to explain what you did and who you are, wherever you move. They will get you fired from whatever job you try to hold down, and they'll burn your fucking house to the ground if I tell them to. They will hunt you, Marta, wherever you go. You will never escape. You will never live this down."

Marta's whole body was quivering now, her breath short and her

171

pupils dilated, a rabbit spotted in the tall grasses. Her arms were still folded over her chest but more to hold herself together, it seemed, than to defend against Evelyn's aggression; but even so, she drew her shoulders back and raised herself taller, if not quite returning Evelyn's molten gaze, then still glaring with considerable force down at her short stilettos.

"I'll sue you, Evelyn," she said, in a tone that would have been assertive if it hadn't been so whisper-quiet. "Expect to hear from my attorney."

Then she turned on a heel, strode swiftly past me and toward the elevator, and pushed the button to go back down to the ground floor.

~

Marta stopped shaking about halfway down the elevator's descent, after a small cluster of businessmen entered the elevator with us and she was pressed again to my side; but then she started again after we entered the parking garage, her shoulders shivering as she pulled open the driver's-side door and I climbed into the shotgun seat across. She buckled her seat belt and wrapped her fingers at ten and two on the steering wheel and then slowly keeled forward, tipping like a jar from a shelf, forming her mouth into an open circle and exhaling in regular huffs at the car horn in the center of the wheel. Tears sparkled in her eyes. I reached out a hand and placed it lightly on her shoulder, but she neither acknowledged my touch nor drew herself away, straightening in her seat with a long sniff and then keeling forward again to puff at the steering wheel. I pulled my hand back.

"It's not true, you know," she said, perhaps louder than she meant to. "What she said."

I nodded, gazing forward at the flat cement supports rising immediately before our parking spot, only inches from the car's bumper. The stone was matte gray but shone slightly, under the golden overheads, despite this. Even the parking garage beneath the tower had expensive lighting, I realized.

"I didn't kill him," Marta clarified.

I turned to look at her a little too quickly. Her face was slightly underlit from the reflection of the lights on the console and the stone outside, shadows extending up above her eyebrows and onto her forehead, shrinking or expanding in reverse of her movements. She took another long inhale through her nostrils, glaring forward.

"It was an accident. It's like I tripped, you know? And fell. I didn't mean to do those things." She shook her head slowly, as though tightly controlling herself, in stark contrast to the continued quivering in her shoulders. "It's like, when you vomit. Bodies just, spasm, sometimes. Your stomach compresses and it forces food back up into your mouth and it's not something that you can help, puking, and it's — it's fucking inane, to blame someone for vomiting. Because it was just their body, vomiting. You see?"

I lowered my head in the first part of a nod and then kept it there, my chin tucked into my neck, as I processed this. Somehow, I'd barely been touched when Evelyn had detailed Marta's actions underneath the water, not ten minutes beforehand; but listening to Marta herself confirming these details now sent a chill down my spine, a dread sinking into the very center of my stomach. I'd long compartmentalized that a large number of people believed that Marta had murdered her husband, but hearing it straight from her didn't fit at all in that same box, or any other.

Marta started the car and pulled out quickly, abruptly, swinging the rear of the car hard into the lane and then reversing forward, slamming the back of my head into the headrest. She slowed only slightly for the turnstile and then zoomed into the downtown traffic, clicking her blinker back toward the lake.

"If someone has an essential tremor, and they drop something — *they* didn't drop anything. Nothing did. Or, their body did, but that person didn't. But that person, is not their body. Do you know what I mean?" A thin stream of tears was trickling from the corner of her eye but otherwise she seemed to be steadying, her shoulders square as she steeled herself against the uproar of honking cars, as she wove through the streets. "If someone cuts off your thumb and then uses your thumb to pull a trigger, you didn't shoot the gun. Right? Because you are not your thumb."

I buckled my seat belt and then held on to it, both hands wrapped around the strap over my chest, as she wheeled the car onto Lake Shore Drive and then toward the leftmost lane.

"Panic—cut my body off from me," she said, but with her voice now trailing off. The car began to slow down underneath her, or to feel like it was slowing down, ceasing finally to accelerate as she settled into the steady sprint of the left lane.

I could feel the pressure of the silence in the car rising as Marta paused for me to make a sound of affirmation and I stayed quiet, my chin still tucked into my neck, watching the traffic rush past. She glanced over, her expression either pained or angry.

"I need you to say something," she said. "Please."

"Yes," I replied at last. I reached out and placed my hand back on her shoulder, remembering to myself that I was falling in love with her, that she needed my help. There was nowhere else to go, without her. "Sorry. Yes, absolutely."

She flipped on a blinker and eased into the middle lane, allowing the other cars behind her to pass. "Thank you," she said, crying more normally now, her face contorted and red with shame. "Fuck."

I squeezed her shoulder and she flipped on a blinker to change into the slow lane, studying the road signs for an exit. I felt guilty for not speaking up earlier and I began speaking freely now, nonstop, repeating her statements and adding my own and then mentioning one of my professors from college and my dream from the night before, relaxing my hand from the seat belt as Marta eased the car onto an exit just outside downtown and then angled into the right-turn lane for the gas station. She nodded along, quietly hyperventilating, her expression teetering on the edge of a panic attack until she suddenly took a sharp sniff and looked straight at me, her eyes wide and alarmed.

"Say that part again," she said.

I looked forward, at the green light above the intersection, and then back at her. She let the car roll forward and then turned toward the gas station.

"About," I said, "my human studies professor? He used to say, whenever someone asked about willpower and—"

"Your dream, I mean. This was last night, you had this dream?"

"Oh." I felt relieved that she'd stopped crying, but felt equally guilty that I hadn't thought through the subject matter a little more closely before bringing up such an obvious analogue for the topic at hand. "Yeah, last night. In the dream I was breathing, sort of, at the bottom of the ocean, only it wasn't really breathing, because it was really the currents in the water moving through me, moving my lungs. I just meant, it was an example of, sometimes it's not even you or your body but actually the environment, 'doing' the thing, and—"

"Huh." She parked the car alongside the gas station and stared at my face, but not at my eyes, her mind entirely elsewhere.

I shifted uncomfortably, crossing my legs toward her. "—but. It wasn't really something I'd thought through, or—"

"Huh," she said again, her eyes narrowing.

We'd made it far enough, on our brief trip through the left lane of Lake Shore Drive, to escape downtown but we were still fairly close to the center of the city, with thick traffic on the adjoining streets and cars in all of the other parking spots, radios playing through open windows and drivers shouting at pedestrians on the road, pedestrians shouting back. Lake Michigan undulated in the near distance, fluctuating like focus.

She finally realized that she was gazing directly at my face and glanced away, squinting up at the nearest red traffic light.

"Shit," she said, leaning forward over the steering wheel as she turned the ignition. She twisted around in her seat to back the car up and then eased us back toward the traffic, squinting now at the advancing cars.

"I think I need to rent a boat," she said.

～

It was a hunch, it wasn't important why, it was a dumb idea that she needed to follow through on like a song you need to sing to get out of your head, it was just something that she had to do, it wasn't a big deal, it wasn't really possible to explain. The more I tried to dissuade her, the more reasons she seemed to have for not being dissuaded and the more urgent it seemed to accomplish this plan now, today and then this morning, before she lost her nerve and so as soon as possible, as soon as a speedboat and diving equipment could be tracked down. It was like all the negative energy of our visit to Evelyn had reversed sign and now Marta was dense with purpose, driving calmly and without disobeying traffic laws toward the highway and then toward Waukegan up north, to where she and her husband had embarked on their dive together one month before. Her skin regained its color and she remarked evenly about how well she remembered the way still, following I-90 to I-94 to 41, and then from there to 137 and the marina. She could see it in her head, she said to me, as if she were looking directly at a map, the lines of red and blue switchbacking up beside the lakeshore as the route wound north.

But I could barely hear her at all by the time we made it to the interstate. That sense of broken compartments, of trying and failing to fit Marta's actions into the boxes I'd established for her, had graduated into a full collapse of anxiety, my limbs rigid and my breathing strained as I tried to convince her to stop and slow down and think it over, as I asked if she had any water in the car. It was less that I began to feel suspicious of Marta so much as I felt suddenly unsure that this person was, in fact, Marta; or at least any version of Marta that I recognized. There was a side of her that I had fallen hard for, and that I was coming to feel that I'd always known, but I was also beginning to realize that there were many more sides to her than I'd encountered so far— remembering the heat in her voice during the ritual with Archie, the reflections of candlelight in her eyes. I wanted her to stop this because I thought it was an awful fucking idea and because I wanted her to stay the version of herself that I was falling in love with, and the version that needed me, whether she admitted it aloud or not. The version that had needed me to comfort her and support her only a moment before. She handed me a water bottle from the seat pocket behind her and I drank the whole thing before I remembered that I hadn't peed yet that morning. I crossed my legs tighter.

She was just going to see if she could find him, she explained again and again to me, in different words and with the same phrases, with an increasing shiver of excitement in her voice. She hadn't thought about Robert's body trapped inside the shipwreck until I'd mentioned the dream but now it seemed so plausible, so obvious: the ritual we'd conducted in their old bedroom might well have worked, exactly as intended, only she hadn't done the basic legwork of locating the body he would return to and so had revived him in situ without realizing, in the same place he'd been left to die: reawakening him to the cold dark at the bottom of Lake Michigan, floating in the pitch black of the ship's hull. Of course she hadn't been able to feel his presence afterward, since his spirit had been sent back into its corporeal anchor—it all made so much sense that she felt like a complete fucking idiot for not thinking of it earlier, for not realizing at the time. Tears entered the corners of her eyes as she wondered aloud if Robert had been suffering down there, stuck back inside his own corpse and potentially drowning all over again, unendingly, for days and days, trying to breathe and choking on the water in the lightless hull and no longer able to escape his body to make it stop, now that the ritual had forced his soul to stay; wiping her tears with the side of her wrist, her eyes bright and her fingers tapping at the corners of the steering wheel, the car accelerating into a turn.

Eventually I gave up on dissuading her and instead just tried to stall her, to convince her to slow down and think it over, but as soon as we got to Waukegan, it seemed she found everything she needed almost right away. There was a whole fleet of speedboats for rent in the marina, managed by two long men with identical haircuts who hunched and smiled over Marta as they guided her to the shiniest gold-and-white launch on the docks and then smiled even wider when she paid them on the spot, and the trip to the diving shop barely took longer, Marta disappearing behind a storefront of scuba-suited mannequins for less than ten minutes before she emerged with a teenaged clerk and a cart of diving equipment in tow, a stack of dull metal oxygen tanks and rubberized clothing and various tubes that they loaded into the trunk in under forty seconds and then we were driving again, returning right back to the rented boat and the water. It was almost too quick to follow. I felt like a time traveler come back to the present in order to avert a future nuclear war, watching everything devolve exactly the way it did in the last timeline despite my warnings, the world hurtling toward its own end; I felt like my window of possibility with Marta was closing in the space of a few scant minutes, and I was watching helpless as she faded away.

"I'll be all right, Peter," she said after parking the car, putting her hand on my cheek to finally stop me from talking. "Really. I'll be back in less than an hour."

Her fingers were cold on my skin and she pulled them away quickly, glancing forward at the windshield. I hurt, looking at her. It was meaningful to feel her touch, but I recognized that it was also a sign that she wasn't feeling the tension between us anymore, that she wasn't worrying that the gesture would mean more to me than she intended. I wanted to kiss her on the lips, to thread my fingers through her hair. She climbed out of the car and popped the trunk.

In the end, she launched off from the pier exactly twenty minutes before noon, without so much as a flicker in her steadfast expression as she revved the speedboat into the wind, her black scuba equipment and three gray cylinders of oxygen glinting in the sun behind her. I stared after her receding figure for a minute or so from the docks and then walked up to the pier's lakeside diner to watch her from a window booth. By the time I was seated at the diner and then came back from using the bathroom, my cheeks hot and my stomach knotted, she was little more than a smooth contrail of frothing wake, a shining spot on the horizon and then nothing at all. The empty blue of the lake against the lighter blue of the sky above.

I ordered a coffee and a beer and a tall glass of ice water, and then as soon as the beer arrived I chugged it down and ordered another, sipping alternately at the hot coffee and the ice water while I waited for the next round.

In my mind, I couldn't stop imagining two parallel scenes simultaneously, branching off from different points of the present but no less vivid for their lack of overlap: I imagined Marta riding toward the dive point and then suiting up and entering the water and I imagined myself waiting for her for years, for decades, waiting for her in this diner by the water and then waiting for her in her house after she came back and I moved in with her, waiting for her to look at me and actually see me where I stood. I imagined her in the jet-black and deep-blue rubber of the scuba suit, the footlong flippers and the mask and the goggles and the oxygen and the backup oxygen, bobbing on the surface as she organized herself in the water and then dipping her head underneath and following her head with the rest of her body, down, and I imagined myself slowly growing toward my thirties and then past as Marta learned to refer to me as Robert and I learned to respond as him, with his tone of voice and his gestures, taking on his hobbies and his peccadilloes and relenting on being loved as myself and instead accepting the love that was available, as a stand-in for him. I imagined my own neural pathways reshaping around Robert's habits as I practiced them day in and day out and I imagined the dark deepening around her as she sank toward the shipwreck, the memories of her first dive layered over and underneath the vision of the masts and the algae-covered deck and the pressure of the water above her, the bubbles rising from the corner of her mask. I imagined her pausing just outside the wooden hull with her chest tight and the light almost too weak to see without a flashlight so far down, checking her oxygen and her backup oxygen and touching lightly on the straps of her mask and her goggles as she looked at the opening, waiting to enter. My second beer arrived and I took a sip of the foam and then took a sip of my coffee and the waiter asked if I wanted a refill or any food and I said yes, thank you, and ordered a sandwich and chips as I pushed my coffee mug to the booth table's edge. I watched him refill the black from the specialized thermos-decanter and I imagined running into my former friends as Robert Forrester and taking too long to recognize them, my face creasing with confusion as they asked Peter what had happened to him and Peter wasn't there to respond, and I imagined

Marta entering the inside of the shipwreck and floating through the intermediate rooms to the hold, her flashlight sweeping across the walls and the detritus and then resting at last on the dead body, the nearly frozen corpse, glinting under the light of her beam. My sandwich arrived and I ate it quickly, feeling my energy begin to restore as the sustenance spread into my stomach and the coffee began to kick in, smoothly accelerating the flow of blood through my veins. The waiter came by with another refill and I gratefully accepted. I imagined Marta approaching the body underwater and then grazing its pale face with her fingertips and I only realized that I was looking right at her through the diner's window, that I was staring directly at Marta's speedboat returning to the docks, when her launch was already fully visible and beginning to slow as it approached the pier. I shot to my feet so fast that I felt briefly dizzy. I threw two bills on the table and ran out the door.

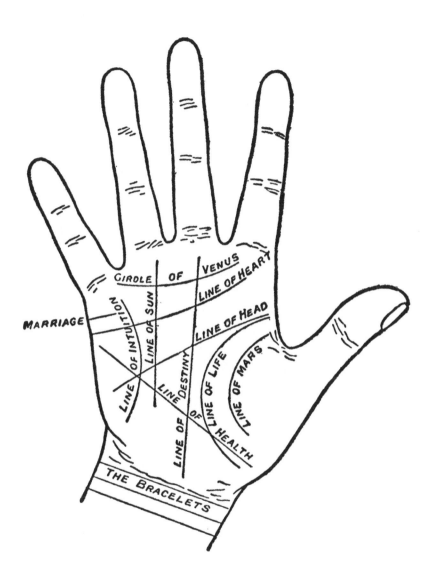

GIRDLE OF VENUS

LINE OF HEART

MARRIAGE

LINE OF INTUITION

LINE OF SUN

LINE OF HEAD

LINE OF DESTINY

LINE OF LIFE

LINE OF MARS

LINE OF HEALTH

THE BRACELETS

THUMB

The shape of a second person in the boat had been visible from the diner window and from the top of the steps leading down to the docks, but it was harder to make out from the pier itself, the speedboat's windshield glinting in the afternoon sun and Marta herself blocking my view behind the steering wheel, her posture relaxed and her eyes shining as she raised her hand in a wave. I stared back, motionless. My whole body seemed to be paused, disbelieving, waiting to see that this moment was indeed real before my blood agreed to resume flowing, before my heart consented to continue beating in my chest. Sweat stippled the exposed skin on my arms and on my neck and across my forehead, my eyes beginning to dry in the light breeze as I held them wide. I felt sick. Marta turned off the engine and then tossed me a rope from the deck, gesturing toward the nearest piling. The rope fell at my feet.

I bent down slowly, my knees creaking, to pick it up.

"Peter!" Marta called out to me, her voice impossibly bright. "Peter, you wizard! You are *incredible*! I mean that. Truly, actually, miraculously good." She hopped off the boat and wrapped me into her arms, her body hot against my cold skin. She took the rope from my limp hands and set about securing the speedboat. "You have an actual gift. An actual gift, though. You know that, right?"

Crumpled in the rear of the boat beside the stack of equipment, propped up as though sitting with its back beside the engine, the body looked like an exhausted passenger, slouched and anonymous underneath its full nylon scuba suit and wide goggles and tall flippers standing out ludicrously like clown feet at the ends of its legs. The only exposed skin was in the small circle of its face, and only the parts that weren't covered by the goggles; just the cheeks, in other words, and part of its jaw. Nothing about it seemed possibly real. Marta was talking on about how she'd found him, about the coffer in the hold's ceiling he'd floated inside and if she hadn't known exactly where to look and my vision began to narrow and then expand, like a head rush of blood to my brain, like tunnel vision. No aspect of bringing a dead fucking body to the middle of a public dock in the broad light of day, with at least a half-dozen other strangers coming and going around us, seemed the least bit possible. Underneath its heavily smudged goggles I could see that the body's exposed skin appeared to be covered in yellowish bruises and the suit all over was filmed with a thin layer of muck, but otherwise the fig-ure seemed almost preternaturally preserved: the cheeks looked slightly caved in and some of the equipment seemed to be weirdly suctioned over the parts they were supposed to cover, but it seemed far more like a life-size doll than a month-old corpse just-then dredged from over a hundred feet underwater.

"Do you see it?" Marta asked me, returning to the boat to unload more of the equipment. The body jostled as she removed the oxygen cylinders and then her own scuba suit alongside, leaning them together into a small heap. "You see it, right?"

I looked at her hands and then looked back up at the body, at its head beginning to loll forward as a wave from another boat passed toward shore. I leaned over the far side of the docks to vomit. After I turned back around, my head still slightly spinning, Marta had lifted the body from the back of the boat and dragged it, as simple as that, until it was lying on its back on the planks between us. I jerked backward, terrified, but Marta stepped around and took my hand in hers and then pulled my hand directly down to the body. I tried to resist, protesting and yanking my arm back, but she only grabbed my wrist in both of her hands and forced my fingers down until all three of our palms were resting flat on the corpse's rib cage, my bare palm pressed beneath hers into the squish of grimy nylon.

"He's breathing," she said. "Just like in your dream."

I jerked my hand away too late, my heartbeat banging against the inside of my ear.

Its chest rose and fell.

~

Sitting in the shotgun seat of Marta's sedan, breathing fast and shallow through my nostrils as I watched the other cars turn through the intersection toward the highway, I tried hard to think about what I should do, about how I could either redirect this day or else escape it. I wanted to come up with some idea of next steps, some plan to move forward and bring the universe back into alignment with its own laws of nature or at least some sequence that would move things in the right direction, some basic tricks for calming down. But I couldn't think at all, really, with the corpse lying flat in the back seat behind me. Marta had covered it head-to-toe with a couple of beach towels while we returned the scuba equipment, but afterward she'd removed them from its head, tucking the towel in instead around its dripping shoulders like a blanket, and now I couldn't stop glancing in the corner of the mirror and seeing the edge of its profile, the corner of its chin just visible around the edge of my own seat back. Its face had become more legible as an individual when seen through less nausea: its soaked black bangs sticking out beneath the edges of the nylon and its mouth, its caved-in cheeks, and the shape of the body just familiar enough to bring to mind the photographs of Robert Forrester I'd scrolled through on my computer screen, the smug grin of his graduation photos, the thumbnail he'd used for a profile shot. It made my skin crawl, imagining something alive inside that dead body; it made me feel like I was losing my fucking mind. It was odorless but I couldn't stop imagining smells. Marta opened her window an inch and stuck the fingers of her left hand through the crack as she navigated the car onto the main road headed west, feeling the wind with her fingertips as she turned and then accelerated.

"I rented a house," she said, anticipating a question that hadn't at all crossed my mind, as she glanced over her shoulder to merge. "A little bit inland from here. Just outside Gurnee, if you know the area."

187

I looked at her, my lips parted. She laughed.

"Sorry," she said, reaching out and giving me a squeeze on my forearm. "I started renting a house a few weeks ago, only a little while from here, when I first started researching how to respond to Robert's presence, how to get him back. I figured he and I might need someplace to hunker down where no one would know us, where no one would know that he had died, after I figured out the rest of the details." She pulled her hand back in from the window and located a hair tie in the center console, wrapped and pulled her hair into a ponytail, cinched the hair tie around. "It's a nice place, right next to a forest preserve. I've been trying to get the money to buy it outright." She switched hands on the steering wheel and slipped her fingertips out the window again, shaking her head slowly with a spreading smile. "I honestly feel like I'm flying right now. I can't remember the last time I felt this good."

I exhaled, wide-eyed, staring straight forward. She glanced at my reflection in the rearview mirror and laughed again at my expression, remarking aloud that I couldn't look this worried when everything had *worked*, and exactly as it was all supposed to, switching hands on the steering wheel to thread her fingers through my hair. A chill ran down my spine. I leaned my head back, pressing her hand between the back of my head and the headrest. She glanced over at me with a complicated smile and then pulled her hand back slowly, tracing the back of my head with her fingers. My heart pounded. She pressed the button to turn on the radio and began to sing along quietly to the pop songs.

～

The house was even larger than I'd imagined, nestled between a pair of ancient white oaks that still didn't look very tall next to its three stories, their topmost branches only a little bit higher than the attic dormers atop the tallest gable. It was an old Victorian, with peeling gray paint and a red-brick chimney rising blunt behind a conical tower room, long-faced windows on the lower levels and a wide veranda sweeping across the front and along the right side, covered by a thick wire screen with holes so large that I could see them from the car as we meandered past to park in the converted barn. It was the type of place where a bitter old grandmother would live, I thought, abandoned by all of her children and left to rot and vicious to the neighbors, a stalwart of the local elections board. Only the nearest neighbor was actually three miles farther back along the road, if not four, because of some historical squiggle in the forest preserve zoning that left this land private but surrounded on all sides by acres of county property, untouched except by the local ranger's walking trails. Marta turned off the car in the converted barn and then swore, remembering, and pulled back up the driveway closer to the front steps. The trees leaned low overhead, crowding at the edges of the road and at the edges of the yard and peering, the leaves rustling as we climbed out and opened the doors to the back seat. She fitted her elbows around the soggy armpits and dragged the body most of the way out of the car, and then looked over at me. I leaned down and picked up the soaking wet feet, holding my breath against my rising dizziness.

The indoors were more lived-in, but unevenly, with the fridge humming in the kitchen and yellow bananas on the countertop next to a basement doorway that appeared to be rusted shut, crusted brown and red-brown around its hinges and all around its edges, and a dining room that was still covered in cobwebs in every corner. We dripped a trail of lake water through each room until we set the corpse down on the dining room table, pushing aside some of the dust-covered chairs with our legs to make space. Marta made a quick circuit of the room with her sleeve, rubbing the top layer of dust from the table beneath the corpse's head and from the headrests of the seats, the tops of the chair backs.

"All right," she said, her shoulders hunched, "all right." She pressed her hair flat against either side of her head, pacing halfway around the table and then doubling back, and then pacing that half circuit a second time. "All right," she said a third time, nodding. "Let's take off the suit, then."

I looked at her. She removed the right flipper first and a small cascade of water fell onto the hardwood floor, smelling of earth, and then another after she took the left flipper off. Then she walked around the edge of the table and removed the goggles, slowly, sucking in a breath through her teeth as though pained, as some of the skin adhered to the rubber edges and peeled off along with the fogged lenses, leaving lines of exposed, skinless flesh where the edges had dug into the face. Marta set the goggles-and-skin down carefully on the dining table beside the head, letting the dripping liquid join the larger puddle already oozing out from underneath the rest of its parts, spreading across the wooden surface and trickling over the nearest edges and onto the floor.

The face was collapsed underneath the mask. The cheekbones looked broken on both sides and the palate was snapped inward, as though impacted. But the eyes were legible, if not even, with eyelids and eyelashes and a kind of implicit expression of intent concentration, it looked like, that bothered me almost as profoundly as the obvious disfigurements. Marta stepped around to look at the face straight-on, and then she reached out a hand and traced her knuckles over the line of the jaw.

"Oh, Bobby," she breathed.

Then she moved her hand farther down to the rib cage, feeling again the steady movement, the slow rise and the slow fall of the lungs breathing underneath. I took a step back into the kitchen, stomach acid burning at the back of my throat.

"It's just, it's so . . ." Marta began, gesturing with her hands at where her words would have continued. She laughed, surprisingly loud, wiping her eyes with her fingers. "It's just such a *freedom*. I've been so, compressed, underneath all of this—the weight of it all. The guilt, I mean. I've been so flattened, so completely flattened, you know? And it's only really becoming clear to me now how much, how much I've been flattened by this, now that it's finally passing." She laughed again, tears still sparkling in the corners of her eyes. "God! I didn't kill him, Peter! I didn't, I didn't. And if—and if I, or if someone thinks I—then I brought him back. I brought him back, and—" She shook her head and made a gesture of throwing up her hands, and then showed me her empty palms. "And he's back. He's also, he's back." She turned around in a circle, her hands still open, a slow-motion pirouette. "Bobby," she said, placing an arm around my neck. She swayed with me, pulling me into motion with her. "Oh, Bobby."

I moved stiffly along with her, an awkward partner at a slow dance. She lowered her head to my chest and took a long, slow inhale, and then let out a long, slow sigh, gripping me tight in her arms. I relaxed very slightly, wrapping my own arms around her shoulders.

"Marta," I said, a tiny voice that barely made it out from my throat.

But if she heard, she pretended not to. She swayed for the space of another long inhale and then stepped back, straightening, and ran a hand along the side of her hair.

"Right," she said. She looked me in the eye and held it, smiling. "Thank you, though, Peter. Really."

I glanced at the ground, blushing. While she was in my arms I'd involuntarily imagined myself kissing her, putting my lips to hers in the same way that I'd stolen a kiss the day before; and now I couldn't get the image, the memory out of my head, despite it all. She floated over to the counter and picked a banana out from the bunch, peeled its sides and took a bite, set the rest back down inside its peel and then walked back into the dining room, began searching with her fingers along the corpse's side for a zipper in the nylon.

I walked to the doorway, my blood surging in my veins.

"What are you going to do now, though?" I said, louder this time.

Marta found a zipper underneath the right armpit and bit delicately down on her lower lip as she pulled it, her expression pained with concentration, down the far side of the corpse's torso and thigh.

"Shoot," she said.

I shuddered, imagining. Her bottom lip curled farther inward.

"The skin," she said, screwing up her eyes.

I crossed my arms over my chest. She lifted up part of the nylon beyond the zipper and I caught a glimpse before I remembered to look away: the soaked-through skin was so loose that it appeared to be coming off in long strips with the suit, patches and scraps of epidermis lifting and tearing with the nylon. I'd never seen a clearer demonstration of skin as a kind of fabric, as just a flimsy clothing to flesh; and I kept seeing it, even after I turned away and retreated to the kitchen, holding myself straight with a hand pressed flat against the wall.

I volunteered to go back to the car and get the rest of our things, to see if there was anything that we'd forgotten that I could bring in. Marta nodded without listening, maybe without hearing at all. I strode through the dust-covered rooms and back through the front door, down the steps and into the disheveled front yard, surrounded on every side by forest.

~

I waited outside for half an hour, maybe longer, before I was able to convince myself to go back indoors. I sat on the veranda for the first while, in the doorway of the covered part of the porch with the swinging screen door propped open on my knee, listening to the stray latecomer birds in the upper branches and the rustling of the squirrels, the snapping of twigs and sticks in the undergrowth. The environment was familiar but more from movies, really, than from my California childhood; the surroundings of an East Coast family vacation comedy, or an East Coast family vacation drama, in the lake of the woods. There was even a small lake nearby, according to Marta; more like a pond, compared to Lake Michigan, but supposedly swimmable. I briefly imagined myself rising and walking along one of the trails until I found the water, stripping off my clothes and wading in and then my body slowly coming apart into its constituent pieces as I breaststroked farther and farther from shore, my arms coming loose from my shoulders and my hips wiggling free from my torso above, my legs kicking. My head floating along on its own. I stood and walked a little to the side to try to vomit again, retching dryly over a pile of dead leaves, but nothing came out other than a little drool, dribbling from the center of my lip. I wiped my mouth with the back of my wrist and then eased down onto my haunches, covered my face with my arms.

Something alive was moving that body. Whether or not it was Marta's dead husband, or whether it thought that it was—there was something at work there, manipulating the body at its behest. Inside that soaked-through, falling-apart corpse, some force of will was lifting its chest and then making it fall in an imitation of inhales, a pantomime of an autonomic response. No air seemed to be moving through it, after all, as far as I could observe: there was no water coughed from its lungs despite the whole body being soaked full of Lake Michigan, no drippings of lake residue from its nostrils, no bubbles in the corners of its mouth: only the motion, the rhythm. The rise and the fall. I was reminded of the appendages of predatory plants, evolved to look like exact facsimiles of other living things to draw prey into their jaws without noticing, without realizing just how many little things were wrong. Its skin coming off under Marta's hands and its chest expanding, contracting, when I touched it earlier with my own palms.

I stood quickly, a little more quickly than I meant to, shaking my head sharply to either side.

"No," I said aloud.

The sun was near the center of the sky, the woods quiet in the increasing humidity of the approaching afternoon. I went over and checked the car, glancing only briefly at the drenched beach towels and seat cushions of the back seat before I reached in to grab Marta's handbag from the center console. The keys were in the cupholder, I noticed. I walked back to the house neither slowly nor quickly, pacing myself intentionally, one foot after the next, one stair at a time and then through the front door and the front room and the kitchen, toward the doorway to the dining room. There was the hint of a smell beginning now, I noticed; not strong, not yet, but something more organic, more putrid than the unnerving odorlessness of before. My heart pounded in my neck. I set Marta's bag on the counter and then walked into the dining room and around the table, around the dead body on the table, toward her.

The corpse had been stripped completely naked, like a cadaver in an operating room. Marta had figured out some superior technique for taking off the suit in the time that I'd been outside and most of the skin on the rest of its body remained relatively intact, with only a few strips and patches removed from its right side where she'd started. The chest was a little bit compacted, I noticed, and the stomach oddly sucked in, the muscles drawn tight around the guts and bones and the legs and penis shriveled, darkened in some spots and yellowed in others, with a strange yellow-purple bloom just beneath the rib cage. But it still looked more human, laid out naked: beaten and malformed, a discarded first draft, its hair intact and flat around either side of its head and its squeezed-shut eyes covered lovingly by Marta's palm, her face a mask of wonder.

"His eyes," she said, her pupils unfocused as she gazed straight forward. "They're moving, underneath his eyelids." She moved her glance a half inch to the left and caught a glimpse of me, it seemed, however briefly. Her lips widened into a smile. "This is—it's. You—this." She laughed at herself, withdrawing her hand finally with a little thrilled shiver, returning to the room that we were sharing. "Have you ever looked at anyone's eyes, when they're in REM sleep? The way they move, back-and-forth, underneath the eyelids? *God*, it's weird to feel."

I looked at her. "Marta," I started, working hard to keep my voice steady.

"I just noticed it, while I was undressing him, and—I was too nervous to try and lift the eyelids, but—"

"Marta." I took her hand in mine, only briefly twitching as I felt how damp it was, the residues on her fingerpads. "What if this is just a dead body?"

She looked at me, her expression completely blank. She understood what I meant, I felt certain, but she was choosing, as a first response, not to.

I took her by the hand and led her back around the table and toward the closest next room with a door that I could shut, pulling her insistently into a heavily cobwebbed library that was nonetheless quite bright in the sunlight coming in through the broad, tree-covered windows. One of the glass panes was broken by a branch punching through and a squirrel scampered away through a far door when we entered, its claws scratching on the wood and into the hallway. But the fresh air was a blessing. Marta crossed her arms over her chest, still playing befuddled, while I reached around and closed the door behind us.

"Why are you closing the door?" she said, bothered.

"Just bear with me for a minute. Just for a minute, Marta." I licked my lips. Marta shifted her weight onto a hip, that single vertical crease enunciating itself between her eyebrows. "I've just, I've been thinking about this, for the last little while, and—what if this is just your husband's corpse? That you've recovered, yes, from the bottom of Lake Michigan. But nothing more. What if it's still—"

She exhaled through her nose. "Peter," she said.

"—but what if it's still, underneath what looks like, what appears to be—breathing—what if it's only a dead body? And here we are, undressing it, and laying it out on the dining room table, but it's only—"

"Peter." She took her hands in mine. "Stop."

I tried to say the same thing again in different words, but she drew sharply closer and then put her hand over my mouth, as if gently, her eyes only inches away as she stared me into stillness. I swallowed, blinking.

"Stop," she said, her fingers cool against my lips. "Please."

I blinked again, my heart beating. She let her hand down slowly and then took one of my hands in hers, nodding as if in response, and threaded our fingers together.

"This is the best thing that could've possibly happened," she said, easing herself down on the back of an ancient leather couch until she was half standing, looking up at me. "I've been so worried that I was just crazy, all this time. Before I met with you for that dinner, I'd never even admitted to anyone, out loud, that I'd been feeling Robert's presence near me. I didn't think that anyone would believe me, and—I didn't really know that I believed myself." She shook her head, swinging our linked hands between us as she recalled. I let my foot slide a half inch closer. "I got so obsessed, and spent all this time researching, feeling him close to me, but I couldn't talk to anyone about it. No one at all, I mean. I started trying to do these rituals in our old bedroom and I felt like such an idiot, such a—and—" She twisted around toward the window, toward the branches scratching at the glass. "—that weight, that I was talking about earlier."

My fingers began to sweat against hers. I opened my mouth and then licked my lips, my pulse racing just beneath the surface of my skin.

"It's funny, though," she said, peering at the splintered hole in the window's glass, "talking about this now—I also didn't really feel allowed to see it, I don't think, before. To see the whole situation, I mean, or to admit that I saw it in certain ways. Like before, it felt too awful to admit that—to notice, even, how much more obsessed I was with Robert, after the accident, compared to before. How much more—how much more typically—in love, I've been. It felt too guilty to even notice the difference in myself, when I already felt like I killed him." She turned almost back to me, her thumb rubbing lightly against the back of my hand. "But now, it's not—it's not such a confession, you know? To admit that yes, I love him, but also, to notice how fucking terrible he looks in there. Honestly."

She grinned and I smiled a little bit also, although the hairs on the nape of my neck rose again at the mention of the body. I was still more unnerved than words could express by the charade of life inside the corpse, and increasingly convinced that it might be a manifestation of some true, elemental evil; but in this other room, and with the door closed, I could hear plain enough that it would break Marta to have this absolution taken from her. And here—in this room, and with the door closed—that could be more important, for now. A breeze picked up outside and the light wind sang softly through the hole in the glass as it entered, a low whistling. I broke my hand free of Marta's and then stepped around her to lean against the couch back on the other side, placing my arm behind her, almost around her waist. She leaned her body into mine.

"It's real, Peter," she murmured, her voice low in her chest. "We've both seen it, and felt it. We brought him back. You did."

I peered down at her as much as I was able with her head nestled underneath my chin. I barely heard her at all except for her voice's vibration against my chest. I knew the question that I wanted to ask, but I didn't know if there existed any way to ask it.

"Marta," I started again. The leaves rustled outside the hole in the window. "What do you think of me?"

She exhaled with surprise, twisting her head around to look up at my face. I felt embarrassment heating under my skin.

"If we were two strangers, I mean. Meeting for the first time." I straightened my neck, furrowing my brow as I focused on maintaining composure. The old library room had been cleared of books but the shelves remained on every wall, floor to ceiling, a pattern of shadows and dim reflections of light on the dusty surfaces that I studied, each shelf in order, as if thinking about nothing else. I should've left a long time ago, I understood—should've stayed outside and then taken the car, should've sprinted in the other direction as soon as I saw her boat at the pier—but I was here instead, with Marta, breathing in the smell of her hair as she rearranged herself against me. My heart beat against her shoulder blade. "Do I seem like the kind of guy you might spend time with, in another lifetime?"

"Huh," she said, her cheek pressed to my shoulder. "That's kind of hard to say, honestly." She adjusted herself again, touching her hair with her hand.

The low whistling in the glass pane waned and then increased, lightly rattling the frame. My whole body was rigid with interpretation, held in suspense as I tried to work this response through.

"But I did—I did, actually, want to ask you," she said, reaching over to take my free hand in hers. "I wanted to ask you something, though."

She stood, still holding on to my fingers, but my heart dropped into my stomach anyhow, watching her rise away from me. Even when I'd been dumped, I'd never felt this painful an ache before.

"You know that—game—we were playing, earlier," she said, standing above me now as I half sat on the couch, her eyes clear, her freckles standing out against her pale skin in the sunlight. "Or, yesterday? Where, you were being Robert, and—I was telling you, how to be him?"

I looked up at her, my eyes wide with alarm. Elsewhere in the house, the squirrel that we'd loosed began scampering again across the floorboards, bumping into things and scratching loud against the wood.

"I, well." She breathed through an open mouth, unable to look me in the eye. "I wanted to ask you—to ask, if—"

"Marta," I said. "No."

She blushed. "Oh," she said, "sure. Right. I was just—"

"No, Marta." My body felt stiff, hurting. I stood up from the couch. "That wasn't real. That wasn't real at all. You can't—this is—" I shook my head, fast and then faster, my hands out. "I was just trying to kiss you."

She made a face, her skin still red, running a hand along the side of her hair to press it down. "No, yes. I know. I just thought—I thought. Well." She put a fingertip in her mouth and bit down.

She was looking at me in a strange way but now I couldn't return her gaze, my neck too strained and my skin too tired from forming expressions, the muscles of my face too fatigued. It was finally hitting me, suddenly and all at once: the rejection that I simply hadn't recognized when it arrived so long ago, that I'd chosen to disbelieve so that I could keep clinging to this idea that I somehow had a snowball's chance with Marta, so that I could keep hanging on around her despite her obvious obsession with her dead husband and her frequent attempts to push me away, to hold me off at arm's length. I'd chosen to interpret that first moment in her kitchen as an indeterminate jumble of signs, as though almost-accepting my kiss in the guise of practicing for Robert had been a mixed signal—when it had always been exactly what it was, plain as day, on the surface. I'd only been lying to myself. I could feel the humiliation cascading down my arms, my sides, as the facts hardened in the very bottom of my stomach. I slumped back down onto the back of the leather couch.

"Shit," I said, with a little huff of disbelief, as I finally saw the whole narrative arranged in its proper order.

Marta stepped forward, her hands held out in front of her. I looked at the lines along her palms. "Hold on," she said, ducking her head down to try and catch my eye. "Peter, slow down. You're not hearing what I'm saying." She clasped my hand in both of hers, her skin cool against mine. "I want us to stay here together. I want to stay here, with you. I also love my husband." I stared down at the floorboards, at our footprints in the dust, my brow deeply creased. "Peter, I haven't even asked a question, yet."

I shook my head. I remembered the increasing smell of the body in the other room and then I couldn't tell, after that thought crossed my mind, whether the stench was indeed reaching through the door in that moment or if it was only my memory of it, or if maybe my attention had summoned it to my consciousness right then. Marta tried to lift my hand from my side and I stood abruptly, rising to my full height above her.

"I think you should bury the body," I said.

She stepped back with a sharp inhale through her nostrils, her shoulders high around her ears.

"Jesus, Peter," she muttered. "Think about what you're saying."

But I was already shaking my head, already gagging in the back of my throat at the putrid stink of flesh in my nostrils and in the air, that oversweet odor of new rotting. I shoved past her and shouldered open the door.

The Hanged Man

It took me over an hour to make it the three or four miles from Marta's house to her nearest neighbor, even with a brief running start, and then another forty-five minutes to walk from there to the nearest bus terminal; and I only barely managed to catch the last bus to the city that evening, the ticket seller calling out to the driver to wait while she counted out my change. It felt like a high-stakes moment from another day, from an earlier version of myself entirely. I couldn't shake the feeling that I'd woken up from a dream and into another dream, so plain and ordinary as to be entirely convincing, on the surface, that I was awake and in the real world. The rumblings and bumpings of the bus underneath me felt too flawlessly familiar, too exact a reproduction of a previous normal and I felt strangely anxious about closing my eyes in case I should open them again in another reality, the world warping as soon as I looked away.

The sky was dark by the time I made it back to Chicago. I disembarked near downtown and then changed to a city bus and stared wide-eyed, my corneas drying, out the window at the sidewalks and the streets and the people, the streetlamps glowing as they slid past, the flashing headlights and the glimmers from the windows, the tiny auras of pedestrians' cell phones. I was thinking constantly about Marta but less in words or in images than in missed recognitions: half the faces of the women I glimpsed seemed to be hers, turning away or disappearing around a corner, staring directly back at me as she drove in the opposite direction and then past. I couldn't stop feeling afraid that I was about to lose her, even though she was already so long gone.

Not all of the stores in the strip mall were closed when the city bus let me off, but the stretch of shops around Jessica Fortune and Apothecary was dark enough that I had the sense that no one could hear me when I began knocking, when I began pounding on the basement-level door. I started with sharp-knuckled sets of three and regular pauses, calling out the Lady Jessica's name and then listening, but after the first minute or so I switched to simply thumping a steady drumbeat into the top panel, hammering with the bottom of my fist on the wood just hard enough that the hinges rattled with every impact. In my head, I imagined myself as a mob, arrayed at her door with torches and pitchforks and the wild violence of an anonymous crowd; as a hooded stranger, begging for food and succor, a god in disguise; as a teenager, banging my head over and over against a wall. I began to suspect that there was no one inside at the same time that I began to suspect that the Lady Jessica was standing inches from the other side of the door, glinting in her strange dark-red shirt and sequins, listening. I pounded harder for a stretch of ten more knocks and then stepped back, my wrist smarting. A group of high school or college kids walked by on the sidewalk above the basement stairs, laughing in unsteady voices, imitating one another in a spiral of higher- and higher-pitched warbles. I turned to squint at their shadows passing. Then I climbed back up the basement stairs and stared into the parking lot, into the circles of light around the streetlamps, as if trying to catch the Lady Jessica slipping away and into the dark.

I was beginning to cry, I finally realized. Snot was clogging my left nostril and a pressure of tears was building just underneath my right eye, even after I squeezed my eyes shut and pressed the bottoms of my wrists into my eye sockets. I had a feeling that it was recent, that it had only begun just now, but I wasn't actually sure. I wiped my nose with the back of my forearm and then pushed my fingertips into my eyes, concentrating.

A car swept its headlights past and I straightened, caught in the brief glare before the darkness fell back into place around me, thick black except for the small reds of the shrinking taillights.

I pivoted on a heel and skipped down the steps to the small land-ing, leaned back and hoof-kicked the Apothecary's door just above the doorknob, feeling the wood give slightly under the blow. Then I kicked it again, and then a third and a fourth time, until my heel broke a hole in the thin wood and punched clean through, sharp splinters scraping painfully against the skin around my ankle. I hopped awkwardly on my other foot and scratched my skin far more deeply as I withdrew, hissing, and reached a hand through to undo the latch from the inside. The door swung open into the musty darkness. I leaned forward and called out for the Lady Jessica, declaring myself and my intention to come inside, but I couldn't see anything at all in the pitch-black hallway except for the reflections of colored light leaking from her office at the opposite end. The smell of animal feces and urine floated out to where I stood; but not, I noticed at once, any animal sounds. There was no squeaking or keening, no scrapings of claws, no rustling at all. I called out again before I stepped inside.

The inner room was empty. The bedsheets that had hung from the ceiling and covered the walls were tied back at the corners and the metal cages were gone while the glass cages were all bare, the bedding still there and the food containers still stacked high with pellets but no rabbits or any other rodents—only the droppings everywhere, in the cages and on the floor and on the carpet, on the little table in the center and on the desk in the far corner, along with scratch marks, smears of blood, crumpled pages from torn books. The bulbs had all been left on, burning monochrome yellow without the hanging cloth to color them, painful and shadowless from every side, giving the strong impression that someone was going to return at any moment. I stepped over to a small shelf stuffed tight with tiny paperback books and flipped through the titles, but they were all in Old English and I had a hard time reading the script. Stepping over to the little table in the center of the room, I briefly shuddered at the conspicuously clean breadboard but found little more in the table's skinny drawers except for beads and marbles and an old Rider-Waite deck. I didn't know exactly what I was looking for, but I was feeling increasingly anxious to find it; the animal stink wasn't getting any easier to bear, and I could feel a headache beginning under those lights. I went to the desk in the corner, previously hidden from view by a bedsheet hanging over it, and opened the old laptop tucked in its keyboard drawer. There was a Google Maps page of directions open on the screen, a red line zigzagging from this address to another, to a building on the same street as Naphtha's. My breath shortened, leaning in to the screen.

"Wait," I said aloud.

~

"Oh," AJ said at the door, his jaw set to one side. His eyes were completely black at the center, dilated so wide that the irises had disappeared. "Yeah, I guess."

He stepped aside with a heavy sigh to let me enter. I shouldered past him and into the party, almost stepping on a brown-and-white rabbit on its own mad dash to escape through the open door, a ball of terrified fuzz shooting around my left ankle and AJ's right calf and then onto the sidewalk and the street and instantly disappearing. I watched it go with my eyebrows raised. AJ rolled his eyes and shoved the door shut.

The warehouse was packed with people, thrumming with music and loud conversations and many different kinds of smoke, the walls thick with blue and white Christmas lights and the crowd on the wide-open floor highlighted in regularly spaced intervals by large glowing orbs, glass balls ensconced in strange sort-of-firepits and pulsing with a soft, even yellow light, just enough to glimmer on the edges of the guests' glasses and earrings and teeth and make everyone look recognizable, as I slid past and between them, if not finally recognized. They were classmates of mine from art school, at least half of them, but most I only knew from hallways and large events and other parties like this one, faces that together conferred a sort of impersonal familiarity to the space but didn't actually give me anyone to talk to, no one to pull aside and ask where Naphtha was, if the Lady Jessica was somewhere here or if she'd simply lent the party her animals. It felt more dizzying, navigating the near-strangers, than I remembered, and not just because there was a surprisingly consistent layer of rabbits and mice underfoot, darting around the orbs and fairly often getting stepped on, squeaking and scampering to every side. I couldn't look at them without shuddering. I waded through the bright coiffures and the perfumes, the industrial chemicals and the snuffling laughs, the back of my neck growing hot and then slick with sweat as not a single one of the other guests accepted my gaze or even acknowledged that I was there except to step to one side or the other. I pushed through to the treated-slab-of-wood/

kitchen area and spotted a pair of my old roommates, two of my former closest friends to whom I hadn't spoken in almost nine months now, and pivoted on a heel to walk instead through the hookah-smoking area and to the backyard outside. Naphtha was hooting with a laugh at the center of a small group on the trash-strewn stone patio, her elbow propped on one arm and her cigarette smoldering at the end of an elaborately long cigarette holder, her smile wide.

"P!" she cried out, lifting her hands above her head at the sight of me. "You made it!"

I put on a smile a little belatedly but she was already striding over and then wrapping me into a delicate hug, carefully keeping the ember of her cigarette away from my hair. She squeezed my butt and I rose onto my toes, surprised.

"I haven't seen you in forever," she said, stepping back and taking an elongated drag. "Have you been crying?"

I caught my breath in my chest. "Oh," I said.

"You all right, P? You look a little—bruised, maybe, too."

I shook my head, swallowing underneath my imitation smile. "I was looking for the Lady Jessica, actually," I said, casting a glance around the patio. I knew already that she was nowhere to be seen among the two separate clusters of smokers, but I squinted at them anyhow, stepping to one side. Byron raised an eyebrow from his group and waved to me. I lifted a hand to wave back.

"Oh, yes," Naphtha said, grinning, "hah. Sorry about that. I know you hate her, I just—I thought it'd be fucking weird, and cool, to bring her out. You know? And with all the little bunnies, too. She's just reading tarot right now, I think, in the basement." She licked her lips, looking at me. If I didn't know better, I might've thought that she was feeling guilty. "Is that why you're . . . ?"

I shook my head again, waving her off. "Thanks," I said, turning to go.

But she caught me on the arm, holding me back for another moment while she studied me, her brow creased.

"Don't be a stranger, P," she said, quiet. "Text me back sometime, okay?"

I started to nod and then stopped, finally returning her gaze with a frank glare. I hated her, I realized, as much as for what she wasn't as for what she pretended to be, my heart beating in the side of my neck. She stepped back, surprised, possibly even hurt. I pushed my way back into the crowd inside.

~

The basement was less crowded than the upstairs, but only slightly, with a nook set up with large speakers and a laptop table and an open area with maybe nine or ten people dancing to the music, Daft Punk with a sample of something more retro, along with a couple, a girl and a boy, holding hands and sitting cross-legged in front of — as I turned the corner, peering underneath — the Lady Jessica, as promised, tucked underneath the stairway and kneeling before a card table. She was still wearing those tiny pitch-black glasses on the end of her nose and a blouse with sequins in each of the button-holes, but this time the shirt was dark purple instead of dark red and there were also sequins glinting in her hair, attached to the sides of her short-cropped bangs in a line of evenly spaced clips.

Something in my chest hardened, a vague memory condensed into a specific muscular tension, seeing her sitting so calm and authoritative behind the table. The boy made a noise in his throat as she murmured something about the tarot laid out between them, and then he turned to the girl and kissed her full on the lips, their tongues briefly visible as they leaned into each other.

The Lady Jessica shifted to one side, gazing dispassionately at the spectacle, and then jerked backward with alarm.

"Egh," she expectorated, apparently recognizing me, or maybe just unnerved by the hunched stranger looming over their nook under the stairs. The couple stiffened, glaring and surprised, as though their privacy had only then been violated. Each of them mumbled their annoyance and offense as they stood. The girl handed the Lady Jessica a sheaf of twenties and they shuffled off to make out against some other wall.

I took their seat with my legs wide, moving the table roughly to one side so that there was nothing between the Lady and me. The tarot cards shuddered and slid along the surface, fluttering over the sides and to the ground.

"I need to know," I said in a low voice, leaning forward with my hands on my knees, "how much of this is real."

The Lady Jessica shook her head and made a wave with her fingers, as if I were a waft of smoke that she was trying to dissipate.

"You did something real," I said, my patience thin, "when you communicated with my brother. You connected with him." I licked my lips, remembering the body, the rise and the fall. "How?"

She twisted her lips into a grimace, observing me. Then she gave a deep sigh and cast a glance around the room, at the kissing couple and at the dancers, the DJ behind the table.

"This," she said, her voice barely audible over the Daft Punk remix. "This is why I hate parties."

I started to quiver slightly, holding on to my knees so hard that the muscles in my arms began to spasm. She scooched back another inch, returning her gaze to me, to the backs of my hands.

"Everything in my life has gone to shit since I first met you," I said to her, loud and clear. "You need to tell me what you did. How it works."

But she was observing me in a different way now that she'd noticed my unsteadiness, her eyes searching my veins where they stood out from my skin and her tongue touching lightly at the corners of her mouth, concentrating.

"No," she said finally, narrowing her eyes at the hairs on my wrists, at the blue veins visible between my wrists and my knuckles.

I clenched my fingers around the sides of my thighs. The Lady Jessica lifted her chin and calmly looked in my right eye, and then in my left.

"That is not what you are here to ask me," she said.

I squinted at her. The song on the dance floor ended and the DJ announced to the nine or ten people that he was going upstairs for a piss and set the music to play automatically from a playlist, pop hits from the

1990s and early 2000s. The room began to empty, the steps creaking behind and above my head as the others filtered out after him.

A rabbit shivered past my ankle and I stiffened, my stomach turning as I watched the Lady Jessica bend down and scoop it up. She cradled it expertly against her right shoulder, petting its ears flat with her free hand.

"A friend of mine," I murmured, watching the bunny shake and twitch in her arms, "brought a man back. After he was drowned. For almost thirty days." The skin on the back of my neck was tingling, my scalp tight. "The body, it looks like—he looks like he's breathing, now. Like he's alive. And his—eyes, apparently . . ." I shook my head, unable to finish.

The Lady Jessica watched me impassively, her long fingers and her long fingernails forming deep lines in the rabbit's fur as she stroked it, as it trembled.

"I need to know if it's possible," I started again, my face crumpled in concentration. "If it's really the same person, I mean. Inside." I made a gesture with my hands and then ran my fingers through my hair, gathering the strands into my fist and then tugging my head forward, like a doll's head that I was manipulating into position.

The Lady Jessica looked at me and then at my hands, and then at the ceiling. She sighed. "No," she said. "That is not your question, either."

I clenched my jaw, trying to catch myself back from saying something I'd regret, from standing and leaving on the spot.

"I think it is, honestly," I said, blinking through the frustration. "It's fucking terrifying. I need to know if I'm just insane, or if it's possible that I'm not."

The Lady Jessica exhaled impatiently. "The man, Lazarus? Returns from four days, entombment. He breathes, he moves, he is Lazarus. Jesus weeps. Et cetera." The bunny made a move to leave but she held it tight, wrapped in both hands. "Albeit, thirty days is longer than four."

I blinked again, but differently than before, processing. It was a strange sort of relief, hearing from her that I wasn't just losing my mind.

"And now, see?" she said, audibly irritated. "You still have to ask. Because this, was not really."

I looked at her, my brow wrinkled. I wanted to say that I didn't know what she was talking about but after I opened my mouth, my lips dry, I realized that I did. It was only humiliating, too humiliating to mention. I wiped my sweaty palms against my thighs and leaned backward, folded my arms.

"You want to know if she can love you," she prompted. "Yes? Or if she is, will always be, in love with the other."

I looked at her, my eyes wide. I felt like a worm, wriggling.

But she only nodded slowly, finally releasing the bunny to bound from her lap and across the floor, up the stairs. She bent down and picked up the loose cards from where they'd fallen after I pushed the table aside, and then added them to a deck of tarot cards that she gathered from the floor beside her chair. She held them out to me.

"Cut the deck," she said.

I looked at the cards and then at her, at the place in her lap where the bunny had sat trapped a moment earlier, trembling. I reached out and picked up the top half of the deck and then slid it underneath the bottom half.

The Lady Jessica accepted the cards back and I reached out and dragged the table back between us, setting it steady on its legs. She placed the deck down and then flipped the top card onto the center. I leaned forward with my breath held.

"This is," I said, studying the drawing. "A strange deck."

"Yes."

"These, those are—"

"Swords."

"—the ten of swords, then."

She leaned forward, tilting her head to the side, and then nodded. "Yes." She touched her tongue again to the corner of her mouth, observing. "It is a daughter, trying to climb back into the boat. But the father has cut off all of her fingers."

I raised my eyebrows. The swords were plunged into the ocean like serrated harpoons into a whale's back, only the daughter's stumped hands visible and waving. At the top of the card, a man whose head was not shown held the bloody knife over the boat's edge.

"Yikes," I said.

She narrowed her nostrils. "Yes."

I slumped down. My body had been tensed for hours, my shoulders and my forearms and the muscles of my face all flexed without relaxing since morning. I could feel the Lady Jessica observing me in either eye, in the veins of my hands.

"It is not always wrong," she said, "to love someone who does not love you in return."

Her tiny black glasses were perched on her nose so as to exactly preclude eye contact with her pupils, but I still squinted up at her. "Is that seriously something that you tell to people?" I asked.

She shrugged. "We can't always help who we love," she said, "and our chances are few. To love is the only reason to live." She picked up the deck and tucked it into a bag hanging over the side of her chair and then stood, and held her hand out to me. "Forty dollars, is fair?"

I drew my head back, dizzy. But I gave her thirty-five dollars and then watched her go, *tsk*ing after a rabbit as she creaked up the basement stairs, its pattering footsteps syncopating with hers. The crowd noise briefly increased as the basement door was opened and then shushed after it was closed, footsteps pounding through the floorboards above.

～

The bass had changed register in the upstairs playlist by the time I re-emerged, shifting from the E string of an acoustic guitar to a thumping heartbeat, holding steady and then accelerating, with the huge orbs now flashing white at regular intervals and freezing the crowd in an after-image of jostling, laughing, looking, looking back. It was completely disorienting. When I'd first arrived, there had been a sort of searing clarity to my anger, to my need for answers, but now I was only at a party and had no idea why. I felt out of breath just being near so much motion. But there was booze there, at least, and I beelined for the cluster of bottles along the far wall, sliding between the thick, flashing mass of bodies without looking up until I was already at the whiskey, unscrewing the top and then pouring the liquid into a red plastic cup. I took a sip and closed my eyes, focusing on the burn as it traced beneath my rib cage and into my gut. The anxiety spreading across the bottom of my stomach felt not unlike like what dogs experienced, I imagined, when they sensed an earthquake coming, or a hurricane—a thickening, physical dread that felt almost like horror, or almost like grief. I slipped the pint of whiskey into my back pocket and asked a stranger next to me for a drag of their cigarette. They refused, but seemed to know me as Jason and gave me a whole cigarette to myself, lighting it for me with a match before asking a question that I couldn't quite understand, maybe couldn't quite hear over the music. I inhaled and then coughed, nodding, and made a gesture like I'd be back in just a second before shouldering my way back into the mass of people. I didn't see the Lady Jessica anywhere but the bunnies were still present at different parts of the building, clustered now into small clumps and groups around the places of lower traffic, shivering and terrified.

I spotted the pair of my old roommates, one of them lounging on a low couch and the other leaning deep into a beanbag chair on the floor, only after I'd accidentally stepped between their conversation and then stopped, waiting for the person in front of me to make room to move forward. Terry was the first one to shout, and then both of their voices rang out.

"Peter!" Terry cried with his arms above his head, accidentally slopping a splash of beer from his Solo cup onto the back of his hair. "Ack! Ack, ack."

I startled, my eyes wide. "Holy shit," I said, slipping the whiskey pint back out from my pocket.

"Yooooo," Anthony intoned, tugging at my pant leg from the beanbag chair. I stumbled back and into a stranger's shoulder, which shouldered me back.

"It's been decades, Peter," Terry said. "We thought you hated us now." He appeared to be trying to pat his head dry with the palm of his hand, the suds of his beer pooling on the little flaps of skin between his fingers.

I took a swig, burning. "What?" I said.

"You never hang out with us anymore," Terry clarified. He wiped his hand off on the couch and then inverted his body to try and wipe the top of his head against the other cushions. "We used to be beautiful together! Remember the *Review Canoe*? You still have those lithograph slabs, don't you?"

I squinted down at him, at his contorted writhing not unlike the girl in *The Exorcist* possessed by a demon, feeling the pit of anxiety dig deeper into my stomach as the loud party crowd shuffled around and past. The week before I moved out, I'd learned that my roommates had all held a house meeting without me, to discuss me; and my subsequent decision to leave had been largely preemptive, anticipating that they were on the verge of forcing me out. I remembered hating them with the full focus of obsession and I felt a strong sympathy, now, for that hatred. Anthony continued to paw at my pant leg and I tried to shake him off and he lurched forward, practically pulling down my pants as he tried to drag me down into a wrestling match. I kicked him off, maybe a little too hard.

"Did you ever figure out," Anthony asked from the floor beneath me, undeterred, "what happened with your brother, and everything?"

The music changed on the speakers and a cry rose out from the crowd around us, hips beginning to sway in a different rhythm, a line forming to funnel people back down to the basement dance floor. I took another swig of the whiskey. "You mean, did I ever figure out why he killed himself?"

Anthony barked out a laugh, loud and surprised. "I guess so!" he said, as if tickled. "You always were so good at knowing when I was secretly trying to be an asshole, when here I was, stupidly thinking I was just trying to be nice."

Terry sat up to kick him and Anthony yelped, moaning about how everyone was kicking him, but I was too angry to continue hearing his voice anymore. I took advantage of the change in crowd flow and stepped to the side, as if to let someone past, and then stepped farther off and into the full crush of human traffic, into the crowd and out of sight.

~

I stayed at the party too long, as usual, but not for the usual reasons and not in the usual way. I wasn't trying to find someone to take me home and wasn't trying to catch a girl's eye on the dance floor, wasn't trying to enter conversations and meet new people, wasn't trying to stay in those conversations after the crowds dissipated and we could actually hear each other speaking, remember each other's names. I wasn't lingering to try and locate the expensive drugs and I wasn't looking to bum a cigarette, wasn't searching for a bottle with some liquor left and wasn't working to maintain my inebriation just beneath that bliss point of almost throwing up, wasn't stumbling around with the spins and aiming for a place to lie down. I wasn't even at the party at all, really, so much as hiding in the building while the party continued around me. I stood on the back patio and found someone with a pouch of rolling tobacco and spent a long time very slowly rolling cigarettes and then very slowly smoking them, not really talking and not really listening to the people around me, and then after the rolling tobacco left and I ran out of rolled cigarettes to smoke I went inside and spent a long time in the bathroom, the latch closed on the sliding door and my hands on either side of the sink, the muffled sounds of people waiting outside slowly growing louder, the intermittent poundings on the door.

~

I didn't actually see the Lady Jessica leaving, but the rabbits and mice were missing from the obvious places across the floor and the corners when I emerged from the bathroom and I guessed that she must have taken them, the glowing orbs set back to their steady yellow radiance without any flashes of strobe-white. And without the terrified small mammals, the room seemed to be drained past some essential tipping point of its energy and was abruptly emptying, a flipped switch that sent an exodus of people to gather around the exits and share out one-last-cigarettes by the front door, en masse. I saw Terry and

Anthony leave and I saw Naphtha waving and hugging her favorites among the departures and I stepped around the edge of the group and out to the back patio, where I knew there was a panel in the sheet-metal fencing that you could lean just-enough open if you shoved at the weak point with your whole body weight. I squeezed myself out and then walked around the corner to where I could see the front door from around the edge of the building, where I could watch the crowd separate into groups of two or three or four and cross the street and into the darkness.

The shadows of the warehouses on the opposite side of the road loomed above the haloed streetlamps, flashing into flatness as a single cab arrived and then sinking back into depth after the headlights turned and receded, the shouting laughter of the first few departing groups fading into more intimate mumbling, jokes and arguments and retorts. Above, the moon was just a stain of white behind the cloud cover, the only color in the otherwise black sky. The stream of departing partiers slowly reduced into a trickle, pairs of strangers waiting for the other to start walking so that they weren't walking too close, faces lit from beneath by the glowing screens of phones. I lifted the back of my wrist to my nose to wipe away the snot, and then pressed the heels of my hands into my eye sockets.

I decided to skip the bus and walk home to my apartment, taking the long way around the highway overpass.

Ten of Swords

There's a version of my brother's suicide where he didn't know what he was doing, or where he didn't believe that what he was doing was real. Where it was a cry for help and it wasn't supposed to work, where he was attempting as a gesture but not attempting to succeed, and it was all a sort of strange, meticulously staged accident, like the kind of workplace disasters that befall daredevils or acrobats after they plummet from great heights or into boiling cauldrons but they never really meant to, they were only supposed to almost. A classic tragedy. Romeo and Juliet only misunderstood each other, Theseus's father saw the wrong sails.

The only problem, when I try to hold that story in my head and keep it there, is Henry himself. Possibly some parts of my brother wanted to be snatched back from the precipice, and had hoped to be caught before he fell; but there was another part, at least, that I'd known throughout our childhood together and intermittently during our adult lives, that would have never considered himself confused. And it was this refusal of confusion, specifically — I don't want to call it clarity, although that's the word he would have used — that was his engine. He burned with certainty. He saw how *shit* the world was and he saw how *shit* he himself was and he refused to stop seeing it, as he repeated over and again to me, his voice lilting with the triumph of a perfectionist in the act of proving himself wrong. Even when he was sitting at the very top of a mountain, his legs dangling over the edge of a rock and his eyes smiling, his face covered in sweat from the hike; even when he was playing pool at the back of a bar, grinning at his own miss; even when he was struggling to form words through his own cresting panic; holding tight to my hand after I hugged him to go. I dreamed that I was pleading with him over the phone, raising my voice louder and louder until I was screaming into the receiver and I woke up with my throat raw, like a stone was wedged underneath my Adam's apple and stabbing, hard-edged and sharp, my sheets soaked through and my face wet, breathing.

My phone was buzzing on the floor beside my mattress but I didn't turn my head to stare at it until it started buzzing a second time, the light of the mini-screen bright in the dark studio with the shades drawn over the windows, a beam of blue that formed a faint square on the ceiling above. On the fifth ring, I heaved myself up and crawled over to the charger and looked at the name flashing on the screen, and then slowly rose to my feet. The universe seemed to be fluctuating in real time, shrunk tight around my tired headache and then suddenly expanding, opening wide in every direction. I stepped over to the window and pulled back the curtain. She squinted up at me, an outline of herself on the sidewalk, and waved.

I opened the front door to my building in my pajamas and a white tee, wearing sandals and a baseball cap for the sun, expecting her to walk over to me and then come inside. She stood next to her car on the sidewalk for a moment and then walked across the street in very quick-small steps, her hands open at her sides. She'd been crying, I saw, and quite recently, and was maybe still crying as she wrapped her arms around my shoulders, squeezing me into a hug. I hugged her back.

"Thank you," she said, breathless, "for coming down. I can't be there alone anymore, Peter."

Things had been going wrong and wronger since I'd left, apparently, the stench growing too strong to abide and things, insects, burrowing, eating. I stepped back and watched her face as she spoke, her skin pale and dark bags beneath her eyes, exhausted and beautiful. She was scared, more scared than she could handle, her hands shaking while she'd driven down to my apartment and she'd had to pull over four times, she said, at four different rest stops along the highway, to get herself under control enough to keep driving. She was sorry, she said. She pulled me in for another hug.

"I'm sorry," she repeated, her forehead pressed warm against my shoulder, her face buried into my chest.

I took another breath, feeling her weight against my inhale.

I don't know that I ever made a decision so much as I always chose, at every point, to decide later on. I allowed myself to follow Marta to her car because I wanted to be near her for now and because she was the only place I could imagine being right now, and then I agreed to drive her back upstate because she wasn't currently able to drive herself and because I could always leave again afterward, after trying one more time, if I decided to then. She was listing from side to side, stumbling to the left and then to the right as we walked to the car and then leaning her whole body in either direction as she rode next to me in the passenger seat, curling into a ball away from me and then toward me. A bird with a broken wing, I thought. We listened to the car radio and she spoke constantly in a low voice and I told her that I was thinking about maybe staying there with her for a little while, at the house in Gurnee with her, and she looked at me for a long time before asking if I wanted to take a pill that she'd brought. I told her sure, and took it with a swallow of water from the bottle in the seat pocket. She started crying again, but so quietly that it took me some time to notice. She unbuckled her seat belt and leaned down until her ear was resting on my near thigh, lying down with her head in my lap, and I felt a warmth move through me at the same time that I felt increasingly self-conscious about my stiffening erection, only a few inches away. I tried to focus on the road in front of me, tried to remember why this exchange from I-90 to 94 West was so familiar, even before my last trip up with her, while she shook with tears against my thigh. My cheeks burned.

"I was going to be a lawyer," she said softly, lifting a hand to her lips to bite down on a fingernail.

I could feel the movement of her jaw muscles on my thigh, the sharp click of her teeth as they came together around the tip of her pinky finger, the pressure of her tongue inside her cheek. She swallowed.

"Have I been this way the whole time, do you think?" she asked, her voice uneven. "Underneath, I mean? Was I always the type of person who would do this, these things, under the right circumstances?" She pushed herself up from my lap, my leg briefly cool after the weight of her cheek lifted off. "Or did I change?"

I looked at her reflection in the rearview mirror, at the rectangle of her rubbed-red eyes in the glass.

"You can still be a lawyer, Marta," I said.

She looked at me and then looked away, crying. "Fuck, Peter," she said, pushing her palms over her face, wiping her cheeks with the sides of her hands even as fresh tears streamed down. "You really love me, don't you?"

I exhaled through my nostrils, my heart beating. "I don't know," I said, feeling a strange glow beginning to spread inside me. "I hope so."

She reached out and took my near hand in hers, threading her fingers through mine.

"I don't know what I would do without you," she said, holding my hand tight as she stared forward, her eyes open above her flowing tears. "God, I hope this works."

My ears pricked up, hearing the negative space around her statement, but the glowing in my chest was already too intense to think about anything else—tingling, it felt like, on the insides of my veins, up the undersides of my arms and along the bottoms of my thighs, heating me. I mentioned to Marta that I was feeling strange and she glanced sharply at the clock, noting that it was only twenty minutes or so since I'd taken the pill, and then asked if I'd had any breakfast that morning. I shook my head, feeling the hairs moving on my neck, the heat increasing. We pulled over and she switched into the driver's seat. I buckled my seat belt in shotgun and then rolled the window all the way down, enjoying the feeling of the fresh air on my fingertips, the smell of exhaust. I asked Marta what this pill was that she'd given me and she explained that it was a kind of tranquilizer, twisting the key in the ignition. A trucker in an eighteen-wheeler thumped past our parking spot and I stared at him, open-mouthed, hearing an entire landscape in the rhythm of his sound.

I began to float outside myself about the same time that we pulled off 94 West and onto the smaller state highway. At first just a couple of inches, like a sort of double image of myself, as though my mind's eye had become cross-eyed and I was coming out of focus; but then I floated out farther, half a foot and then a full foot, far enough that I could look down and see the space between us, see my body underneath. I looked small, I thought. My hair was sticking out in many more directions than I'd realized, now that my baseball cap was removed and hanging from my knee, and my bruises and cuts from the Garys hadn't healed as much as they'd felt: there was still a yellowish blotch on one of my cheeks and visible pink lines where the cuts had healed around my mouth. My hand rose to my face and traced the corners of my lips with my fingertips and I saw the sensation, saw the touch and feel of my stubble against my skin as though reading a needle on a meter, observing the phenomenon from above and noting its friction, its muted intensity. Then my hand lowered back down to my side and I floated up and through the car's ceiling and gazed at the scenery around us, at the trees standing stiff along the edges of the highway and far beyond, extending out and to the edge of Lake Michigan and then the serenity of the surface behind it, the dazzling bright of the reflected sunlight, the crisscross of other roads and streets and houses and towns extending out from the highway's artery, the intricate expanse of human life around the water. I briefly wondered if this was what my mother had meant when she'd talked about astral projection, when she'd described traveling to the in-between world while still alive. The towers of the city shone in the distance, back the way we'd come.

The house was hard to make out at first, nestled in the thick trees as it was. I saw the town of Gurnee with its daisy chains of highway off-ramps and on-ramps and I saw the forest preserve, stretching out in an even oval around its puddled lakes, but it wasn't until the car was past the gravel road and turning into the driveway that I could finally see the three stories of the old Victorian, the gables and the tower room, the converted barn beside. My body tingled with emotion, far below. I descended from the sky until I was close enough to see Marta rising from the driver's seat, her body lithe and nervous, walking quickly to the veranda and then through the front door; and then myself, getting out more slowly behind her with my hands held out like a blind person, like I was trying to feel my way forward without losing my balance. But I tripped anyhow, lurching and minuscule, onto my knees on the forest floor. I was moving like a toddler, I thought, still navigating that unsteady period of walking on my own two feet. The birds fluttered in the tall branches beside me and I felt absolutely transcendent, floating so close to them, able to see the texture of the individual feathers underneath their patterning, their hues. I lifted my consciousness over and into them, imagining wings.

Marta reemerged from the house and made a sound of concern, seeing me on the ground, and she dropped her bag of things and rushed over to me, lifted my arm around her shoulder and then dragged me with her, step by step, to the converted barn. She set me down by the door, slumping me briefly against the outside siding like a rag doll so that she could open the latch and then heft me back up and in, and then she came out to fetch her bag and close the door behind her. I descended my awareness from the treetops slowly, loath to leave behind the outside. I slipped through the gabled roof from above.

The dead body was already there atop the dining room table, set up exactly as it had been before, in the far corner of the barn where stalls for animals must have once separated the space into small compartments. But I floated over to Marta instead, at the other end of the huge room: over next to the barn door, only ten feet or so from the entrance, where she was pushing my body flat against the wall and arranging my feet onto a bench, but as if standing, with my back to the wooden wall and my knees held straight by her hands. My neck drooping. She climbed onto the bench with me to hold me in place while she secured my ankles to the wall with a thick rope, and then my legs, my shoulders, my wrists. My chest glowed as I hovered, my awareness so close to her that I could feel the heat of her breath, the trembling in her fingers as she pulled the ends through the knots.

After she was finished securing my body to the wall, she stepped off the bench and then removed it, allowing the rope ties to take my weight and hold me aloft. It was quite painful, I could see, but not so painful that I lost feeling in my ankles and wrists right away. I saw my skin begin to prickle in my extremities, my fingers starting to fall asleep, but my attention was more preoccupied with following Marta as she returned to her bag and then set about lighting a series of candlesticks, placing them into holders and then arranging them in a straight line between the dead body on the far table and myself against the near wall. I wanted to tell her that I did know whether I loved her — or if I didn't love her yet, then

I was going to. That I wanted to love her more than anything or anyone I'd ever wanted before. She came back to the bag and removed a large knife from a plastic holder, took a step and immediately dropped it down onto the floor beside her, swore and bent to pick it up.

But then she paused before her fingers quite reached the handle, drew her hand sharply back, and crouched into herself on the ground. She sank her weight back onto her heels and lifted her forearms over her head until her face was completely hidden behind her elbows.

For a long time, she only swayed there, rocking back and forth, breathing ragged through her arms.

Then she stood, her eyes freshly reddened, and took a careful breath through her nose.

"All right," she said.

She exhaled slowly, intentionally, and then turned back to her bag and removed an old book, flipped to a particular page, and traced her finger down.

"All right," she said again.

She bent down to pick the knife back up from the ground.

THE REMADE MAN

~ ~ ~

The young widow starts with the thumbs. She cuts off the corpse's thumb with the steel knife and then attaches it to the young man's stump, watches it move and wiggle, and then carries his fresh thumb over and sews it to the corpse, watches it flex and turn. Like mortise and tenon. She swaps out the hands finger by finger and then palms, forearms, biceps and shoulders, the corpse flexing its new arms at the elbow now while the young man begins to keel forward from where he's strapped to the wall, his torso drooping under the weight of the stiff dead limbs. She ties his forehead back with a scarf and then exchanges the legs, stomach, spine. She strokes the corpse's cheek for a long time while its head is still on the table before she carries it over and replaces it on the young man's open neck, and then carries his head back. The eyes blink slowly, like they're either very bemused or very surprised. The young widow spends a long time sewing the edges, getting the joints tight.

The remade man sits up for the first time that evening, after the young widow comes back from picking up dinner. She spots his perpendicular shadow in the window when she's stepping up the walk and she runs inside, shouting, and he holds an arm out in her direction. She takes his hand and twirls and twirls, holding his fingers aloft above her while she turns. The sunlight is orange in the room, the air moving. By the following day he's standing on his own and on the third day he begins eating, chewing and swallowing, the pupils in his eyes beginning to focus when he looks at objects and his skin regaining its color, except around the edges that still leak. He begins to make noises at the end of the first week, squawks and moans that sound like migratory mammals calling for the herd, and by the start of the second week he's already watching television in his free time, in between standing and staring out windows and walking in circles around the backyard. The young widow sets up a small camera and puts it on a bookshelf in the kitchen to see what he does when she's out and later she shows him the video of himself sneakily eating Snickers from the candy cupboard. For the first time since reviving, he laughs.

She notices the burly men in a white van taking photographs of them from the second day on, but there's nothing to be done about it, she determines, and so she stops noticing them as soon as she can.

Their first conversation occurs in the third week, while they're practicing walking together on the paths near their house. The remade man remarks about a mail truck careening especially quickly down the lone road and the young widow laughs and asks if he'd been hoping to send a letter, and he replies that he might've been. It's the first time he's been able to match a response to a prompt, to follow in sequitur from a preceding statement. He asks his first question shortly after, and she begins to answer. He has a new name now, she explains to him, and a face that won't match the face he remembers; she walks him to the bathroom and shows him the mirror and points out his scars, his jawline. She can't tell if he remembers the death and then the operation, the swapping of each of the individual parts, but in any case she doesn't quite have the words to remind him. He traces his fingertips over the edges where the pieces came together and says his new name aloud.

They move back to Lincoln Park, in Chicago, shortly thereafter. She takes him on a tour of the house and describes to him all the things they used to do there, his habits in each of the spaces and when they usually sat down for dinner, what they each liked to eat. On the first night she helps him cook nachos in the oven and chops the onions and tomatoes for the homemade guacamole while he slices the avocado and accidentally cuts off his left hand. He stares at it blankly but she laughs, startled, and sews him back together. They throw out the homemade guacamole and nachos and order takeout from Taco Bell. For the first time since the remaking, she begins to feel anxious that he doesn't remember himself more easily, that she has to teach him so much of what defined him: she begins to feel anxious that she might not have gotten all of him back. That night she cries on his chest—his strange, new chest—while he pets her hair with his good hand, his fingers tracing the outside of her ear.

The following afternoon she comes back from an errand at her law school and finds that he's gone shopping by himself, bought new onions and new avocados and new limes and made a big bowl of homemade guacamole before she arrived. She kisses him and kisses him. He pushes the rest of the things on the table aside, lifts her skirt and fucks her until she accidentally squeezes him too hard between her thighs and he begins to bleed through his seams.

~

The young widow reenrolls in law school that spring semester, with an eye toward graduating the following winter. One of her friendlier professors warns her that the powers that be are looking closely at her file, that she'd do well to give them no excuse to come down on her, but it's easy to avoid trouble and she passes with flying colors, and lands an internship that summer at a county prosecutor's. She brings home case files and sad stories of repeat offenders, of ludicrously stupid crimes and similarly stupid juries, and the remade man grins and asks for sensory details, what they looked like, sounded like, walked like, smelled like. She laughs and tells him that's the wrong type of question, that that's not the kind of question he would ask. They go on picnics on Sundays and wave to the burly men in the white van as they snap their photographs, visiting the lakeshore and the park.

He starts to study to remember what he used to know, enrolling in courses at the community college that the young widow recommends to him in order to come away with a degree. He sits in the back and sleeps, mostly. She graduates and they move downstate and he reenrolls there but keeps failing his classes, eventually because he stops showing up. He and the young widow take up biking instead. They cover the whole state over the course of a single season, long highways and farm roads, evenings and dawns. Their rented apartment becomes a house, and then a house undergoing a renovation. The neighbors don't speak to them and they don't wave. A woman comes to the front door one day claiming to be the remade man's mother but he's able to close the door on her, even with her fingers gripping the edge.

I love you, he says to the young widow, over and over again, until she finally smiles and kisses him back.

He begins drawing birds at the end of the second year. The young widow likes them at first, cartoon sketches that soon become heavily crosshatched, outlines of motion. He hangs them up in circles around their first-floor rooms to show the complete cycle of a bird's descent and then photographs the hangings, photographs her. She blushes. They take a trip back to the house in Lincoln Park to recover his old expensive cameras from the basement and spend a weekend there, walking through the steps of their old life, having sex under a blanket on the grass. There's a pile of mail on the front step that they burn together in the barbecue the last evening, warming their hands as the sky purples overhead.

But the birds increase, and increasingly quickly, as the weather cools. He refuses to leave the house except to buy paper and pens and Scotch tape to attach the sketches together, a long stitched-up scroll that he hangs in the bare branches of the trees so that it blows in the wind, that he unfurls out of the upstairs windows. The young widow ignores it for as long as she can. One of the neighbors walks over to complain about the scattered trash and she receives a ticket from the town and she tries to stop leaving money around the house, to keep him from buying new drawing supplies, but then he's arrested for stealing from the hardware store and she has to pick him up from the county jail on her way home from work. She collects him with her stomach empty, a high-pitched ringing in both ears.

She begins with a series of questions, sitting across from him at the kitchen table that night. She asks him about himself and about his past, about his childhood and his family and his university and his friends, about his favorite movies, his most instinctual pet peeves, about their past together. She holds his hand between hers and asks him what food tastes like, which music sounds good, asks him if he can remember being a seven-year-old, asks him if he can remember the color of his hair. He can't answer any of it but she keeps asking him anyway and he nods, as though taking instruction. *I love you*, he says to her. She asks him if he can remember any moment before the last two years and he tells her that he remembers running into a wall, and believing in God.

Her hands start shaking at the kitchen table and he wraps them in his own, clasping her, his fingers tight around her knuckles, his palms pressed against her wrists.

ACKNOWLEDGMENTS

THANK YOU to my teachers at Oberlin, Iowa, and Brown, to my classmates and my workshopmates, and to my irreplaceable wife, Amanda. Thank you to my family, my sisters and brothers, and to all of my strange friends. Thank you to Disquiet International and the Iowa Writers' Workshop for their generous support. Thank you to my editor, James McCoy, for believing in this book all the way to the end, and to Emily Forland, for believing in it from the beginning. Thank you to my parents, for this life and the next.